A CRUISE FLING

A CRUISE FLING

LAURA BROWN

This book is a work of fiction. Names, characters, places, and incidents are the product of the author's imagination or are used fictitiously. Any resemblance to actual events, locales, or persons, living or dead, is coincidental.

Copyright © 2023 by Laura Brown. All rights reserved, including the right to reproduce, distribute, or transmit in any form or by any means. For information regarding subsidiary rights, please contact the Publisher.

Entangled Publishing, LLC
644 Shrewsbury Commons Ave
STE 181
Shrewsbury, PA 17361
rights@entangledpublishing.com

Amara is an imprint of Entangled Publishing, LLC.

Edited by Molly Majumder and Lydia Sharp
Cover design by LJ Anderson/Mayhem Cover Creations
Cover images by Tetiana Lazunova, rtguest, and kbeis/Getty Images

Manufactured in the United States of America

First Edition March 2023

At Entangled, we want our readers to be well-informed. If you would like to know if this book contains any elements that might be of concern for you, please check the book's webpage for details.

https://entangledpublishing.com/books/a-cruise-fling

To the survivors of the Boston Marathon Bombing, and anyone else whose life was impacted by that day.

Day 1: Florida

When life hands you lemons, don't wait for them to rot.

The boat swayed beneath Mackenzie Laurel's feet as she walked along the outdoor promenade of the luxury cruise ship, the warm sun melting her troubles away. Or trying to. She squashed those pesky burdens down into the depths of the ocean surrounding the ship, determined to make the most out of this last-minute impromptu getaway. And when she returned home…

Nope, not going there.

She'd been wandering for a bit, learning the layout of the ship, making notes on important things to revisit, like the ice cream shop where she planned to spend her onboard credits. She hoped that when she returned to her room, her luggage would magically have arrived. She wanted to unpack, change her clothes, and settle in, but no luggage. She prayed it wasn't a sign that this trip was doomed and she really shouldn't have splurged while her life headed into a tailspin.

Worries for another day. A menu hung up in the shop window, and she scanned the flavor options, from the standard vanilla and chocolate, to a fancier black raspberry chip, to—oh my—a lemon sorbet! Would it be wrong to try them all? Not in one sitting, of course, but a valid goal for her vacation.

As soon as she could unpack. She headed out of the promenade, leaving the warm sun behind for cool air conditioning, winding her way back to her stateroom. Fewer luggage pieces sat outside doors than before. She knew the cabin stewards sometimes put the luggage inside the cabins, so the hall visual could be misleading, and Mac didn't want to get her hopes up. This entire trip, her being here contemplating ice cream under the hot sun rather than huddled under blankets on her friend's couch, felt like too much. It tempted her bad luck, probably the sole reason why her luggage was MIA.

Please don't still be MIA.

Thanks to last-minute availability and a pushy friend/travel agent, she had found herself in a suite, a balcony one at that. She was used to tiny inside cabins with no windows. Small by hotel standards, this cabin was the lap of luxury for the typical cramped cruise space. The rectangular room, complete with a couch and queen-size bed, had a place to sleep and sit and a balcony to escape from it all.

Her life had gone down the drain, and there might be no recovering from this bad decision of epic proportions, but she planned to get the most out of her impromptu getaway.

Thank you, Dani.

Mac arrived at her cabin. No luggage outside. No luggage for any of her neighbors, either, which did not fill her with hope. She pushed into the room, momentarily dazzled by the ocean view greeting her, unable to help the smile on her face. She'd left the sliding door open, and the ocean smell filtered through, better than any candle she had back home. Her cell phone rang, blasting "Single Ladies" into the air.

Dani's theme song. Mac put the phone on speaker, staring at the blue ocean outside her balcony, wondering what kind of cell plan she had to work over the Atlantic Ocean. Or what the charges would be, charges she could no longer afford. Her worries climbed out of vacation mode and took over once again as though they aspired to be flesh-eating bacteria. "Dani, I shouldn't be here."

"Relax. I told you, the cost of that tiny nosebleed inside cabin was the same as this lovely balcony stateroom. None of which should matter since this is a gift. And you deserve it. You can't seduce some unsuspecting hunk in a nosebleed cabin." Dani was co-president of the "Get Mac Laid" club with their other BFF, Susie. Reason number one why they forced her to pack all her sexy underwear. Dani was also not her conscience.

Mac, on the other hand, was not in the club. She wanted to relax, and after being dumped she'd be fine without a man hogging her bed or failing to bring her to orgasm.

"And what do I do at the end of the week?"

"You get your shit out of storage and return to my couch. I'll keep you well fed in tons of ice cream as we ponder the direction your life should head. But only if you enjoy yourself." Her voice turned serious. "Don't let that a-hole destroy you."

Mac swallowed against the emotion clawing up her throat. "Chad's history."

"Yeah, thanks to himself. You let him walk all over you."

"Dani." A headache, she was going to start her vacation with a headache.

"All right. I'm done. We can have this conversation next week. After you get that sexy little bod of yours laid."

Not likely, but Mac would deal with that later. She disconnected and discovered the mystery as to why the call had come through in the first place: wifi calling. Imagine that. Her life was in the toilet bowl, yet she watched the ocean tumble past. Sounds of music and chatter waved in from the open balcony in every direction. Except hers.

Make lemonade, Mackenzie.

She'd find a way, somehow. She turned back to her cabin, her gaze landing on two black bags nestled by her couch. Luggage. Just not her luggage. Mac sighed, contemplated calling Dani back, positive this idea was destined to fail. But the ship had set sail; she couldn't exactly leave.

The black luggage held no personality to it, except that it appeared beat up, as in been through a car wash more than once. A strip of gray duct tape covered a small portion. Mac wasn't even sure she wanted to touch the pieces but had to admit luggage didn't stay clean.

She shifted them, finding the tags, complete with the stateroom they were supposed to be in. Several floors down. How the hell had they managed to get into her room? It would be one of life's great mysteries. But maybe, just maybe, this person had her luggage?

Stranger things had happened. Case in point, this cruise vacation.

Mac poked her head out her door, but no staff members lurked in the hall. She turned back to the luggage. She could put them outside or lug them down to customer service. Both worked, but which one was right? She had a thing with decisions, namely that she sucked at making them. Hence the reason why she'd ended up in her current unemployed-while-on-a-cruise-ship predicament. She'd learned long ago that there always was a right and wrong answer, and she and her rotten lemon luck had a penchant for the wrong answer.

So which one would the right answer be? Leaving the bags outside or customer service? But, a little voice nagged, if she made it down to customer service, then she might as well dump them off where they belonged. Not like she had anything better to do. And maybe, just maybe, she'd manage to acquire her own luggage along the way.

Right or wrong, it gave her something to do. Mind made up, Mac grasped the handles, noting that for a beat-up pair of luggage, it moved easily on wheels. She checked the tags again. They both belonged in the same place. Time for a little adventure.

* * *

Cole Matterhorn pulled out the piece of paper tucked in his travel folder, a not-so-subtle reminder from his employee that his vacation did not provide an escape from the deadline two weeks away.

Have a great trip! And remember, we need a decision on going remote or renewing the lease ASAP. You know my vote, but this isn't my decision.

Yeah, he knew. A frustrated sigh escaped him as he shoved the paper back in the folder. Because he had no good answers. A damned if you do, damned if you don't situation, each option worse than the first. As a travel agent, remote made sense, but he'd worked hard to set up his office. He had long-standing customers that preferred those face-to-face visits. On top of that, the office was in a busy area, and he got regular leads that just happened to see his sign, the reason why he'd established himself there in the first place. He'd lose all of that if he went remote.

Tell that to the person raising his rent. New owners, decided he'd been paying too little and now wanted a big chunk more. Either decision guaranteed him a loss. He needed to sit down and crunch the numbers and figure out which loss looked best.

Not that he hadn't crunched the numbers more times than he could count already, each time hoping some magic loophole he'd missed would appear. A loophole hell-bent on avoiding him.

Cole rubbed the back of his neck. This postage stamp-size room in front of him would not aid him in any decision making. Nothing screamed "loss" like a tiny inside cabin. He could have upgraded, gone for something with more breathing space, or at least a goddamn window. No, he was "roughing it." As much as one could rough it on a cruise ship.

He was used to much more luxurious accommodations and was willing to wait until the last minute to book said accommodations. Had been since…well, since. No use planning for a future he damn well knew wasn't given. He once gave himself less than twelve hours to pack and board a plane.

Not this time.

This time he planned. Booked. Months out. He coordinated with Trent, his buddy, on the best phase of Trent's latest six-month cruise contract to party. And here he was, on Trent's final week. Trent understood him, one of the few people who had known him since before. Back when he had two legs and didn't use a prosthesis. Trent had been the lucky one and kept all his limbs.

And Cole didn't want to think about that recurring nightmare. Not on a crowded ship where someone could be plotting nefarious things. All passengers and luggage were x-rayed prior to boarding, but one never knew.

Cole's motto. Always be prepared.

He dropped his carry-on bag in the corner. The rest of his luggage had yet to arrive, but he knew to expect delays and planned accordingly. Still, not much to unpack, and his visitor was running late.

The conditioned air nipped at his skin and climbed up his right pant leg, cooling off his covered calf. A chill tickled his left ankle. Now was not the time to feel sensations from body parts he no longer possessed. It reminded him of things he didn't want to think about, about the fragility of life. The reason why he kept his circle small—less people to worry about.

If it left a hole inside, well, that blame belonged to the traumatic backstory he refused to let ruin his vacation.

Where was his damn friend?

As if on cue, a knock occurred at his door. "About damn time," Cole grumbled and headed over to open it. On the other side stood Trent, with his brown hair neatly combed, pristine staff shirt and pants, arms propped on the doorjamb.

A wide grin spread across Cole's face. "How the hell are you?" He reached out and then did the hug/back tap thing even if it became more hug than tap. Once released, Trent stepped into his cabin.

"I'm good," he said, sliding his hands into his pockets.

Cole laughed. "Tell me how you really feel."

Trent sighed and glanced at the now-closed door. "That I'm fucking relieved there's eight days left and then I can stop smiling and being polite to every goddamn person out there."

Cole patted his friend's shoulder. "There we go."

Trent shook out his hands, people-pleasing face back in position. "You got luggage? I'm hearing it's more messed up than normal this week."

"Nope, not yet."

Trent opened his mouth, but another knock occurred at Cole's door.

"Maybe your cabin steward found them?" Trent suggested.

Cole shrugged and moved to the door, opening it. No cabin steward on the other side. No, the person standing there had coppery locks framing her face, blue eyes popping out from stylish, black-framed glasses. Spellbinding. Her black top dipped low in front, revealing lush cleavage he had the sudden urge to bury into.

He forced his gaze back to her face, warding off the quick burst of lust that took even him by surprise. Only instead of regaining his composure, he got lost in the myriad of blues in her eyes.

"Umm, hi. This might sound strange, but I seem to have gotten your luggage delivered to my room, and I was kinda hoping maybe mine made it to yours?" She bit her lip, and his brain had trouble remembering how it worked.

"Hi." *No, say something better than that!* "Uh, no, your luggage isn't here. I haven't gotten any. Though I do appreciate this." He glanced down at the bags by her feet. Those were definitely his. He probably should have checked those out first, if his brain hadn't hung up an out-of-order sign.

She pushed the handles his way, and he grasped them, colliding with her hand for a second. A spark, a connection, a desire for skin, *something* occurred, and he knew he wanted to spend this next week getting to know her better.

Not his plans. Not his normal MO, but tell that to his out-of-order brain.

"Maybe we can help you find yours?" he asked, gesturing back to Trent and not wanting to know what his friend thought of his behavior. Cole had perfected the unattached method to life and didn't usually fumble over himself.

The woman glanced behind him and gave a small wave.

Trent moved Cole's bags into the room and reached a hand out. "I'm Trent Decker. You'll see me at a lot of the activities. And I was just telling Cole that the luggage situation is a bit of a mess this week. I'm sorry about that."

The woman shook his hand. "Well, that explains it. Mackenzie Laurel, but my friends call me Mac."

"Nice to meet you, Mac," Trent said.

"Mackenzie-Mac," Cole whispered, enchanted by her name. He really needed to get his brain back online. "I'm Cole Matterhorn."

She studied him. "You don't work here."

He chuckled. "Wouldn't be in a room if I did. Trent is my friend, and I'm...visiting, you could say."

"Preparing to bust my balls more like." Trent pressed his mouth closed, and Cole held in a laugh. His friend had great people skills, but after six months, his edges grew ragged.

"So why don't we help you? What does your luggage look like?" Cole asked.

Beside him, Trent scoffed. "Asks the man with boring black luggage."

"Hey! That duct tape comes in handy for identification purposes."

"Which would work if that's why you put it there."

Cole decided to ignore Trent and focus on his luggage goddess instead. Mac's cheeks pinked, and he feared he'd spend the next week following her around just for a glimpse of her smile. "My luggage actually shouldn't be too hard to find. It has lemons on it."

Trent leaned forward. "Lemons?"

Mac's face turned a deeper shade of red. "Yeah, sorta an inside joke and easy to find."

Cole clasped his hands together. "Well, then, why don't we head out and see where your lemon bags have migrated to?"

...

Mac didn't know whose luck she somehow managed to borrow, but walking down the halls with two nice and insanely good-looking men did not usually happen to her. Maybe the universe was attempting to make up for Chad?

Cole walked beside her. He had a slight limp, but she struggled to get her own sea legs and didn't pay it too much attention. Not when a black T-shirt covered his broad shoulders. Her sandy-haired new friend had the most amazing set of green eyes she'd ever seen.

Trent had jogged a few paces ahead and chatted with another staff member. He fit the description of tall, dark, and handsome, with light skin and dark hair. Really, there were worst ways to spend an afternoon.

"I have a theory. Indulge me in a few questions," Cole asked.

Mac nodded, eyes volleying from the luggage lining their perimeter to him so she could hear better. Not even anything yellow to steal her attention, never mind her set.

"People travel for one of three reasons, and I'm curious which one you are."

He paused, and she didn't know if it was for dramatic effect or not. "I'm going to need you to tell me those options in order to answer."

He laughed and held up three fingers, stopping along the side of the hall. "One, to meet up with friends or family, bonus points for a special occasion. Two, to get away with a loved one. Or three, because they need a chance to get away."

Mac mulled those options over. "I wonder, are you really curious about your theory, or trying, not so subtly I might add, to find out if I'm travelling with others?"

Cole held up his hands. "I am genuinely curious. I can't help it if it also has a nice ulterior motive."

His face held a faint smile and a ton of mirth in his eyes. Mac should be wary. The man was a total stranger, after all. But she wasn't going to make any friends if she didn't take chances. "If I had a companion, don't you think we'd be searching for luggage together?"

His smile grew. "Fair enough." He leaned in. "For the record, I'm a bit of one and three. While seeing Trent is my initial reason, he's busy, so my plan is to be an annoying pest any chance I get."

Mac laughed. Trent took that moment to jog back to them. He started talking far enough away that she couldn't hear him, though Cole didn't appear confused. Frustration wanted to simmer, but this was life for the hard of hearing. Doubly so when her companions didn't know she needed any accommodations. "What was that?" she asked once he got close enough.

Trent stopped two feet away. "Sorry about that. My friend over there did report a colorful piece of luggage that he thinks was heading one floor up. I'd check it out with you, but I've been called in. If you don't find it by dinner, definitely let customer service know."

Mac nodded.

"It was nice to meet you, Mac. I hope you'll take advantage of some of the activities on board. Cole, you bastard, I know I'll see you heckling me later."

"Admit it, you'd cry and pout if I didn't."

Trent shook his head. "You see what I have to put up with?"

Mac grinned. The lighthearted banter between the men spoke of years knowing each other and made her want to know both more. "I'm not buying this as a hardship."

Cole laughed, as did Trent.

"I see I'm leaving you in good hands. Pick on him. He needs it." Trent patted Cole on the back and gave them both a wave before taking off.

"Shall we try one floor up?" Cole asked.

"Ignoring your friend's request to pick on you?"

He shifted closer to her, warming her up with his presence. "I think more time together gives you the opportunity."

"You still want to help me?" Mac wasn't sure what to make of this. If Chad had been here, he'd be unpacking his own stuff while Mac looked for hers.

"Yes. I do."

His face seemed so serious for a moment, then he blanked it, back to the more jovial expression he wore. Her luggage pal intrigued her, more so than she would have thought.

"I'm not sure how to pick on someone kind enough to help me find my luggage."

"Spend some time with me and I'm sure you'll come up with something."

It was tempting, the time together not the picking on him. She followed him up a flight, glad he didn't talk along the way. Or at least, she didn't think he talked. With other passengers wandering up and down, she ended up behind him, noting that his limp grew more pronounced on the stairs. Maybe it wasn't as simple as sea legs? She pushed those thoughts down. She'd just met the man and doubted that was the teasing either Cole or Trent had in mind. They went back to scanning all the luggage pieces they could find, including catching a rolling cart with a bunch crowded in. A few random colors here and there, but still no lemons.

"Best to travel alone or with others?" Cole asked.

Mac considered as they shifted to one side, allowing a family of four to pass them. The narrow halls were even more problematic with the luggage. "Depends on the crowd. Both known and unknown people come with pluses and minuses."

"I hope new friends fall into the plus category."

"If we meet again on day eight, you can ask me."

"Maybe I want a chance to see you again before then, help make this vacation a good one for you."

She didn't know how to respond. A fling was in Dani and Susie's plans, not hers. Her life needed less complications. But she couldn't deny this man attracted her to him, both in looks and personality. Didn't she deserve some fun?

Up ahead, a flash of yellow caught her eye. "Wait, what's that?"

Mac jogged ahead, and just around the bend, she found

her two lemon-covered suitcases waiting for her.

"Unless someone else has your affinity for lemons—and if so we'll need to establish a meeting—I'm guessing these are yours."

Mac squatted down and hugged them. "Yes, yes they are."

Cole laughed. "I'm glad I've helped reunite you with your children."

Mac stood, grasping the handles of her bags. Relief washed over her. Now she could unpack and finally start relaxing.

"Before we part paths, would you care to accompany me dancing tonight?"

Mac hesitated. She wanted to see more of him, yes, but it went against her goal. Another decision, and she'd already chosen the bold one early.

He clearly caught her unease. "Or not. I will be doing trivia tomorrow to harass Trent. Maybe you'll show up and help me." Then he waved and turned, walking off in the opposite direction.

A pang of sadness hit her at his departure. She shook it aside. Nope. She did the right thing. Didn't she?

. . .

Two hours later, Mac stood in front of the mirror, fluffing her bangs so they fell to the side, no longer covering her dark-rimmed glasses. She took a deep breath of the vacation air, smoothing down her dress. She'd unpacked and felt much more settled in; nothing like knowing all her belongings were with her and she no longer had any "chores" to do until the end of the cruise. She hadn't accounted for being tempted by the dancing offer. The thought kept circling back to the front of her mind, poking at her resolve. She didn't know the where, but thanks to the luggage meeting, she did know how to find Cole again.

Maybe after dinner.

She wandered onto her balcony, needing a moment with the waves and fresh air. Leaning over the railing, she watched the white peaks of the small waves floating off the side of the moving ship. Point for Dani, because her breaths came easier in this environment. She almost hated how much she needed it, and that only made her more grateful for her friend's gift.

Her cell began to ring, and she answered it a second before the music connected with her brain cells. "Before He Cheats" had begun. *Shit, abort, abort.* Too late to abort.

"Mackenzie, where the hell are you?"

Mackenzie, her full name. Chad hadn't used her full name since he asked her out to dinner after her first week at the job. She could have said yes or no. She chose wrong. "Hello, Chad. Are you really going to be formal with a woman you once went down on? Poorly, I might add."

The silence gratified her until the murmur of voices and muffled laughter floated through. Speakerphone. Which meant he was on site at the most recent construction zone. She glanced at the water and wondered if it would be better to jump.

Chad cleared his throat, and the murmurs died down. "Why aren't you at work?"

"Besides the fact that you fired me?" And why did it take him this long to follow up?

"Mackenzie, sweetie." His voice dripped with fake concern. "That was just a lover's quarrel."

Was she still on speakerphone? Who cared? "No, dumping me because you're fucking the boss's daughter was a lover's quarrel. Is Kit there? Can I say hi?"

"Mac." Chad's voice came out strained, and she could all but see his clenched jaw and vein popping on his forehead.

Not a good look on him.

"Look, you cheated. You dumped me. You fired me. And you moved all my belongings out of the house. Where exactly do you expect me to be?" Certainly not surrounded by water.

"I need you to help finish this project."

Her hands shook as she thought of all the hours she put into helping him design and construct this latest building, how she practically had her own architecture degree with everything he ran by her. "No."

"No?"

She could almost see his pompous eyebrow raised.

"Yes, Chad. No. I understand you're not familiar with this word. Become familiar."

She hung up her phone and raised her hand to toss it in the water. Bye-bye, Chad. But that would also cut off both her BFFs.

The breeze ruffled her hair as she remained frozen, hand raised like a humorous millennial statue. The warm wind encouraged her to break free, be spontaneous for a change. Live. She could do all that and keep her phone. She went into her settings and disabled wifi calling. She'd explain to Dani later, via email. With a push off the railing, she headed out of her cabin. A nice, carb-heavy meal was exactly what she needed.

And absolutely no dancing with her luggage friend. Just look at what happened the last time she said yes to a date. She shuddered. And it had nothing to do with the cold interior hall.

Down on the third floor, Mac trailed after a waiter named Dei from Indonesia, as her nametag informed. Dei wore a crisp white dress shirt and black pants, the same as all the other waiters and assistants regardless of gender. She led Mac through the posh dining room, a silent two-person game of follow the leader. Mac smoothed the lace edge of her yellow top over her black pants as the woman weaved through tables draped in long, snowy cloths. The few tables with occupants had people talking and laughing. The noise blended into the atmosphere, where a piano played in some distant corner unseen. Everywhere she looked she saw groups of people together. Mac's good feeling faded, another bitter reminder she was alone.

Beyond being alone, she'd forgotten the acoustics of a large dining room. Between the piano and talking and dishware clatter, her ability to hear would be questionable. The last time she cruised, she'd spent most of the time at the buffet with her friends. Still as loud but quicker, and more control over who they sat with.

Now she was on her own. She should have gone to the buffet, but that would have made her feel even more alone than she did at this moment, walking through a dining room, following a waiter, with no one waiting for her. The temptation to veer off in the opposite direction and get the hell out brewed, but she stuck to her guns. No sense confusing Dei and she was hungry. She silently prayed for a table in a quiet area and loud people to interact with.

Dei stopped in front of a round table set for eight people. Two had already arrived: a woman with short, spiky black hair contrasting with her light yet tanned skin and a man with cropped dark hair, dark skin, and a goatee. They were deep in conversation, smiles on their faces, and looked up as Mac sat down.

Dei put Mac's napkin on her lap and handed her a menu. She thanked her and turned back to her dinner mates. They eyed her curiously over their menus.

"Hi, I'm Quinn, and this is Rob," said the woman. Mac didn't know if it was dumb luck, the mostly empty tables surrounding them, or Quinn's voice, but she thanked her lucky stars she didn't have to start her dining experience by asking, "What?"

Rob smiled.

"I'm Mac."

Quinn leaned forward. "You scoping out the single scene like me? Tell me what you've found." Her eagerness was as apparent as the dip in her low-cut top.

"Please excuse her zeal. It's her thirtieth birthday, and she's determined the stars have aligned and she'll find her 'one true love' on a boat somewhere over the Atlantic Ocean." Rob dramatized his statement with wide hand motions.

"Single, yes. Haven't seen *too* much." Though Mac tried to push it aside, she couldn't help thinking of Cole's brilliant green eyes.

"Oohhh, that's something." Quinn squirmed. "See, she's found someone already."

Mac nearly choked on her own saliva. "I had a luggage debacle and had a nice stranger help me find mine, that's it."

"Your smile tells a different story, but I've got all week to harass you," Rob said.

Quinn thumbed her friend. "He thinks he's the relationship guru. Except I keep reminding him that, hello, he's failed with me." She displayed her empty left ring finger.

"Because you, darling, are impossible. I'll be lucky to get you paired off before you dry up."

The easy camaraderie lifted Mac's spirits yet again. "What about you, Rob? If you're so good at relationships, why aren't you in one?"

"Oohhh, I like her," Quinn said.

Rob smoothed the napkin in his lap. "I recently ended a relationship."

"Bastard cheated on him," Quinn stage whispered.

"On that, I have personal experience," Mac said.

"Go on," Rob encouraged.

"My ex cheated on me, dumped me, and, since he was my

boss, fired me."

"Well, damn, that takes the cake from Ethan." Quinn placed a hand on Rob's shoulder.

"Honey, you deserve whoever put that delicious smile on your face."

"I deserve a fun trip and new friends, that's it."

"Right there with you."

"New friends are great," Quinn began. "But I want a mate. And he's on this ship."

Rob patted Quinn's head. "She's delusional, but really a sweetie."

All through dinner, Mac chatted with Quinn and Rob. Their table filled up with an older couple and a similar-aged group of three, but mostly they chatted amongst themselves, ignoring the younger patrons. At times she needed some repetition, but not as often as she feared. She still suspected this was another epic case of spoiling lemons. But at least she'd have fun while they spoiled.

Napkins settled on empty dessert plates when Rob leaned forward. His lips moved, but Mac missed whatever he said. She shook her head and prepared to explain, but Rob shifted closer and spoke again louder, without any further prompting from her. "Any plans for the evening?"

"None yet."

"We were thinking of going dancing." Quinn bounced in her seat.

Mac laughed. Dancing—the secret word of the day. And her laughter had her new friends giving her curious smiles. "My luggage friend had offered dancing earlier, but I said no."

"Well, why did you do that?" Quinn asked.

Rob nodded. "I have to agree with Quinn."

Mac flailed her hands, flustered. "I don't need a rebound, but I do need time to get over my ex."

"Then you'll have to go dancing with us." Quinn stood and grabbed Mac's hand, pulling her up. Mac contemplated protesting, but what else would she do? Besides, she enjoyed Quinn and Rob's company.

Maybe she needed less decision making and more going with the flow?

Quinn laced her arms through Mac and Rob's once they got into the open area of the hall. They navigated across the ship, making small talk about the things they passed, until they arrived at the intimate lounge. Inside, the dimmed atmosphere had a large dancing area in the middle, with small round tables along the side. Music with heavy bass hit them, a live band providing the ambiance. People danced and sat at tables, and waiters wandered around, taking orders and delivering drinks.

"Singles," Quinn squealed. "Lots of singles. I bet my future hubby is in there."

Rob patted Quinn's head. "Down, girl. They might not be singles. Check for cheating bastards first."

Mac heard them since they still stood by the side, but the deeper they ventured into the room, the harder it became. She shifted her attention to checking out the area, all the happy people enjoying the first night of their vacation, letting them chat amongst themselves. She was the third wheel, after all. Let them rope her back in when necessary.

Her gaze connected with one table, and she stopped walking. Cole sat there, nursing a drink in a short glass. He had one leg crossed over the other. Beige pants, green polo, and slicked-back hair. He'd taken her breath away when he answered his door earlier, but seeing him refreshed was even better.

"What have you found?" Quinn said into Mac's ear.

Mac shook her head and turned away from Cole. Which was good, because the man surely would realize someone had been staring soon. She tried to find her voice. "That's the luggage guy."

"Oh! Where, where!" Mac gestured and gave a brief description. Rather than comment on her friend from earlier, Quinn and Rob both grabbed one of her hands and, before she could register, had pulled her over to where Cole sat.

So much for avoiding him.

The noise grew louder, then softer as they got close, and her ears registered Rob talking. "...and this is Quinn. Mac tells us you helped her find her luggage."

Mac's cheeks felt hot, and her fair skin and red hair meant she knew she'd be blushing right down to her cleavage.

Cole smiled and shook Rob's hand. "Yes, I had the pleasure of meeting Mackenzie-Mac earlier."

His eyes lingered on her, no mistaking a hunger there, one she felt pulsing more than the beat of the music. He'd done that once before, combining her name and nickname, and something about it felt like an endearment.

Quinn sat down, and so did Rob, forcing Mac to sit next to Cole. "What are the odds we all came to the same lounge?"

"While there are several places for music at the moment, this is the only one offering dancing. So the odds are decent if the activity is the same."

Cole looked at Mac as he spoke, a curve to his lips, as though she came here looking for him. And she didn't. She came because of Quinn and Rob, and she'd been looking around because... Crap, maybe she had been looking for him.

"I met Quinn and Rob at dinner, and they wanted me to join them."

Cole nodded, though she doubted he believed her. He leaned forward. "Then will you allow me a dance?"

This man's eyes could eat her up, and she'd let him. Mac swallowed and tried to find the rational part of her brain, but it currently drooled over the man in front of her. She glanced at her new friends, both gesturing for her to go.

Not my decision then, so maybe it won't be wrong.

"Will one dance satisfy you?" she asked.

His grin turned lavish, and she squeezed her legs together. "I highly doubt it."

She swore sparks flew as he reached out a hand for her. When was the last time she'd experienced sparks anyways? Too long, certainly not with Chad. And that thought settled it. She turned off her brain, determined to simply enjoy herself this evening.

. . .

Cole laced his fingers between Mac's, his warm palm against her cold one. He should stop, and let her go. The woman he met earlier gave off the indication she didn't want more than a new friend. Yet he wanted more, from her in specific, be it a dance or trivia or something more sensual. He held on to her hand, guiding her to the dance floor. He didn't often consider himself a lucky man, but he appreciated the chance at having this dance with her.

A new song began, slower than the last, and he didn't pause to figure out what song it was, simply used it as an opportunity to place his free hand low on her back and pull her close. With her heels on, she was nearly his height. Something settled in him at having her close, but he pushed that thought right out of his mind. He wasn't good for anything but a good time.

He'd been in the lounge, looking around, seeing if anyone captured him the way Mac had. And then she was there and no one else mattered. It didn't match his typical unattached relationship status. At least a cruise came with a clear end date, regardless of how she felt in his arms, they'd part paths on day nine.

And if that caused a strange sensation in his chest, he'd

ignore it. No one would be looking at him for a happy ending, because he couldn't give them one.

Cole leaned in close to Mac's ear, pulling on the charming vacation guy most people knew him for. "Is this your first cruise?"

He pulled back, and she faced him, brows furrowed. "What did you say?"

He must have been too soft. He leaned in and repeated himself at a higher volume.

This time a smile graced her beautiful face, and he nearly forgot why he preferred to remain unattached.

"Not even close."

"What's the tally?" He continued swaying, their bodies close but not touching. He wanted touching.

The hand on his shoulder began tapping, one finger at a time. "Eight. You?"

A fellow cruiser and frequent vacationer. Granted, the odds of finding that while on vacation increased dramatically, but it warmed him to her nonetheless. "This makes ten for me."

"Favorite vacation spot?"

He spun her around, then brought her in a little closer. She'd taken the reins of his standard intro conversation and damn if that didn't turn him on. They continued to sway with the music, their thighs bumping along with their chests. *Combustible* was the word that came to mind.

He did a quick review of his favorite trips, though the answer came easily to mind. "Italy. Great romance, amazing architecture. And…gelato."

Mac laughed. "True, the gelato is to die for."

"Worst vacation spot?" he asked.

She scrunched her nose. "Mexico."

"Ahh, but the ruins are magnificent."

"I'm sure they are. I only got to spend time in my own bathroom."

He stopped swaying, waiting her out.

Her cheeks flushed. He liked the look on her. "I, uh, ate something that didn't agree with me."

Poor dear. He shook his head, laughed, and held her closer as he resumed swaying. "Oh no."

"I remember eating something that looked like a delicious donut but did not taste as expected. And then...hello toilet, my old friend." She rested her forehead on his shoulder for a moment, and he gave her back a light, comforting rub. "I want a do-over one day so I can enjoy the beauty I only got glimpses of before. And this is not a conversation to have while dancing."

"Any time with you is fine by me." And he meant it, more so than he'd meant anything in a long, long time. It nagged, threatened to scare him right off the boat, but Mac remained in his arms, and he didn't want to let that go.

The song stopped, and they broke apart to clap. The sudden air between them made him miss her warmth and want to reach for her again. When the music started up again, he pulled her close. "Surely you're not finished with me already?"

Her blue eyes volleyed back and forth between his. He figured he'd either played his final card and she'd be gone or he'd be ignoring the other single women for the rest of the cruise. He feared the latter would be true regardless.

Mac reached out, placing her hands on his shoulders. "I think I can give you one more dance before finding my friends."

"At least?"

Her smile rose her cheeks. "We'll see."

Relief uncoiled as he collected her back into his arms. He'd have to figure out what strange magic possessed him. For now he planned to enjoy it, and he'd worry about the rest when he landed back in Massachusetts.

Day 2: Bahamas

Cole woke up in a pitch-black room. His body rocked from the ship, much like a baby being rocked by a parent. Heavy eyelids yearned to flutter closed. Before he succumbed, he grabbed his cell and checked the time.

Seven a.m. He bolted upright and rubbed his eyes. Damn inside cabin. No natural light shined through. It could be two a.m. or two p.m. and he wouldn't know the difference. Without that familiar glow of morning sunlight, it felt like the middle of the night. And he had less than half an hour to meet up with Trent at the gym.

But first, he'd lay his head down for five more...

With a gasp, he jerked awake and checked his phone again. Seven fifteen. No more time to pretend it was still the middle of the night.

He hated inside cabins.

Hand slapping the wall, he searched for the light and flipped the switch. The sudden onslaught of bright light burned his retinas. "Son of a bitch," he shouted into the empty room. "This is not a fucking vacation."

When his eyes stopped tearing, he swung his legs over the side of the bed. His right foot touched the carpet. His left leg ended below his knee and hung in the air, even if his brain still thought his missing foot should be on the floor with his right. He stretched the left knee and ran his hands over the bottom of the stump. A little reality check to stop the phantom sensations. Then he grabbed the smooth liner and rolled it on. Once secured, he collected the prosthesis and fit the stump into the socket. With two working legs, he threw on jogging shorts and a T-shirt.

By the time he made it to the gym, Trent was already on a treadmill, pounding away the miles. "Sleep well, sunshine?" he teased.

"Blow me." Cole got on the treadmill next to Trent. After he tested the surface, he began a slow warm-up.

Trent allowed Cole a few minutes of warming up before speaking. "No running leg?"

Cole punched up the speed. "How many legs do you want me to pack?"

"So you finally got one?"

Cole rubbed his neck and ignored his friend. "Not much of a runner anymore." Although the little running he allowed did wear down his prosthesis at an accelerated rate. His longest barely made it to two-and-a-half years.

Trent increased his speed, showing off his two working legs. Cole waited for him to rehash the age-old debacle. Trent didn't. "How did things go with Mac? Did you find her luggage?"

Cole started a light jog. "Yeah, your informant was right. We found it a few minutes later." He almost wished her luggage had taken longer to find, but it didn't matter, as long as he saw her again.

Trent studied him as only a decade-long friend could. "I thought I saw sparks. You saw her again, didn't you?"

"Bumped into her again in one of the lounges and got to dance with her." He could still smell her floral scent, feel her waist under his hand. No need to mention to Trent she'd initially declined his dancing suggestion.

Trent shook his head, sweat forming on his brow. He said something under his breath. All Cole caught was, "this one."

"This one what?"

Trent didn't look at him. "Nothing. What's up with the lease situation?"

Conversation swerve. Trent would share his piece when he felt like it. The problem with going through hell with someone, it forged a bond thicker than blood. "I haven't decided yet."

Trent hopped to the stationary side of his treadmill to look at Cole. "I thought you needed to make a decision before the trip?"

Cole punched up the speed. "I have two weeks."

"Oh man." Trent resumed running. "You are so screwed."

"How am I supposed to make a decision? They both suck. Either I lose my best clients or I hand my profits over and cut paychecks. Damned if I do, damned if I don't."

"Ahh, so that's why you saw Mac again. She's a distraction."

Cole rummaged over that. He certainly wasn't thinking about rent or business while staring into her blue eyes. But it was more than that. It was…her. He just wanted to be around her.

Strange foreign sensations.

"What if she is?"

"You like running from your problems."

Cole tapped his prosthesis. "I'm not running anywhere."

"Not as long as you don't get a running prosthesis. And as long as you don't, then you don't have to worry about it."

"So what am I running from here?"

"Making a serious decision."

Steam threatened to come out his ears, and not due to physical activity. "I run a successful business. I make decisions all the time."

"So what's the problem? Decide. Pay more for rent or go remote. Easy."

Cole grounded his teeth together. "Not easy, it's a lose lose situation."

"No. It's a decision that comes with risks in either direction."

Trent let the final word hang there, the fact that they both shied away from risks. Nothing like being in a terrorist attack at twenty-two to change, well, everything.

"Okay, maybe I do want a distraction. Or maybe I just like Mac and want to spend time with her."

"That's the other thing. I'm used to you playing the crowd more first, waiting a day or two."

"What does it matter which day I hook up with someone?"

"You've been a one-note man for nine years. I'm only pointing out a stray from character." Trent glanced around, then leaned toward Cole. "Now me, when I get back on land, I'm staging a month-long boink-a-thon."

"Didn't get enough while on board?"

"Can't, unless I want to be dropped off at the nearest island."

Cole slowed down. "You've been celibate for six months?"

Trent kept his eyes forward and his voice down. "Not quite. Passengers are forbidden, coworkers more lenient. Both have their ways."

Cole shook his head and punched up the speed. "I think I'll stick to being a passenger and not a crewmember."

"And keep distracting yourself when you need to make a decision."

"What happened to my friend?"

"Long six months."

After the workout, Cole's grumbling stomach demanded food, and lots of it. He would have preferred the dining room, but his stomach pulled him toward the speed of the buffet. He managed the crowd, ignored the stares and whispers his leg drew, and weaved his way in and out of lines. With his plate piled high, he found a small table by the window.

He devoured half his plate and ordered a coffee before his stomach let him lean back and relax. Outside the water zipped past the boat, white tops rustling far below. From his position, he watched the chairs by the pool fill, mostly with young women in string bikinis angling their chairs to get the best sun. None of the hot babes were as tempting as one redhead with black-framed glasses named Mackenzie-Mac.

Distraction, thinking about Mac when he needed to focus on business. He had data to compile, advertising to research, and enough numbers to crunch that his head already swam.

He dug his phone out of his pocket and checked his emails, finding nothing from his employee back home.

From: Cole Matterhorn
To: Dani Martin
Subject: Update

How's the office? What happened to that big family trip I was working on before I left? Any information on that advertising program we were looking into?

P.S. I really wanted that suite. You should have let me have it.

He rubbed the back of his neck. That suite would have prevented his late morning start. But Dani had held fast to Trent's "roughing it" orders.

His phone dinged before he could put it away.

FROM: DANI MARTIN
TO: COLE MATTERHORN
SUBJECT: RE: UPDATE

THE FAMILY TRIP IS BOOKED. TOLD YOU I COULD CLOSE IT AND I DID. COMPLETE WITH UPGRADES SINCE THEY GOT TO WORK WITH ME. ADVERTISING DETAILS DID COME THROUGH. I'LL FORWARD THEM. YOUR TIMING SUCKS, MATTERHORN. I'D LIKE TO KNOW IF I'LL HAVE A JOB IN A FEW WEEKS.

AND YOU STAY AWAY FROM THAT SUITE. I FOUND A MUCH MORE DESERVING OCCUPANT.

He laughed and quickly typed a response.

FROM: COLE MATTERHORN
TO: DANI MARTIN
SUBJECT: RE: UPDATE

GOOD JOB ON THE FAMILY TRIP. YOU'LL STILL HAVE A JOB. IT'S ONLY THE LOCATION THAT'S UP IN QUESTION. AND WITH ALL THE SUITES ON BOARD, HOW WOULD I EVEN FIND YOUR MYSTERIOUS PASSENGER?

He'd been ten minutes away from swapping his room to the sole remaining suite when she booked it for a friend and refused to say anything more. On a ship this big, he knew even if he remembered which room it was, he'd never meet the person. Another email came in, one with the advertising details. He'd settle in and analyze it later.

"Hey, Cole, right?"

He looked up to see a dark-haired man with a goatee standing in front of him, full plate in hand.

Cole now had a perfect distraction to the email. Damn, Trent was right. "Rob, nice to see you." He gestured to the empty chair across from him, and Rob sat down.

"You looked quite friendly with my friend last night."

He'd managed to turn two dances into three before finally letting her go, and even then he had been reluctant. "Mackenzie-Mac is..." What? What could he say to capture how light he felt when around her? "She's amazing."

"I've only just met her, too, but a friend is a friend," Rob narrowed his eyes, "and I stick up for friends." He gestured with the knife he used to cut his pancakes, not quite a threat, but Cole would be smart to stay on his good side, just in case.

Cole leaned back, sipped his coffee. He could hardly do much damage in a week. Nothing to worry about. "Good friends are hard to come by. I'm here visiting one of mine."

Rob looked around. "Where is he?"

"Working. He runs a bunch of the activities."

"You meet on a ship?"

Cole resumed eating his breakfast. "Nope, back home. We went to college together. And you're here for a friend, right?" he asked.

Rob put the silverware down. "Yeah, I am." His voice held a note of mistrust.

Cole did his best not to grin. He read people well, part of why he succeeded at his job. "I'm getting the vibe that she's happy to be here. You, not so much."

Rob chuckled. "Good catch. This is only my second cruise. Not really my thing, I prefer resorts on land. But it's Quinn's birthday, and subsequent manhunt. Why she thinks a cruise will land her a husband I don't know."

Cole choked on his food. "Husband? I understand a fling, but a husband? On a ship with international passengers?"

Rob shrugged. "Never said she was the brightest crayon. She follows her gut. Her gut says this ship. Of course, her gut isn't always right, but that's a story for another day."

With no other response in his head, Cole laughed. "Looking for someone yourself?"

"Maybe a fling. I'm here to enjoy myself. Bad relationships take their toll."

Cole raised his coffee mug in salute. "Well said." Not that he stayed long enough for a relationship to turn bad, though he suspected a few of his exes had him labeled as such.

"And you've already found your fling, have you not?"

Cole choked on a piece of egg. "Perhaps." He pushed down the awkward and unfamiliar resistance to Rob's statement.

Rob studied his face and was silent for a full minute. "Well, okay then."

Cole waited for more, but Rob focused on his pancakes.

"You have something to say?" Cole asked.

Rob shook his head. "Nah, not yet. We'll see if I have something to share in a week."

Cole didn't know what to make of his new friend. A fling was a fling. He wasn't looking for anything more than a good time. He no longer had the capacity for more.

・・・

Mac woke up with daylight pouring through the heavy blue drapes. She stretched and took in her surroundings. Nope, she hadn't dreamed the previous day. She was on a cruise.

She wanted to feel bad about it, she really did; after all, her post-cruise life was most definitely in the toilet, and she needed to start looking for a new office administrator job ASAP. But the smile grew, and she snuggled under the blankets, breathing in the conditioned air that tasted of over-purification and vacation.

She really needed to find Dani a suitable souvenir.

Mac reached for her phone, squinting at the small icons since she hadn't bothered to grab her glasses. Nine a.m. She had an hour before trivia, an hour to decide if she wanted to see Cole and Trent again or not. And who was she kidding? She wanted to see them again. Especially after a night dancing with Cole. Maybe Dani and Susie were on to something with the fling thing.

She clicked over to her email and scanned through the growing messages. Spam, advertisement, spam, a message from Chad—delete—spam, and a message from Susie. Open.

From: Susie Patel
To: Mackenzie Laurel
Subject: Vacay!

How's the vacation? Meet anyone yet? I know you'll find some happiness on this trip. Nowhere to go but up from where you are, right? Make that lemonade, sweetie.

Hugs,
Susie

Mac loaded a response.

From: Mackenzie Laurel
To: Susie Patel
Subject: RE: Vacay!

Yes.
Love, Mac

And hit send. That should have Susie shitting her pants in anticipation for the next few days. Which, perhaps, was not a nice thing to do to her pregnant friend.

The next message was from Dani.

FROM: DANI MARTIN
TO: MACKENZIE LAUREL
SUBJECT: CRUISE GOALS

GOALS FOR YOUR TRIP: 1) HAVE FUN. 2) GET LAID.

REPEAT BOTH OFTEN.

LOVE YA!

Mac smiled and typed up a reply.

FROM: MACKENZIE LAUREL
TO: DANI MARTIN
SUBJECT: RE: CRUISE GOALS

WORKING ON IT. AND MAYBE I'M STARTING TO SEE YOUR POINT ABOUT GETTING LAID…

Sent. If her two BFFs talked, they could put together a few small puzzle pieces. Maybe she should split the story and give each half? Thoughts for the remainder of the cruise.

A quick shower later, she was on a hunt for breakfast when she bumped into Quinn, who somehow managed to run to her in what looked like four-inch heels. Mac had to admit, the heels did show off her killer legs. Then again, the daisy dukes helped.

"Oh thank God, someone I know!" Quinn clutched onto Mac's arm like a life vest. "I'm lost. I could get lost in the stateroom. I don't know why I ventured out on my own. Actually, I do, since Rob was already out and I was hungry. But this ship is so huge I don't know where I'm going. I stopped to ask one of the stateroom attendants but his limited English meant I ended up by the theater."

Mac patted Quinn's arm and steered her toward the chart on the wall with a map of the ship. "Meet your new

BFF. These exist on every floor."

Quinn braced two hands on the wall and stared at the chart. "I could kiss this." She studied the chart. "But this still makes no sense." A sob escaped her lips.

Mac explained the chart and then led Quinn to one of the small eateries. With a little food in her system, Quinn calmed down. "Your date last night was a hunk."

Mac smiled, warm thoughts brewing of her sandy-haired dance partner.

"You seeing him again?"

Mac checked her watch. "In about fifteen minutes."

Quinn squealed. "You two looked so cute together." She sighed dramatically.

"We just met yesterday. If anything, we'll have a light fling and go our separate ways." She had no bandwidth to handle anything else after this cruise. She needed to arrive home refreshed and ready for battle.

Quinn ate a piece of fruit. "What if it's more? Nothing wrong with that, is there?"

Mac lost interest in her muffin. Her life couldn't handle more. She already had enough on her plate. "What about the guy I saw you dancing with last night?"

"Nice guy. No spark. When it's right, I'll be swept right off my feet." A faraway, dreamy look entered her dark eyes.

"What? Like love at first sight?"

Quinn waved a fork in Mac's direction. "Exactly."

"You know it doesn't always work that way, right? An instant spark can turn sour, or no spark can develop into one."

"I know it sounds foolish, but all my life I've always known one day I would look up, and boom, there he'd be. Then we'd spend time together and find out if the spark is real."

"And have you had a spark before?"

Quinn sighed. "A few. But that's what dating is for,

learning if it's the right spark." She took another bite of fruit. "And what about your guy? Are you going to tell me there was no spark?"

Mac forced herself to pull a piece off her muffin and pop it in her mouth. Thoughts of meeting Cole made her breath hitch. "Spark? Definitely. But one that will last only for the cruise."

"Don't sell yourself short."

Nope, she was done with her muffin. "I've just ended a relationship, badly. I'm not in any position to find something more."

Quinn cocked her head to the side. "Leave your options open. You may surprise yourself."

• • •

Cole leaned against the closed piano in the nautical-themed lounge. Trent reached into a big bag filled with papers. "Psst, where's the answers?" he asked.

Trent pulled the papers from the bag in a way that blocked Cole's view. "If you want to win, you'll have to do so fair and square. These keychains are precious commodities." He dangled one in front of Cole.

"A keychain, because cruisers carry keys?"

Trent shrugged. He took in the crowd, a few teams already in the seats and a handful of people walking in, either passing through or stopping to participate. No one joining them at the piano. "Your date standing you up?"

Cole ignored the twinge in his gut and checked his watch. "Not yet." Though the ship had been cleared to disembark, she could have opted to head out to the island instead.

"I hope she does. That would be sweet," Trent murmured as Cole caught orange and yellow out of the corner of his eye, reminding him of the marigolds his mother loved so much.

A fleeting thought floated to mind, that he'd found his own marigold. He stuffed that thought down into the depths of the ocean.

"She's here," he whispered to Trent and nodded in Mac's direction. She wore a yellow halter top that brought his attention to her cleavage and shorts that showed off her curvy legs. He puffed out his chest as she came close, wondering when he got to be so foolish, and plastered a smile on his face with surprising ease, since it was already there. "Mackenzie-Mac, we meet again."

She blushed, and the freckles on her nose and cheeks intensified. She held up her coffee mug. "I come with coffee, so in about ten minutes I should be moderately helpful." She grinned and took a sip.

He stared at her lips as she licked an errant drop of coffee. Trent cleared his throat.

Mac smiled at him. "Hi, Trent, thanks again for helping me find my luggage."

"All in a day's work, happy I could help."

She glanced at Trent's nametag, which displayed his name and country. "Not that the accent doesn't give me a clue, but whereabouts in the US are you from?"

Trent gave Cole a look that spelled trouble. "New Hampshire. Hudson, to be exact."

Recognition warmed her eyes, and Cole's stomach did a funny flip that he didn't understand. She knew the area. She wasn't asking how she knew Trent, but dammit, she was local. And the raised eyebrows Trent passed his way said he wasn't the only one figuring this out.

"I'm just over the border into Massachusetts. Methuen."

One town over. She lived one town over from him. And their paths hadn't crossed until they were on a boat on the Atlantic. It should have scared him, should have sent him running in the opposite direction, ready to ensure that this thing between them remained on ship only. Instead, it filled him with something strangely akin to hope. There lay potential between them, and the fear he'd become so accustomed to was strangely absent.

Hell of a time to want something different.

"How's the weather back home?" Trent asked, grinning a bit too much for Cole's liking.

"Cold," Mac joked.

"I've been here for six months. I'm in for a rude awakening when I get back," Trent began. "This is my last week. I keep reminding myself fall in New England is no worse than the theater empty, but I'm going to feel like a snowbird."

Mac laughed. "You'll grumble like the rest of us."

A passenger came up to them, and Trent shifted his attention. Cole waited for Mac to ask where he lived. She didn't. He followed her to a table and sat down.

"Methuen, huh?" he asked, unused to the nerves swimming in his system.

Mac held up a hand. "Look, I get it, you're probably local. But my life is in the absolute gutter right now. This trip is for me to relax and recharge. That's it. I don't want anything longer than this vacation. So it doesn't matter if we're local or not."

Hope hadn't deflated this fast since the doctor told him they couldn't save his leg. He shook it off. He didn't do commitment, she didn't want it, no problem.

And yet his brain had already jumped to the possibility of going remote and having more time to spend with her. What the hell was wrong with him?

"You okay?" Mac asked, placing a hand on his arm.

He hadn't realized any of his internal chaos had been visible. He opened his mouth, then closed it, realizing he wanted to tell her where he lived, just like he wanted to find out what demons possessed her.

"I'm fine." He needed to chill out, get back to the happy-go-lucky guy he showed everyone, none of this other bullshit.

Clearly she took his fine as his full answer. She spun a cushiony chair. "I want a chair like this in my home." She sighed.

She stopped twirling as her eyes drifted down his body and settled on his legs. Since he wore shorts, he knew she saw his prosthesis for the first time. He'd seen wonder, shock, disgust. Mac was the first one to display curiosity. Before she could ask a question, before he could answer, the speaker system kicked on.

"Good morning, ladies and gentlemen." Trent's voice filled the room. Cole glanced over to see a microphone in his friend's hand. "It's ten o'clock on our lovely first full day. My name's Trent, and I'll be your host for the morning. I need you all to break into teams." He moved items on the table in front of him. "Each team grabs a paper and pencil and comes up with a unique name." Trent put down the microphone as a few stragglers decided to join and others moved about and collected their supplies.

Mac rose. "I'll grab the papers." He watched her sashay over to the table.

Did she do that because of the leg? *Let it go, man*, he told himself. *It doesn't mean anything.* She didn't want anything more than a week, so where he lived or how he lost his leg didn't matter. *Relax, enjoy her company.* The relationship could fizzle before the end of the cruise, anyways. And they'd never bumped into each other on land. Who was to say anything would change?

No need to operate any differently than he had for the past nine years.

Mac arrived back at the table. She began writing at the top of the page before her rear landed in her seat. Once finished, she shifted and turned the paper in his direction, giving him a grin that made his mouth dry.

He looked at the paper. At the top of the page, her curvy handwriting spelled out: Strangers.

He locked eyes with hers.

"Our team name. Okay, it's not that creative but—"

"Perfect," he responded.

The top of her nose crinkled when she smiled, and he had the sudden urge to lean across the small round table and fit his mouth against hers. Taste her shiny lip gloss, her coffee, her. When had anyone ever gotten under his skin so quickly with so much ease?

"You're dangerous, Mackenzie-Mac."

"Only to my own welfare."

Any further conversation was interrupted by Trent. "All right, ladies and gentlemen, let us begin our first round of trivia. Today is general trivia, and we're playing for this lovely keychain." He held up the aforementioned object. "Can I get an 'ooh'?" The audience obliged. "Can I get an 'ahh'?" Again, the crowd ate right out of his hand. "These are hot commodities, folks. The only other place you can get these is in the gift shop, so don't miss your chance."

The audience laughed as Trent smirked, right at home in front of a crowd. "Here's how this is going to work. I'll read a question and you'll write down the best answer your team can come up with. Let's begin."

Cole scooted closer to Mac. She leaned toward him, eyeing him over the rim of her glasses. "Now would probably be a good time to warn you: I'm pretty bad at trivia."

"I'm not here to win."

He held her eye contact, all that blue uninhibited without the lenses in front of them. Lost in the best ocean he had ever seen, he missed Trent's first question.

So did Mac.

"Ahem," Trent said, standing by their table, microphone

by his hip. "The first question was: in the English language, what letter begins the most words?" He smirked and walked away.

Mac flushed pink and angled her pen on the paper. Cole couldn't think. He could only watch her. Vivid images came to mind of different ways he could get those cheeks to pink and he wanted to try every single one. "Probably *S*, right? Or *T*...maybe *P*?" She pushed her glasses up on her nose. "What do you think?"

That he had limited blood supply to his brain. "No clue."

"*S*, it's gotta be *S*." Her hand froze over the paper. "No, *T*, definitely *T*." She wrote it down, then bit her lip and looked up at him. He wanted to soothe that dented lip.

Cole cleared his throat. "*T* works."

The microphone kicked in. "All right, folks, next question, this one cruise-themed: what is the largest body of water in the world?"

Mac looked at him expectantly.

"I think, it's rather possible, the answer is your eyes."

She blushed and blinked. "What, do I have anime eyes or something?"

Crap, he was off his game. Way off. "Umm, err, I..."

She burst out laughing. "Relax, it was sweet. A bit creepy, but sweet."

He forced his brain into working order. "The answer is probably the Pacific or the Atlantic."

"Pacific," she burst out, blue eyes racing across the ceiling. "No, it's probably the Atlantic, I mean, if you're looking at a flat map the Pacific covers two sides, which has to be misleading."

"Atlantic it is."

She wrote it down as Trent ambled over. He looked at the paper. Shook his head. "You two are not having a good start. Zero for zero."

Cole glared.

"What?" Mac asked, glancing at the sheet. "Aren't you not supposed to help?"

"My rules, I change them as I want." He flipped his microphone around and continued visiting the tables.

Mac blew a flyaway hair off her face, all happiness fading away. Cole wanted to make it his mission to keep the happiness swirling around her for the entire vacation. Not that he had any right to do so, but he could try.

"Hey, I thought we were having fun?" he asked.

"Sorry, two older siblings. I'm a bit competitive."

"Third question," Trent began, back at his perch. Cole forced himself to focus on the questions and not be distracted by the freckles on Mac's nose as she scrunched it in concentration. For two more questions she had an immediate answer, then changed it. Cole hadn't a clue so he followed her lead.

Trent came around and squatted at their low table. "Are you two even trying?" he asked, an evil glint in his eyes. Cole resisted the urge to punch him. "Wrong and wrong. What I am going to do with you?" He pushed himself up and walked away.

Mac flung the paper at Cole, slumping in her seat. "That's it, I give up. There's no way we can catch up from here."

He caught the paper to his chest, determined to not let her mood spiral over a simple trivia game. "Then you're looking at the game wrong." He snatched the pencil and waited for the next question.

"Question number five: humans are identified by our fingerprints, but dogs are identified by their what prints?"

Cole bent the paper over the armrest of his chair, out of Mac's view, and scribbled down an answer, only poking through the paper twice. Once finished, he gave her his most convincing smile and slid the paper under her nose.

She let out a gasp of a laugh and put her hand over her face. "You can't be serious."

"Life's too short to be serious."

"Their butts?"

He grinned, coaxing her smile out. And just like that, the cold room grew warm.

"Question number six, ladies and gentlemen." Trent's voice didn't break their stare. "The thickest part of the human skin is located in which area?"

Still holding Mac's eyes, Cole shot his eyebrows upward several times.

"I really don't think the answer is eyebrows," she teased.

He leaned forward, into her personal space, close enough that he got a whiff of her slight floral scent. "I was thinking of someplace quite a bit lower. And a great deal more enjoyable."

Her breathing changed, and he had the sudden urge to lick where the pulse now beat erratically at the base of her neck. Was it too soon to drag her back to his cabin?

Before he could lean back, Trent appeared at their side. "I don't trust this man," he said. "Keep it clean."

"So the answer does not involve a pleasure organ?" Mac asked with such sincerity Cole nearly fell off his chair.

Trent stood still. "I expected this from him, not you."

Mac's nose crinkled. *Oh yeah, this one's mine.*

Trent left, and Mac grabbed the paper and wrote in a hurry. Cole scooted closer to her, just because, and read over her shoulder: erogenous zones.

Cole was definitely bringing her back to his room, his own erogenous zone perking to life just looking at her, laughing with her. Christ, no one had ever gotten to him like this woman.

"Next question." Trent and his microphone, a serious cramp in Cole's side. "A little trivia from my home state: what is the state bird of New Hampshire?"

"*You* don't even know that," Cole called out.

Trent didn't miss a beat. "Meet my buddy, folks. He's trying to impress a woman over there. I don't think it's going well."

Mac's cheeks reddened, again, accentuating her freckles as the crowd turned to look at them. She leaned in close to him, away from the stares. "Shows what he knows."

Cole eyed Trent, which took a great deal of willpower to tear his gaze away from Mac, and found his friend sporting an evil grin, very proud of himself. "Give me the paper."

He wrote, "Big Bird." Mac laughed. They continued to bullshit their way through the answers, having a ton of fun in the process. He waited for her to mention the leg, but she didn't.

Cole scooted closer to Mac, until his real leg brushed hers. Their arms caressed each time one of them wrote down a funny or sexy answer. He never thought of trivia as foreplay before and was rather afraid he'd get hard the next time he played.

Unless he was playing with Mac, then it would be perfectly acceptable to get hard.

"That was the last question, folks. Now I need you to swap answers with another team for the answer round."

Shit. An older couple turned and handed over their sheet. Mac squirmed but held out their answers. "Umm, just so you know, we aren't really good at trivia and started to put down silly…and inappropriate answers."

The husband glanced at the sheet and laughed. "Good answers." His wife jabbed him in the side. Cole leaned back and relaxed.

Trent tapped his microphone. "All right, question number one: in the English language, what letter begins the most words? The answer is *S*."

Mac marked up the other couple's paper. Cole paused.

Her first response was *S*. She changed it.

Second question, the largest body of water, the answer was Pacific. Also Mac's first response. The next few questions followed the same pattern.

"You got all of those right," he whispered.

She looked at him like he sprouted a second head. "No, we got all of those wrong."

"You second guessed yourself. Your first instinct was right. You don't trust yourself. Why?"

She focused on Trent and the paper in front of her. "Little deep for a fun cruise thing, Cole."

He opened his mouth and closed it. She was right. Of course she was right. He was fling material, nothing more. His scars ran deeper than his missing leg. One terrorist attack meant the next one could catch him at anytime, anywhere. He didn't want to be someone's loss, or be the loss, even if one spunky redhead had him questioning if it was time to reevaluate his outlook.

He let Mac handle the rest of the questions as his mind spun on a high-speed train (maglev, according to question number twelve). The bombing had changed his life, in every way. He'd stayed detached on purpose since then. Even his career was set up to allow him to live in the now, because later wasn't a guarantee.

No, he wouldn't risk it. Too much at stake. Nothing he was ready to handle. A fling was better. Safer all around.

...

Mac settled on her bed, legs crossed under her. She pulled a piece of paper from her growing stack of cruise memos, turning each over until she found one with a blank side.

"All right, Mackenzie. You can start putting your life in order now, no need to wait until you arrive home."

Something about the swaying of the ship, and the tropical atmosphere, had her feeling like standing in Chad's office, throwing a stapler at him as he fired her, was a million years behind her. Another point to Dani on making her come on this trip. Now she needed to make it worth her while.

She removed the lemon cap from her pen and wrote at the top of the page: *Things To Figure Out*. Below that she listed three items: *Job, Housing, Cole*.

It felt strange, putting Cole on the list, but she needed her game plan, and that included how she handled the rest of the cruise and their mutual attraction.

She'd deal with him later, because the big one came first, her employment. Chad clearly wanted her back, so she wrote that down as her first option. Her stomach coiled painfully, but an option was an option, and she'd do good to make sure she explored all of them. Didn't prevent her from being tempted to cross it right out.

Mac tapped the lemon cap against her lip, thinking about what else she could do. What could her skills handle versus what might make her happy? She added two more, then looked at her list:

Job:

Get old job back

Find a different administrative assistant job (bonus if in architecture)

Find a different job in architecture (what am I qualified for?)

The list had her hovering around what she knew. Sure, she had enjoyed her job, Chad be damned, but did she stay because she wanted to or because it felt safe?

Things to consider. She had a week, after all.

She moved on to the next item: housing. The easy one: crash with Dani until she could afford her own place. If she overstayed her welcome, she could always check in with her parents or her siblings, but Dani was much better company for failing at life. The rest needed to wait until after she'd found a new job.

That left her with her final item. Cole. A smile stretched her face and butterflies danced low in her belly. She'd laughed at Dani and Susie and their fling ideas, thinking that it would take her a long time after Chad to want a man again. Cole proved her wrong.

"Don't I deserve to have some fun?"

The room had no answer, but she realized she didn't need to write anything down. Between Cole and Quinn and Rob, she had people to hang out with and didn't have to spend her cruise feeling alone. She could enjoy her time with Cole, rebound, and be ready to tackle the other items on her list when she returned home.

A fling had been the last thing on her mind, but she couldn't deny she wanted to see him again. She would make lemonade out of the rotten lemons of her life, and she'd start by enjoying her time with Cole.

Mind made up, she got off her bed and changed into her bathing suit in preparation for meeting up with him. Much better than leaving him waiting for her and not showing up. How foolish she'd been to think she could end things before having her fill.

Ten minutes later, Mac pulled up the top of her red strapless maxi dress as she ventured down to deck two, searching for Cole. After their epic fail at trivia, he suggested they enjoy some time on the island together, soaking up the sun. The idea worked for her, as she wasn't keen on wandering around off board alone. She felt comfortable flying solo, but it often made the loneliness factor triple.

No, this vacation would not be about loneliness, she'd make sure of it.

A few passengers wandered about as she descended the

final step, but the man waiting for her would have been hard to miss even in a crowd. Cole leaned against a wall, hands in his pockets, his prosthetic foot against the wall, knee bent. For a man with one leg, he looked calm and casual in a tight tan T-shirt and brown trunks. She took a moment to study the leg, to see if it changed things. It didn't.

When she locked eyes with him, he sent her a white-toothed grin, accentuating the angles of the sexiest square jaw, and everything in her wanted to liquefy. Sooner or later someone was going to ask why he settled for her and not—

A size-two blonde in a string bikini that barely covered her D cups and Kardashian ass walked past.

Mac hitched her cover-up once again. She checked on Cole, expecting to find him drooling over the blonde.

He drooled all right, eyes still locked on Mac. Her stomach did a somersault, and she finally made her way over to where he stood.

"Mackenzie-Mac, sunshine in this dark, enclosed space. Shall we head over?"

He did something funny to her insides; she wondered if it was the magic of vacation. She nodded, and Cole pushed off the wall. He took a moment to regain his footing before they swiped their cruise cards and exited the dark interior into the bright sunshine. The warm Caribbean air wrapped around her, fluffing her hair and filling her lungs. The air exuded peace and relaxation. The blinding sun would take some time to adjust to. Mac reached into her oversize bag and pulled out her sunglasses, swapping them with her regular ones. Beside her, Cole pulled down his own from the top of his head.

Bright colors lined the pier connecting their ship to the island, water rustling below. Passengers walked to and fro and staff lined the path, including photographers. Mac ducked past one dressed as a pirate, feeling a small amount of pity for the long sleeves and pants in the eighty-degree weather.

Cole hadn't managed to escape. Mac turned, finding the pirate with his hook aimed around Cole's neck. Cole feigned a look of terror as the pirate scowled, and Mac laughed in enjoyment, until the pirate turned on her.

"Would you like a picture, m'lady?"

"No thanks." Mac grabbed Cole's hand, tugging him along.

Once they were past the bad picture quadrant of the vacation, she went to release his hand. But he spread his fingers between hers, resting their palms together. Her fast pace slowed, even as her heart kicked up. The gesture was simple and intimate, yet they hadn't even known each other twenty-four hours.

"You don't like to have your picture taken?" Cole asked.

Mac shrugged. "Not to a hate extent. It's more that I have no need to get a picture taken with a fake pirate, so why should they spend the time and finances to print me out something that will end up in the trash at the end of the cruise?"

"Fair enough. What if I might want a picture?"

Mac's flip flop took that moment to make her stumble. At least, that was her story and she planned to stick to it. "You can use your phone rather than pay a lot of money for my windblown hair."

Cole laughed. "Fair enough."

Two kids ran past, calling for their parents to hurry up, as they headed toward the waterpark. The brightly colored equipment resembled more amusement park than tranquil beach.

"Have you been here before?" Mac asked.

Cole nodded. "Once, before all this." He spanned his hand out in front of him. "It used to be a quiet place, beach, greener, nothing that cost an extra night."

Mac looked around, trying to picture the island as it used to be. She couldn't. "That makes me sad. I mean, this place looks like fun. A bit like Disney on water steroids, but fun."

Cole propped his glasses up to his forehead. "Did you want to try it?"

Mac bit her lip. Did she? She'd have to take her hearing aids off, and she'd rather enjoy Cole's company. "Not today."

Cole replaced his glasses. "Maybe some other time you can splurge."

She tried to picture it. Perhaps one day she'd be the woman chasing after her kids. She drew a blank. She had no clue where she'd be in a month, never mind a year. The unknowns crawled up on her, threatened to be a dark cloud on this gorgeous day, so she turned her attention back to her fling contender. Wallowing in her troubles wouldn't do her any good, not when she'd been sent to enjoy herself.

They left the path for the sand, and Mac marveled at how the change in terrain didn't pose much of a problem for Cole. Curiosity about how he moved and what he'd been through stirred, but she didn't know how to ask without being rude. She let the warm wind carry her troubles away, content to be in the moment with him.

He gestured to two empty beach chairs under an umbrella that didn't provide much shade. "Sorry it's so far away from the water. I should have known it would be crowded by now."

Away from the water meant Mac didn't have to worry about her hearing aids unless she decided to swim. She smiled. "Actually, that's perfect for me."

They laid towels out on the chairs, and Cole yanked off his shirt, bunching it in a tangled mess. She fought to keep her gaze on his face and failed. His arms and chest were too well defined to look away from. A single trail of hair started at his belly button and traveled down, down, down, into the brown bathing trunks sitting low on his hips.

She swallowed a moan and sat down without removing her cover-up. She couldn't find an ounce of fat on his body;

meanwhile she carried ten extra pounds and felt lumpy in her green tankini.

Cole leaned back and placed his hands behind his head, staring out into the ocean. He crossed his legs, his prosthesis on top. Mac had never seen one up close and personal. Strange how it only intrigued her. "Gorgeous view." He turned to her. "Your eyes are still better."

She blinked and licked her dry lips. A nervous habit. Curiously enough, his pupils darkened with heat. She hadn't meant to bait him. But she liked the reaction. She sucked one small section of her lip into her mouth.

He leaned forward and brushed her sideswept bangs behind her ear. She hoped for a kiss, wanting to learn his taste and texture, ready to see where this fling went. But he maintained his distance. "Mackenzie-Mac, you are a treasure."

Uncomfortable with the compliment, and so not used to them, she shifted away, her eyes landing on his legs again. "What happened?" she blurted out before she could stop herself. He hesitated, and she cringed. "Sorry, shouldn't have asked. Don't mean to be rude."

He laughed. "No, don't do that. I'd much rather people ask than point and stare." He tapped his knee, or what she assumed was his real knee inside the contraption. "Would you believe a sword fight gone bad?"

She laughed.

"Or a bad encounter with a shark? I fought hard, but he got a good grip on me and refused to let go."

She held up her hands. "Okay, okay. Lesson learned." She turned to the ocean view.

"You aren't going to get much sun in a long dress," he said while eyeing her up and down in a way that made her breath hitch.

She pointed to her freckle-covered nose and red hair.

"Hello, my skin sees daylight and it competes with my hair color."

"I'll cover you with suntan lotion."

You would, wouldn't you? And damn, that sounded good. "Took care of it before I came."

"All those hard-to-reach places?"

"Yup."

He looked genuinely disappointed. She almost promised him an up-close-and-personal view of her body later but caught herself in time. She did, however, brave the elements, and the ten extra pounds, to remove her maxi dress.

Cole's gaze heated her more than the sun. Her ego sufficiently stroked, she settled back onto her chair. Who was the last guy to stroke her ego? Chad, *old* Chad. Back when they first started. He hadn't even seemed turned on by her in months. Blamed it on those pesky extra pounds. The truth was probably that he'd been screwing Kit.

Cole's hand on her shoulder stopped the snarling she hadn't realized escaped her lips. "You okay?" he asked.

She grabbed his hand and squeezed. "Sorry. Not used to this much attention."

"Why not?"

She closed her eyes and took her hand back. "You could say I'm here running from an ex. An ex who cheated on me."

He reached for her hand and held on. His large hand encompassed her smaller one. "Then he wasn't very bright."

She forced her eyes open. He looked at her, and only her.

He rubbed his thumb over her palm. When he spoke again, it was so soft she barely heard it. "If given the chance, I'd never stop showing you attention."

She would have thought she heard him wrong, except the truth of those words shined in his eyes, clear as the sky. She was on vacation to get away from someone. Why did it feel like she was getting into a deeper mess with Cole?

She didn't care. She spent too much of her life worrying over every little detail, making the right choice, the sensible choice, and ended up worse for it. No more. Her gut wanted to be here, with Cole. For the week, nothing else mattered.

...

Cole watched the waves crash against the shore as people young and old played in the water or the wet sand. Most chairs were full, and chatter and laughter filled the air. Crowds always gave him a bit of a pause, but he enjoyed bathing-suit territory: less places to hide nefarious devices. Even if it was a backpack that resulted in him losing his leg, and plenty of beach bags dotted the area.

He pushed those thoughts aside. The ship had metal detectors. Odds of an attack were a lot less than standing in the middle of Boston.

The hot sun beat down on them, and a swim would be nice, especially getting Mac wet. But that would involve taking off his prosthesis and no way would he risk losing it. He might be hard on his fake leg, but he avoided letting it rust. Accelerating wear and tear was the most he'd do.

Voices raised from the chairs in front of them, and Cole caught glimpses of an argument from a couple roughly ten years older.

"So you just went and charged how much to our account without even asking me?" said the woman with a large straw hat on her head.

"It was supposed to be a surprise!" The man flailed out his hands, clearly exasperated and clueless as to why his wife was upset.

Cole placed a fist near his mouth, trying not to burst out laughing. Mac leaned into Cole. "What's going on?"

He gestured ahead of them. "You hear this?"

Mac shook her head.

"Apparently the guy with the shark shirt charged something expensive without telling the woman in the straw hat."

Mac studied the couple in front of them, who continued to yell. Straw Hat remained composed, an icy voice. Meanwhile, Shark Shirt continued to flail his arms. "I don't even have to know what is being said to know he's already in the dog house. And considering we're on a ship, he'll be sleeping in one of the lounges."

Cole laughed. "I suspect you might be right."

Voices raised again. "Because I don't want to go to the waterpark, Bill."

"But you keep saying how we never do anything spontaneous!"

"I didn't mean a fucking waterpark."

Mac poked Cole, so he repeated what he heard. She shook her head. "Poor Bill. Day two and he's already ruined the entire trip."

Cole ignored the continued fighting and faced Mac. "What should he have done?"

"Talked with her first, obviously."

"What if it was meant to be a surprise?"

Mac studied the couple in front of them. "Look at her. Her hair is teased and she's wearing makeup. She's not dressed to get wet. She's dressed to lounge in the sun and tan and look a hell of a lot more put together than the rest of us. Image is important to her. She'd want him to splurge on specialty dining, not water slides."

Cole studied the couple. Mac was right. "But he's dressed to go on an adventure and is probably bored."

"Probably, but then he should have talked with her and gotten a ticket for only himself."

"And leave her alone?"

"She's got a drink and a book. I don't think she'd notice."

The guy stood, face red in a way that suggested anger and not sun.

"What's going to happen now?" Cole asked.

Mac tapped a finger to her lip, and for a moment Cole forgot about the bickering couple. "He's about to stalk off, return the tickets, and then grumble his way through a beer." She paused. "No, he's going alone. Might see if he can find someone to take the wife's ticket. It's probably non-refundable."

Cole crossed his arms, studied the pair. "I think he's going to try to convince her, make a few lame threats, and then stalk off and wait to cool down and probably miss his entrance time. And since he's wasted money, the rest of this vacation might not be too pleasant for him."

"Poor Bill." Mac shook her head.

The shouting drew Cole's attention. "Well, fine then!" Bill stomped off, taking long strides, as his wife tipped down her hat and picked up her drink.

"Whew, that was nasty. I hope I never get into a fight like that." Bonus points since Cole had no plans to. His luck he'd walk off and one of them would be too close to an attack and the last thing said would be, "Well, fine then." Sucky-assed way to go.

"Fights are part of life. If he makes amends, they are going to have wall-banging sex tonight."

Cole studied Mac and the way her bathing suit accentuated her cleavage. He leaned forward. "Would that be something you'd like?"

He caught her swallow, her gaze hidden by her glasses, but he felt it on him. "Maybe someday. But it's make-up sex."

Right. Couple and relationship stuff. Things Cole wouldn't be experiencing.

Sometime later, the guy returned. Dry, so he hadn't

gone to the park, with a beer in hand. He settled down next to his wife and pulled out his phone. Cole suspected Mac's first idea was correct, and like in trivia, she pushed it aside. His redheaded beauty had created a bit of a puzzle, one he planned to unravel.

...

Mac finished piling her plate at the buffet, waiting for Cole to catch up to her. She glanced around at the picnic benches, looking for an empty one or one with plenty of room. No free tables, not with this many people, but she did catch Quinn and Rob sitting by themselves.

Something touched her arm, and she nearly jumped, risking her food tumbling to the ground. She steadied her plate as she took in Cole next to her.

"Didn't mean to scare you, thought you heard me."

Hearing wasn't exactly her thing, and she wasn't ready to find out if he'd be the type of douche not to want to bother with her. She'd deal with that later. "My friends are over there. Mind if we join?"

He gestured with his drink. "Lead the way."

They wove around the tables. The chatter and Caribbean music had Mac crossing her fingers the table would be quiet. The noise wasn't as bad when they got close. Before she could say "hi" Quinn spotted them.

"It's Mac! And Cole! Don't you two look chummy?" Quinn beamed.

Mac rolled her eyes, setting down her plate next to Cole's.

Quinn leaned forward. "You would not believe the chaos we observed."

Rob stabbed at his salad. "Quinn takes far too much pleasure in others' misfortunes."

"Oh hush. The policies are clearly posted. It's his own

damn fault." Quinn faced Mac and Cole. "This guy was ranting and raving, claiming he had just purchased these tickets and he wanted his money back."

Mac exchanged a look with Cole. It couldn't be?

"It really was quite a scene," Rob said. "Didn't he say something about the poor staff being responsible for his divorce?"

Quinn laughed. "Yes, he did! Who does that?"

Cole put down his silverware. "Tell me, was this gentleman a tad older than us, wearing a shirt with a shark on it?"

"Yes! Were you there, too?" Quinn asked.

Cole shook his head. "No, we caught the original fight between him and his wife."

"Okay, now I'm curious," Rob said.

Cole recapped the earlier fight as Mac marveled at the odds of them both catching parts of the same issue for one poor guy.

When Cole finished, he touched her arm. The touch was simple, more to get her attention than anything else, yet the sparks seeped through, traveling up and down her arm. "You were right."

Mac paused with her fork and knife poised above her chicken. "What?"

"He returned the tickets, or tried to, then got a beer and sulked by his wife."

A chortle worked its way up her throat. She put her hand over her mouth. "Oh my, I did suggest that, didn't I?"

"You did. But then you changed it. Wonder why." And he went back to eating, leaving her sitting there, fighting off a feeling that whatever he hinted at would come back to haunt her.

· · ·

Cole shifted in his chair next to Mac as the comedy show started. A tall man stood at the mic. "You know how you can tell all the drunk passengers on a ship? They're the only ones walking straight." The room burst out in laughter, Cole joining in, until he noticed Mac wasn't laughing.

She had a smile on her face, but even in the dim lighting he knew it didn't meet her eyes. He leaned into her, ignoring another round of audience guffaws. "What's wrong?"

Mac shook her head, a slew of emotions crossing her face. He waited, eyes on her, not giving a damn about the performer on stage.

It took a few beats, but Mac blew out a breath, head shaking. She reduced the distance between them. "What?"

He angled closer to her ear. "What's wrong?"

She faced him. He waited for the debate he somehow knew occurred inside her to play out. Finally she raised her hair and pointed to her ear. He almost leaned in to ask again when his eyes registered on something in her ear. A hearing aid.

He caught her eyes as comprehension dawned. She had hearing loss—that's why she didn't laugh. It suddenly made sense that neither of them even mentioned going into the water earlier that day. "You can't hear?"

She grimaced, and nothing on her face showed she understood over the loud comedian and the louder crowd.

Cole stood, holding out a hand for Mac. She placed hers in his, allowing him to pull her up and out of the theater. Once they stood on the other side of the closed door, she let go and leaned against the wall.

"I'm sorry," she whispered, eyes closed, shoulders slouched.

He placed two fingers under her chin and raised her head until she opened her eyes and met his gaze. "You've got nothing to be sorry about."

"I thought I'd be able to follow the show, I'd been able to follow enough of the other events so far, but the sound system is choppy and the audience drowned out the comedian and—"

He put a finger to her lips, cutting her off. The softness of her mouth made him want to soothe her in other ways, but now was not the time for a first kiss. "It's okay. I didn't realize you had hearing loss."

She lifted a shoulder. "It hadn't come up. You don't go around telling people about your leg, right?"

Touché. "Fair enough." He reached for her hand. "Come on, let's do something else."

She followed him into the elevator and out onto the quiet pool deck. The inky black sky held a host of stars. Sure, he'd been interested in the show. But this moment, being out here in the beauty of the night with Mac, meant more to him than an hour's worth of jokes.

They settled onto chairs, Cole stretching out his prosthesis. Mac's head tipped back as she took in the night sky. "It's gorgeous."

Cole watched her and the wonder across her face. "Not compared to you."

She faced him, eyebrows lowering. "I've got my issues. My hearing loss is only a small part of it."

He raised his amputated leg. "I'd be a hypocrite if I had a problem with that. Believe me, I've got more problems than missing the lower half of one leg."

She opened her mouth, and he expected her to ask more questions, but she closed it and settled into the chair. "Thank you."

"We're here to have fun. If you can't understand something, we can always try a different event."

"I don't want you missing out."

He leaned forward. "This isn't my first cruise, and it won't be my last. I've either done it before or I can do it again. The only thing I can't repeat is time with you."

Perhaps that came out heavier than he anticipated, but her eyes lit up and her shoulders relaxed. Worth it.

"Okay. I'll tell you if I can't understand."

He grinned, feeling like he'd won more than one of Trent's silly keychains. "You're a treasure, Mackenzie-Mac."

She shook her head, but no tension crossed her face. "It's the vacation goggles."

"Vacation goggles?"

"Yeah, everything looks better while on vacation."

She turned to the sky again. He couldn't imagine her looking any less beautiful, even if she lounged on his couch in sweatpants, eating chips and watching TV.

And that line of thought was so off course he'd end up at the wrong island. Cole shoved that into a box. Vacation goggles were perfect for a cruise fling.

Day 3: At Sea

The morning sun lit the room, casting shadows on the wall. Mac stretched out in bed, letting her muscles reach just a little further in complete lazy relaxation. It felt so good to stretch out and have an entire bed to herself. Chad had been a bed *and* cover hog. For ten months she had slept in a sliver of the bed, shivering.

No more.

Her open shades displayed a blurred blue horizon. The waves rolled past as the ship wouldn't be on land today. No better way to relax than by staying on board. Mac took in a deep breath. Vacation. She needed this.

On that thought, she pulled out her phone. Still cuddled with her blankets, she let her messages download. She ignored the spam and deleted the one from Chad titled: WHERE THE FUCK ARE YOU? before opening an email from Dani.

From: Dani Martin
To: Mackenzie Laurels

Subject: Cruise Fling

Yes! Cruise fling in action! I'm soooo proud of you, Mac! Details. Details. Details!

Love ya,
Dani.

Mac grinned and responded.

From: Mackenzie Laurels
To: Dani Martin
Subject: RE: Cruise Fling

Cute as hell. Makes me laugh. Nothing more to tell…yet.

Having fun. Thank you, thank you, thank you for making me do this. I owe you.

~Mac

The next message was from Susie and proved her friends talked.

From: Susie Patel
To: Mackenzie Laurels
Subject: Fling: Lemonade or Rotten Lemons?

We need more info! Tell me more about this hunk Dani says you want a fling with. Is he a rotten lemon or lemonade?

From: Mackenzie Laurels
To: Susie Patel
Subject: RE: Fling: Lemonade or Rotten Lemons?

Jury still out on lemonade vs. rotten lemons. I think I can make lemonade before it runs sour. <wink>

Love ya, Mac.

Mac held her phone to her chest. What was Cole? For once in her life, she wanted lemonade, not a rotten lemon. Odds were not in her favor. Example A: Chad.

On that sobering thought, she climbed out of bed and headed for her bathroom.

After her shower, with a towel holding her hair, Mac returned to the main area of her cabin, noticing a light flashing by her phone.

"That's odd," she muttered as she picked the phone up, pressing it hard against her ear so she could hear without her hearing aids on. She had a message. From Cole.

"Hey, Mac. My morning feels gloomy without my current favorite redhead by my side. Please meet me on the upper pool deck later this morning. Or if you are done with me, I'll understand. But I hope to see you soon."

Mac's grin stretched her cheeks, and she repeated the message, just to hear his sexy voice once again.

"Oh no, Cole, I am not done with you yet." After all, she still had a fling to achieve.

• • •

Cole tapped his foot as he sat on a pool chair, searching the crowd for the redheaded Mackenzie-Mac. What the hell had he been thinking? He should have given her a time, at the very least, or asked her to confirm, rather than sitting there like a fool, hoping she'd show up.

She could be done with him; he wouldn't blame her for that. The whole one-legged thing didn't work for everyone.

Sure, he got a few pity fucks out of it, which worked fine for him, since he didn't want anything more.

Cole shifted to watch the whitecaps float past the ship. Nothing but water and sky. He should be living it up, tracking down Trent, flirting with someone new. Instead he'd wait a little longer and maybe be rewarded for his patience.

He laughed and shook his head. She had him so intrigued he might wait a really long time for her to grace him with her presence. Not because he was looking for anything more than this week with her, but because he wanted this one week.

Life didn't allow for much else.

The clouds continued to float past, the water rustling below, when movement caught his attention.

"Waiting for someone?" Mac asked, placing her bag down on the chair next to him. She pulled off her red cover-up, and he followed the exposing of her legs, her yellow bathing suit, the swells of her breasts, all creating a primal drumbeat low in his groin.

"I believe I am," he croaked out, kicking his ass that he sounded surprised she'd joined him.

She swapped her glasses with her sunglasses, then settled in and turned his way, the sunlight dancing across her skin, touching each exposed part. He wanted to be that light.

"Wouldn't want you getting lonely out here."

He shifted to face her and the sly grin on her lips. The urge to lean in, taste her, grew strong. But a crowded pool deck with a young child crying below was not where he wanted to steal a first kiss. Instead, he traced the contours with sight, not touch, and reveled as her breathing quickened, as though he really did touch her the way he wanted.

Cole adjusted himself and shifted back before he embarrassed himself. When had anyone made him crave like this one redheaded wonder? Never, that's when. "You are something special, Mackenzie-Mac."

"I'm here, no use buttering me up."

"You're wearing yellow and you're worried about buttering?"

"Yellow is a bit of a thing for me, which you should get after seeing my luggage. Not asking for compliments."

He suspected she needed the compliments. Worse, he wanted to be the one who changed things for her. *Don't get off course, Matterhorn. You're not going to be in her life for long.* But he could do his best to make the week a good one.

"What do you think happened to that poor couple from yesterday?"

Mac flipped her bangs out of her glasses. "Either they managed to kiss and make up, or they are cruising separately today. You?"

Cole scratched his chin, glanced below, and focused on something familiar. "Or they continue to bicker." He gestured, and Mac followed his finger to Straw Hat sitting below, getting her sun, while Shark Shirt—now Octopus Shirt—waved his hands and seemed to be yelling or pleading a case that his wife ignored.

"Ohh, poor guy. That is not a good vacation."

"Not at all. But I hope I can make yours a good one."

Mac stopped watching the troubled couple, turning to face him. He wished she hadn't switched to her sunglasses so he could see her blue eyes. "What are you saying?"

"Spend the cruise with me. A weeklong date. What do you say?"

She studied his face, and he had a momentary fear that he'd misjudged the situation. Then she smiled, cheeks rising high. It filled him with some foreign form of happiness.

"I'd like that."

• • •

Mac took a final bite of her salad before leaning back in her beach chair. She'd spent the morning in the sun with Cole, then they grabbed lunch at the nearby buffet and returned to their chairs. She felt lighter than she had in a long time, helped by the attentive date who served as a reminder of how badly her ex had failed.

She shook those thoughts aside. Those were for deep reflection and possibly counseling at a much, much later date.

Cole had finished his lunch and placed his plate on the floor. He leaned back, hands behind his head, shirtless. Mac had been thoroughly enjoying this particular view all day. Her companion had a fit-and-trim body, and she rather liked the idea of getting her hands on him.

He swung his legs around, facing her, and she wondered if he somehow knew her thoughts before it registered his gaze landed over her shoulder. "I spy Trent. Want to have some fun?" He bounced his eyebrows, and she couldn't help wanting to laugh.

Mac turned, catching Trent holding a large bag and wearing his cruise staff clothes and sunglasses. "What did you have in mind?"

Cole knocked on his knee covered by his prosthesis. "Random shark attack?"

"On the pool deck? And didn't you try and claim that as to the true reason why you lost your leg?"

Cole had the good sense to grimace. Mac should feel something about not knowing the truth. But for a fling, what did it really matter?

"Okay, no shark attack. I need to think faster next time." He cupped his hands around his mouth. "Is that for me?" he yelled in Trent's direction.

Trent raised his sunglasses, and Mac caught the two-second glare he sent his friend. Cole simply laughed until Trent stood over them, dropping the bag to the floor. "Only if you want to be the target in dodgeball."

Cole grabbed the bag and peeked inside. "Those look like basketballs."

Trent grinned. "They are."

"That would hurt."

"Exactly."

Cole leaned in Mac's direction. "Translation, this man has been on his best behavior for six months and he's ready to crack."

Mac covered her mouth before she laughed out loud. Trent reached up and scratched his cheek with his middle finger. All the confirmation Mac needed to know Cole wasn't exaggerating.

Cole settled back in his seat. "They let you out of your cage?"

"Every once in a while. They feel it promotes better enthusiasm."

"Wouldn't want you missing the sunlight. Vampire staff might only appeal to the younger passengers," Mac said, joining in on the fun.

The two men shared a look. If they expected her not to play ball, then they had a thing or two to learn.

"Mac! Mac!" a familiar voice called. Mac turned and caught Quinn heading over in a bright pink triangle bikini top and shorts that barely could be considered pants. Mac would show off that body, too, if she had it. Quinn plopped down on the edge of her lounger. "How is it I can't find anything on this ship but you?"

Mac patted Quinn's shoulder. "I'm magic, apparently." Not that she ever felt like magic, but on this ship, surrounded by her new friends, she'd take it.

Quinn looked up, and did Mac catch her bat her eyelashes at Trent? She held out her hand. "Hi, I'm Quinn."

Trent's face morphed into a grin, and thanks to the

interplay between him and Cole, Mac caught something off. Confirmed when Trent grabbed his water bottle like a lifeline after the handshake. Cole's friend just got more interesting than Hat Lady and Shark Guy.

"That's Trent, Cole's friend," Mac said, since Trent hadn't even managed to babble. Beside her, Cole laughed, proving she wasn't alone in noticing the sparks.

"Where are you from, Trent?" Quinn asked.

Trent pulled himself together. "I'm from New Hampshire."

Mac glanced up as a fifth person joined them and grinned when she found Rob.

"Quinn, you can't find anything and you found Mac?"

Quinn squeezed Mac's hand. "Mac's my compass."

Mac snorted. "Trust me, you don't want to use me as a compass."

"I'm beginning to think you sell yourself too short," Cole said softly.

Mac darted her eyes to her date for the week, a bit amazed she caught the soft words. Cole held her gaze, those green eyes claiming he spoke the truth and planned to prove it to her. Many had tried, none succeeded, because her luck really did hate her. It would take much longer than a week for him to learn this, and by then, they'd be long over.

Quinn kicked Trent's bag with a silver sandal dangling from one toe. "What's in there?"

Trent patted the material before hefting it to his shoulder. "Basketballs, clipboard, prizes. I'm running a three-on-three tournament in ten minutes." He eyed Cole. "You in?"

"Hell yeah, I'm in." Cole turned to Mac. "It's a thing. He'll pout if I don't play."

Mac glanced at the prosthetic leg.

Cole knocked on his lower apparatus. "It's sturdy."

She didn't know the ins and outs of prosthetic wear,

even if the slight shaking of Trent's head indicated that her gut reaction held some truth. Didn't matter. She sent Cole a megawatt smile. "Go, I'll come watch. See if I'll still go out with you tonight."

Cole opened his mouth but didn't get a word out.

"No," Quinn exclaimed. She grabbed Mac's arm. "You stay here, with me, and sunbathe. I need girl time."

"I'm girl time," Rob said. He shielded his eyes from the sun to see them.

"You also like basketball. Go, be a boy. You can be a girl again later."

Trent scratched his head. "You two might be the strangest couple I've met yet. And that's saying something."

Rob patted him on the back. "We're not a couple. We play the same field."

"Which side are you on, Trent?" Quinn spoke with a certain flair, a certain flirtatious flair. She flapped her sandal against the sole of her foot. Mac swallowed a laugh.

"Ours," Cole said, standing up. "Let's go. I think Trent has a keychain with my name on it."

Mac watched the men as they headed toward the basketball court. Cole hadn't put on his shirt, and she couldn't stop ogling his broad shoulders and narrow waist. She shifted to taking in how he moved, curious after all the basketball talk. He had a slight limp to his walk, as if there was a pebble in his shoe. A stockier way of moving, which she now knew had nothing to do with the ship. He hadn't revealed even a clue as to the real story and she didn't push; he obviously didn't want to share. But it only increased her curiosity.

She shook herself back to her senses and turned to stare at Quinn. Lost in her own little world, Quinn laid out the towel and settled into the chair. "Ahh, this is the life."

Mac continued to stare. Quinn ignored her. "Hello," she finally exclaimed. "What was that?"

Quinn turned and looked Mac. "What was what?"

"You. Trent."

"Me...Trent... What?"

Mac laughed and threw her head back.

Quinn sat up. "What? What am I missing?" She checked her itty-bitty bikini and boy shorts. "I'm not exposed."

"You may as well have been, but I'm not talking about that. I'm talking about a spark that the people in the pool below felt."

Quinn's mouth dropped open. "Spark?" She turned in the direction Trent had left. "You're getting me confused with yourself."

"Nope. Trent was speechless. You were flirting."

"I...what?" Quinn leaned forward. Her wide eyes didn't reveal even a hint of teasing.

A realization grew within Mac. "You don't even recognize your own sparks?"

"That wasn't a spark." Quinn rubbed her hands together.

Mac's good humor faded. Could have fooled the charged air molecules between them. "It wasn't?"

"No, it wasn't. He seems very nice, but—"

Mac cut her off, baffled by this whiplash. "Is it because he works here?"

Quinn straightened in alarm. "What? No, don't be ridiculous."

Mac tapped the side of her chair, debating her next words. "Quinn, does your husband search have a checklist?"

Quinn picked at the nail polish on her thumb. "No... Well, not much of one."

"Quinn?"

She sighed and turned toward the sun. "I want a family. I love my job, but I want the option to stay home with my kids. And I want to actually see my husband."

"This is Trent's last week. He goes home when we go

home."

"And then what?"

Mac shrugged. "Don't know, you'll have to ask him. If you keep cutting off options like this…you might pass on the one person you shouldn't."

"Like you aren't in danger of going against your own wishes."

Mac faced the ocean. Thought of a certain tempting man with a limp. "Plenty of danger. Fortunately I'm the queen of bad decisions. So whatever happens, the only given is that I will fuck it up sooner or later." Her past, heck, her entire existence had taught her that. She'd been teased about her rotten luck so often the words still lingered in the recesses of her mind.

"And you wonder why *I'm* unattached."

Mac fiddled with the bottom of her bathing suit top. "I told you my ex cheated."

"So he was a bad decision. Maybe Cole is a good one."

Too deep for a vacation, for a fling. Mac noticed Cole's shirt had fallen to the floor. She picked it up. "I guess they're playing shirts and skins."

Quinn sat up straight. "Then why are we sitting here?"

Mac laughed as Quinn shoved her feet back into her sandals. "So you admit there is something there?"

Quinn opened her mouth. Closed it. Opened it again. "Trent is good looking. But me and signals are a bit…off."

Mac pulled on her cover-up. "It's a vacation. I know you have your plans, but if you were just here to have fun…"

"And that is why we are heading over to watch them play. You can watch Cole. I'll be soaking up Trent."

Mac followed Quinn, suspecting her friend might want to give Trent more than just a visual soak.

• • •

Cole dribbled a ball back and forth between his hands. The warm sun overhead beat down on his bare back. His stump already felt slick in the lining—nothing new there. He'd need a wipe down after the game or risk a high stink factor.

He'd already demonstrated to Rob what he could do on a court, two working legs or not. Now the only holdup was Trent. "Come on, take off your shirt and be the third player," he called out.

Trent glanced up, pushing his sunglasses off his nose to check his watch. "Someone will come along shortly and we'll begin." He let the glasses fall back as he checked his clipboard again.

Cole clucked. The other group of three players stood nearby, chatting amongst themselves as they waited for the game to start. Rob had his shirt tucked into the back of his pants and stood in a wide stance. He joined Cole in the clucking.

Trent grabbed the ball from Cole mid-dribble. "You want in the tournament, you play by my rules." He tossed the ball back with enough force that Cole lost his breath.

"Bitchy," Rob muttered. "You treat all the passengers this way?"

Cole grinned and high fived Rob. "Yes, another partner in crime."

Trent checked his watch and exhaled. "No, I treat Cole that way because he's a prick."

"What about cute brunettes with short, spiky hair?" Rob asked.

Cole grinned wider. His friend didn't often get caught off his game, but Quinn managed it enough they all noticed.

Trent stared at Rob, then pulled off his shirt. "We're playing." He called the other team over and reviewed the rules. Before long, sneakers squeaked on the court as they ran back and forth under the hot sun. Cole moved slower than before the amputation. He couldn't get the speed or agility he used to. The difference was subtle to others, even as it perturbed him. Nine long years had passed and his body still expected to move like it had before.

A running prosthesis would help. But he wasn't a runner, not anymore. Besides, he'd be fine for a short game. The ball passed back and forth, the score slowly climbing. Yet they were still losing.

Cole prepared to take a shot when he caught sight of Mac at the edge of the court. Her skin glistened and the sun had made her cheeks rosy. He missed.

"Guess it's a good thing your girlfriend isn't here to watch you fail," Trent said before he turned and caught Mac and Quinn. "Well, well, well, I guess she is here to watch you fail."

"Blow me," Cole grunted out. But the sting wasn't good enough. He moved to steal the ball from Trent, just as Trent moved into a fast layup and tripped over Cole's prosthesis. The action threw Cole off-balance and he stumbled to the ground, his hip hitting the pavement hard. A foot away, Trent lay face down.

The other team caught the ball and stood still.

Cole checked his prosthesis, amazed to find it still on. He fixed the socket, best to be sure he wasn't about to fall back on his ass. Trent swore a string of profanities in what appeared to be several different languages.

"Good thing this is your last week." Cole pulled himself up, air hissing as his stump settled back into the socket. He reached out his hand for Trent.

Trent gave him a look that promised a toss over the edge. He refused the hand and pushed himself up, dusting his hands on his shorts. "Let's play," he grumbled and reached for the ball. The other team remained still.

"Uhh, Trent," Mac called out. "You're bleeding."

Cole looked down and noticed a gash in Trent's knee and

a trail of blood reaching for his sock.

Trent looked down as well. "Son of a bitch. Six months, I've been here six months. Haven't seen the medical department once for myself. You're on board two days and what happens, what happens?"

"Relax, shit happens," Quinn said as she pulled a tissue out of her back pocket. She squatted down in front of Trent and wiped up the blood.

Trent froze, and Cole couldn't help the smirk. He'd never seen Trent off his game in front of a woman before.

Mac tossed Cole's shirt to Quinn. "Cole tripped Trent. Use his shirt."

Quinn wrapped the shirt around Trent's leg. "At least it's already red."

Trent, hands on hips, glared at Cole. He said nothing, and Cole knew he couldn't. Customer service and all that bullshit. The look in his eyes said, "I'm going to kill you."

"Careful, I have your blood on my shirt," Cole said.

Trent shook his head and laughed, his shoulders relaxing and the look of murder leaving his eyes. He hobbled over to his bag and addressed the other team. "Sorry about that. You win by default of the saboteur over here." He pulled out three keychains and tossed them to each member.

Rob wiped his forehead with his shirt and pulled it on. "You're bad luck, Cole. Mackenzie, be careful."

Mac grinned.

Cole shook his head before he forgot about his injured friend. "Come on, Trent, let's go visit medical services for the first time."

...

Mac arrived at her stateroom and leaned against the door. What a day. She'd been onboard for a little over forty-eight hours and it felt like weeks. Everything that led to her being here—her fight with Chad, their breakup, him firing her—a mere hazy memory. And why would that particular memory be clear, when through her open curtains dark blue water passed by? Nothing but ocean and blue sky and a calming sense of tranquility.

She pulled off her cover-up and walked out onto her balcony. The warm air whispered across her skin. She fixated on the steady horizon as she leaned on the railing. Life had endless possibilities. What was she doing with hers?

More importantly, what did she want to do with hers? Dead-end jobs, dead-end relationships, none of them were working out. She needed to stop heading down the wrong paths, the paths that didn't open more doors and potential for her. A career, something she loved to do, something that would have her waking up each day excited to go to work. And her next relationship—after her fling with Cole, of course—would be with someone who had long-term potential and most assuredly was not her boss.

The answer to both existed, and Mac would find it. No more rotten lemons for her.

A smile on her face, she walked back into her room in time to hear the knock at her door. At least she thought it was her door. And the first knock. She opened it a crack and found Cole, still shirtless and alone.

Definitely her door, then. And that gave her a little thrill he'd come to her. The smile spread before she could help it.

"I figured you'd give me a call." Mac tried to go for nonchalance but couldn't keep her eyes on his. Not with his chest so bare and so...there. Cold, too, by the looks of it. She could warm him up... *Down, girl.*

"After listening to Trent bitch at me, I wanted more than your voice."

Her body moved without her brain's permission. She

stepped back, allowing him into her room. The door closed behind him with a loud bang, signaling they were completely alone, for the first time.

"How's Trent?"

"He's fine. It was a bad gash, but he'll be fine."

"Good."

This close, she could practically feel the heat emanating from his body, and not just from his gaze. The air grew thick between them. Cole crossed over to her in one step, brushing her hair back. "I can't get enough of you," he said with his eyes on her lips.

"You haven't had me," she whispered.

"Yet."

Before she had a chance to respond, he crushed his mouth to hers. The connection electric, his lips fitting to hers like a lock and key. He took control, the sting of his stubble contrasted with the softness of his lips, a combination she wanted to drink in and savor. She reached up, grasping onto the smooth skin of his shoulders. He filled her senses, taste and touch. Neither overly pronounced, but still alluring. The heat built inside her, desire resorting to begging, as she pulled him even closer.

As far as first kisses went, this one would be near impossible to beat. She fell into him and the promise of the moment; screw everything else. He continued to seduce her with his lips, and the slight swipe of his tongue at the seam of hers had her gasping for more. Somehow her leg ended up on his hip, reminding her of one very real fact: they were both in their bathing suits. Lots of skin and very little clothing. Before rational thought could stop her, she allowed her hands to roam over his body, his smooth chest, flat abs, and stopped as her fingers danced over the band of his trunks.

With one hand in her hair, the other on her thigh, Cole broke the kiss and put his forehead against hers. "You're killing me, Mackenzie-Mac."

Reality took that moment to sink in. Flings had never been her thing, and she knew next to nothing about this guy. Her bad luck had yet to work its magic to ruin her vacation, and maybe some caution wouldn't be a bad thing. "Tell me something truthful about yourself, Cole." Just one fact, that was all she needed. One fact before things got too real.

His breaths were quick. "Like what?" he asked.

"How did you meet Trent?"

He cleared his throat. "College." His eyes volleyed back and forth between her own. "You're wondering if I'm local like Trent."

Was she? She hadn't been looking for anything specific, just some little truth nugget she could hold onto. "I'm not looking for anything beyond this cruise."

"Even if I live one town over from you?"

Her eyes grew wide, but she shook the shock away. "Even then. When my plane lands back in Massachusetts, I only have time to put my life back together, nothing else."

"Fair enough. I don't do relationships."

She swore a "but" lingered there. She paid it no mind. They both wanted the same thing. It really didn't matter where he lived, only that he happened to be on this ship with her.

He brushed a lock of her hair back. "You need more truth or are you done with me?"

Her body wanted her to crush into him and forget words existed. "I'm not done with you."

He leaned forward, pressing his lips against hers. "Good, because I meant what I said earlier. I want this week with you. And only you."

She practically purred. What did it matter what she knew or didn't know about the man or whether flings were her thing or not? She liked him, he liked her, and she deserved a good time. "I'm good with that plan." She wrapped her arms around his neck and kissed him again, sinking into the heat, until nothing outside of this vacation mattered.

She was back to playing with his waistband when he pulled apart. "I should go," he whispered.

Huh, Mr. I Don't Do Relationships wasn't taking it further. Which worked for her, gave her time to be sure of this fling thing before jumping into bed. "Okay." She leaned back until their bodies no longer touched.

But he pulled her to him again, in a hot and frenzied kiss. Her knee bumped his prosthesis, cool where the rest of his skin was warm. "Until later." He turned and walked out of her stateroom, the door clicking closed behind him.

Mac slid down to the floor. The taste of Cole lingered on her lips, and she almost wished she'd never asked for a truth. If not, they could be on her bed right now, rather than separated. She needed her friends, needed their support. Flings were so not her thing, but giving this chance up was not on the menu.

She rose and gathered her phone, finding emails from those she needed already waiting for her.

From: Dani Martin
To: Mackenzie Laurels
Subject: RE: Cruise Fling

What do you mean there's nothing more to tell yet?! Come on, girl, you're only there for a week. Live it up! Do not come home with an unopened condom package!

Mac laughed and typed out her reply. Exactly the pep talk she needed. *Thank you, Dani!*

From: Mackenzie Laurels

To: Dani Martin
Subject: RE: Cruise Fling

Cute as hell. Kisses like a God. I think I'll put that package to good use.

~Mac

She clicked over to Susie's message.

From: Susie Patel
To Mackenzie Laurels
Subject: RE: Fling: Lemonade or Rotten Lemons?

Yes! Make that Lemonade, Mac! You deserve it!

Mac grinned as she responded.

From: Mackenzie Laurels
To: Susie Patel

Subject: RE: Fling: Lemonade or Rotten Lemons?

I plan to. Would tomorrow be too soon?

~Mac

That really was the question, wasn't it? Did she want to savor it or exploit it? Her body was all for the exploration, and she dragged herself off to shower. She needed to calm down and let things progress as they would.

...

Cole had never walked away from a sure thing before in his life. Never stared at a beautiful face and wanted more than a specific time frame. Not like staring at Mackenzie and wanting her to be on his next vacation.

"What the hell is wrong with you?" he muttered out loud. Not his best idea while walking down the hall and still revved up from Mac's kisses. She didn't have time for him after this trip, needed to get her life back together, the details on which he hadn't learned. And he had to either pack up his office and do the legwork to switch to remote or bust his ass to make the increase in rent work.

Nothing there said, "Start a new relationship." Heck, nothing there said, "Maybe it's time to actually attempt a relationship." Beyond the no-time facts, he didn't do commitment because it meant risking losing someone or being that loss for them. He'd seen the look on his parents' faces after the attack, saw the devastation around him. No way would he put anyone through that.

A fresh wave of terror took that moment to crash into him, and he had to pause and lean against the wall. What if something happened to Mac? Today or tomorrow or next year? And he might not be there to hold her hand or…

Cole scrubbed a hand down his face. What happened to him? He connected with a person, that's it. No use jumping off cliffs or drowning in fears that didn't need to matter. Local or not, they'd go their separate ways after the cruise and all would be right in his world.

It didn't settle well, and that just made him want to punch something. He'd somehow gone and changed the rules for himself, and he'd had no intention of ever doing that.

He made it back to his room and grabbed his carry-on bag, where he had enough paperwork to properly distract himself. He loaded the documents Dani had sent him, and for the next hour he crunched numbers about the lease, advertising, and average sales. He pushed aside all thoughts of Mac or relationships, focusing solely on the task at hand.

When he resurfaced and accessed the damage, he stared at the same results he'd been staring at for months. Both options sucked.

Cole checked his email one more time, finding a response to a possible new location. He scratched his head. Less visible, but still an office, and lower rent. Worth it or not? At this point, he should flip a coin since none of his research helped. Still, he flagged the email. He could compile data on it as well. Call it option C.

He backed out of the email and meant to stop, but another message caught his eye, one from his top clients, the Andersons. Empty nesters who travelled half the year. They always made an appointment and came in to go over their options.

Cole read the email, standard "it's time to book something new" even if they had the next two years already mapped out. And yet he felt an opening, and perhaps a way to make a confident decision. He loaded a response, scheduled a visit, and then added a line, *How would you feel if I took the business remote? We could still find a way to meet in person.*

He stared at his words, debating deleting them, not his clients' problem. But without their bookings, he'd surely flounder no matter what he chose.

Cole sent the email. Then he cleaned up his mess. He had evening plans to get ready for.

• • •

"Will your ears be able to handle this?" Cole asked as he entered the karaoke lounge with Mac. The music felt loud to his ears, and he didn't know how that would translate for her.

She bumped his hip. "Is it really a bad thing to miss a few things at karaoke?"

He laughed and pulled her into him, stealing a quick kiss. Now that he'd had a taste of her, he wasn't sure he could stop. Her hands settled on his shoulders, allowing him to deepen the kiss, not giving a damn where they were. He had half a mind to screw the karaoke—and his earlier resolve—and take her back to one of their cabins when she pulled back and licked her lips. He nearly went all cave man on her.

"I think you promised me some bad singing with the occasional *American Idol* contestant."

"That I did." He cleared his throat and let the cool lounge air do the trick to cool him down.

They settled in at two chairs with a small round table between, ordering drinks from a waiter passing by. A young twenty-something woman took the stage, smoothing out her dress.

Mac leaned in to Cole. "What do you think? Nerves or confidence? Is she going to be good or bad?"

Cole studied the woman, the way she didn't shift at all and kept her composure. She appeared at home on the stage. "She's got the poise. She might not be the best, but she'll be entertaining."

Mac stopped watching him to turn to the performer, who had started to sway to the opening cords of her song. "I'm torn. She's either already had a few drinks, which has her calm but also unfocused, though she will be entertaining. Or she's got the chops and a scout is going to snatch her up from the back." She turned, as though looking for said scout who happened to be relaxing on a cruise ship, waiting for his next big money maker.

He didn't see anyone that looked to have an air of importance about them. The lounge held several groups of varying ages, a mix between dressed up for dinner and casual. "I don't think it'll be the second one."

Mac snapped her fingers, a playful frown on her face.

The woman began singing, some Taylor Swift song, angry Taylor Swift, and her words slurred together. She spat the words out, eyes trained on one area of the lounge, and the crowd turned to see what had spurred on the song. A guy roughly the same age scrunched down in his chair, hand shielding his face. Next to him a group of women cheered the singer on.

Mac leaned in close. "Not a good cruise for relationships. Are you sure you want to try this with me?" Her lips held a tease, one that drowned out the loud noise.

Cole angled close to her ear, not sure where he needed to speak to be heard with her hearing aid snaking behind her ear. "I'll take my chances." If Mac sang angry songs about him on day eight, that still gave him five days to thoroughly enjoy her. A pulse point ticked in her neck, and he wanted to taste it.

The singer finished to a standing cheering section from her friends. The guy stood and walked off, but the singer didn't go after him. She grabbed his drink and knocked it back to more cheering.

The next singer took the stage, doing a surprisingly good Prince interpretation. Mac and Cole's drinks arrived, and they sipped and watched through the next two performers.

"You going to perform a song for me?" Cole asked during a quiet moment as performers changed.

Mac picked up her drink. "Absolutely not. I am much more the clap-and-cheer audience member than a public singer."

"Suit yourself. It could be fun." He leaned into her space. "A fun duet?"

She shook her head, hand not as steady putting her untouched drink back on the table. He liked her reactions, liked playing and joking with her. But karaoke was for singing, and even though he wasn't the best, he enjoyed the fun.

Cole flipped through the song options, trying to think of what he could pull off and keep the flirting vibe going. He stopped when he found an Ed Sheeran song. That could work.

He waited for an older couple to perform "I Got You Babe." Both men, but one wore a long, Cher-type wig. Cole wasn't surprised when they were good, because who else travelled with costume pieces unless they planned to make good use of it?

He took the stage, the spotlight temporarily shielding the audience from him. Until Mac cheered, and he followed the sound, finding his little spot of sunlight out in the crowd. "This is for my companion for the week," he said as the music started. Mac grinned, and in that moment, he would have sung anything to make her happy.

"The Shape of You" started, and he did his best Ed Sheeran impression, gliding to the beat. He wasn't as good as the Sonny and Cher couple, but he could carry a tune and add enough flair to entertain the crowd.

Then the chorus started, and he wanted to kick himself. He knew the song was sexy and adoring of the female form, and that's what he wanted to show Mac. But singing about love to someone he'd known for two days should have been a light-and-fluffy joke.

He felt it. Felt the live wire between them, as though the other audience members didn't exist. Felt more than a song, more than a fling. Felt more than he had in so damn long that it wanted to climb up and choke the hell out of him.

He couldn't stop, not if he wanted to, couldn't stop singing about loving her body. Or thinking of having her. For the week, nothing more. But in that moment, in that song, it didn't feel like the truth.

The song finished, and he nearly stumbled making his way back to her, not hearing anything but the roaring pulse beating in his ear. The crowd could have cheered or booed, and it wouldn't have affected him, not in the slightest.

He reached Mac and pulled her into a kiss, bent over

awkwardly, but not caring with her lips against his, her hands in his hair, and all that heat swelling around him.

His blood slowed, and the cheers and whistles registered. He stopped the kiss and sat down next to a flushed Mac.

"That was quite the performance." Her fingers touched her lips.

"Maybe one day you'll let me show you more." He wanted to drag her away, finish exploring where their chemistry would lead. But at that moment he needed to cool off and figure out where the hell that song came from.

Day 4: Haiti

Cole lounged in a beach chair, teal water teasing the shore mere feet away. The sun beat down overhead, the occasional light breeze floating past. The air filled with the mingling scents of suntan lotion, sand, and water.

Hands behind his head, he was in heaven. He tilted his view toward the water, where Mac stood calf deep with Quinn. The water slapped their legs as they laughed. Mac's marigold hair was picked up by the brilliant sun, blond hues shining. God, she was beautiful.

She wet her hands, rubbing her arms and neck with a fresh sheen of water. He nearly drooled, wanting to be her hands or the water now clinging to her skin. Cole's gaze drifted to her cleavage, accentuated by the tight top of her black-and-white bathing suit. He no longer cared about the paradise view, because he only wanted to see her.

Someone sat down next to him. "Do you need a bucket of cold water?" Trent asked.

Probably. Cole peeled his gaze off of Mac. He eyed his friend's knee and the fresh white bandage. A stab of guilt hit him, a light one since Trent only needed a bandage, not an amputation. "How's the leg?"

Trent glanced down at his knee, and Cole knew the image that played in his head, the same that played in Cole's, of that awful day when it had been Cole's leg covered in blood, never to be used again.

Trent shook his head, and the smoke-filled memories faded back to teal water and clear skies. "I'll live."

Out on the water, Mac laughed with Quinn. Trent glanced out to the water at Mac, and back at Cole. "I know your reasons for keeping things light, but she might be worth it."

Cole snorted. "You damn well know as well as I do that nothing in life is guaranteed."

Trent tapped his unbandaged knee. "Look, this is the wrong time to get into it, but it needs to be said. Losing your leg was bad enough, but then you closed yourself off. You were dealing with a lot, so I got it. But now…" He squinted at Mac. "How you act around her is closer to the person you were before the bombing, a person that's been missing since."

Cole stared at his friend, ignoring the twist in his gut. He wanted fun. Plain and simple. "Your point in telling me this?"

"This doesn't have to be a fling. You do the fling thing to ensure no one gets close. Always holding them out at arm's length, ready to run at a moment's notice. Take a chance. Let her in."

"I don't run," Cole grumbled.

"You swapped running with your legs to running with your heart."

Did he really? Mac pulled her hair off her neck, revealing skin he wanted to kiss. Whether he ran—figuratively—or wanted a fling or not almost didn't matter. He wanted her. And he needed to shift this conversation fast. "What about

Quinn?"

Trent shot his gaze to Quinn and her itty-bitty bikini. "What about her?" Only he didn't move an inch, not shifting or even attempting to look back at Cole.

"Gonna take a chance?"

Trent laughed and stood up. "Can't, there's a difference."

Mac and Quinn made their way back over. Mac was dripping from her shoulders down and very much a wet dream. Cole followed the droplets of water down her curves and had to bite his tongue. Quinn remained dry except for her legs.

"You'd be a lot cooler if you took a dip," Trent said to Quinn when they got close.

Quinn wrung her hands together. "Mac can't get her hearing aids wet, and I don't like the feel of dripping water." Either proving her point, or because of her point, she picked up her towel and dried off her legs.

"You don't?"

Quinn shook her head. "It's a neurodiverse sensory thing. Ever wear a pair of stiff pants that are really uncomfortable and you can't wait to get them off and can't think of anything else until they are off?"

Trent patted his pockets and held out his hands. "These are stiff, but I'm used to it."

"Talk to me when you have something you can't get used to."

Cole watched Trent, suddenly a great deal more interested in watching him stumble at Quinn's feet. Curious if he was willing to stick his neck out. Because while he would admit he'd been distant since the attack, Trent wasn't that much better.

"There's got to be a way to get used to it," Trent said.

Quinn shrugged. "Not for me." Her gaze locked on Trent, her lips curving. "I'd rather go naked than be uncomfortable."

Trent grinned, and Cole saw it, bait taken. At least they could start a support group.

"Well, lovely chatting with you folks," Trent said to the ladies, ignoring Cole. "I'm off to do my job. Enjoy the island."

Mac settled back on the towel-covered chair beside Cole, water droplets still clinging to her skin. Quinn sat down on Mac's other side and fixed her bikini top.

Cole rubbed his hands together and kept his eyes on Mac. "I've got two surprises up my sleeve. You need to pick one."

"You don't want me to choose something," she said.

"Ahh, but I do. One is the zip line, over water. The other is the aqua park." He pointed out to the blue-and-yellow inflatable contraptions, floating between the island and the ship.

Mac's gaze traveled down to his leg. "You can do both of those?"

Cole stretched his amputated leg out. "Sure. The aqua park might be best if I took the prosthesis off. I don't let it slow me down." Much.

Mac looked at him, her eyes wide behind her glasses. "Those both need to be purchased. Did you learn nothing from Shark Shirt?"

Cole laughed. Unlike Shark Shirt, he didn't mind spending the money, and he didn't share finances with Mac.

"Don't ruin a man willing to spend money on you," Quinn offered.

Cole knocked fists with Quinn. "She's right. Say thank you and pick one. Or do you not like a little adventure?" He leaned forward and let his gaze collide with hers.

"Adventure, sure. But I always choose wrong and—"

"Don't overthink. First one that interests you, first instinct. Own it. Zip line or aqua park?"

She bit her lip as she looked over the island, head shifting left and right. "Zip line."

"Is that your first choice? Because Cole here is right. Let him be your cruise hero." Quinn reached into her bag and pulled out an ereader.

"Excuse me?" Mac's cheeks matched her hair. She grabbed the device from Quinn. "What exactly are you reading? *Fifty Shades of Making Mackenzie Blush*?"

Quinn grabbed her ereader back. "If you must know, I'm reading a young adult fantasy."

Cole shoved his right foot into his sneaker; he hadn't bothered taking the left off. "Young adult?"

"The books are good, and the characters are young. And they all have names like 'Cole.'"

"Or Quinn."

She grinned, pulled down her sunglasses, and began reading.

"So what do you say, Mackenzie-Mac? Zip line?"

Mac took a deep breath and eyed the aqua course again. "Yes. First instinct. Zip line. You'll regret it."

He highly doubted that. It was clear she would have changed her mind. He wanted to see what going with her first choice would do for her.

...

Mac stood on a platform high above the ground. Through the mesh of the white floor, she looked down, down, down to the microscopic sand and trees below. Over the railing, trees and water lined the zip line's path, leading up to a sand dune.

Adrenaline skipped through her veins, her normal life a mere figment of her imagination. Why had she ever doubted this vacation? She took in a deep breath of the salty air, her lungs filling, and closed her eyes in the gentle breeze.

Her pulse kicked, again, as warm hands grasped her waist, and an even warmer chest pressed against her back.

"Scared?"

She grinned and opened her eyes. "Not the slightest bit." She turned in his arms. "You?"

"What's there to be afraid of?"

"A five-hundred-foot drop?" a shaky, squeaky voice from across the platform said. "And faulty wires?"

Mac turned to a twenty-something man with hair even redder than hers and a breathing pattern a tad too close to hyperventilation. A pang of sympathy coursed through her.

"Come on, man," said one of his buddies. "Don't be such a wuss."

Mac turned to Cole. "Nice friends."

He lifted a shoulder. "Guys."

She pointed. "If he flips, throws up, or creates a scene, my luck proves right."

"If it doesn't affect you, then it doesn't."

She didn't have time to dwell, as it was their turn to climb into the individual seats connected to the zip line. She got in, and a nice Haitian man with limited English and an accent she couldn't quite comprehend secured the harness. Cole got into the seat next to her with its own cable attached overhead, and on the other side of him the scared man and his buddies. The scared man struggled to get a breath, and the zip line operators attempted to calm him down with their limited English.

Or, at least, she hoped they tried to calm him down.

He only gasped harder.

"See?" Mac said to Cole.

He turned to the man. "Look, do you want to have a fun ride down to the sand, or wet your pants and make your friends laugh at you?"

The buddies laughed harder, but the scared guy steadied his breathing, a determined expression crossing his brow. The staff didn't take any chances and sent him down the tracks, his screams filling the air.

"Are you a screamer as well?"

Mac laughed and held her hands wide to the side as instructed. "I enjoy my thrills in silence. Some even say I look bored." It was true. She once got off a roller coaster and her older brother asked her why she didn't have fun. She did have fun. She just didn't need to scream.

"All thrills?" Cole arched an eyebrow. "I bet I could make you scream."

With her breath knocked out of her, the line above her head released. She let go of the anticipation running through her veins, the kind that had nothing to do with the zip line. The wind rushed past her face, rustled against her microphones, and filtered through her open hands. She took in the island sights, all appearing miniature from her position high above the curved tops of trees—a life-size model in teeny tiny form, one that could fit in a gift shop snow globe. She sped toward the ground, and the landscape grew bigger, sand clearer, rustling water stronger. In the moment, her own thoughts didn't exist, only the rush of the experience.

Funny, she sat in a safe contraption, but she felt as though she flew through the air. Toward a better future. Intense thoughts for a zip line but there it was. A better future.

All too soon, sand came up close to her feet. She toggled the brakes and slowed down. Refreshed and rejuvenated, she got out of the harness and moved back in time to see Cole land. He had a huge grin on his face and hooted as he came to a stop.

He walked over and pulled her close, fitting his mouth to hers. Still on a euphoric high from the zip, she melted into him. His tongue teased her lips, forcing her resolve to puddle at her feet. He pulled back. "How about I get some noise out of you?"

Her knees wanted to buckle. She locked them. "You

could try. You may not succeed."

He laughed and kept one arm around her. "Let's go."

As they walked away, the redheaded man's friend threw up into the shallow water, to laughter from the redhead and a bit of a commotion from the men working the line.

"See, you had a good time, even if they didn't."

Mac paused, and Cole stumbled over his feet at the action. "Huh, you're right. Maybe it's you?"

He brushed a lock of hair behind her ear. "I'm just a little birdie on your shoulder."

"Funny, you look more like the devil."

His gaze drifted down to her lips and lingered. "Sounds a lot more fun."

She bit her lip and resumed walking, pulling him along. Time to go for what she wanted, and right now, she wanted him.

...

Back on the ship, Cole followed Mac like a lovesick puppy. Trent's comments be damned. He held her hand, thumb brushing over her knuckles, keeping that tension simmering between them. He wanted her with a need he hadn't known before. He chalked it up to the anticipation; no other answers made sense. She led him right to her stateroom, the invitation clear without a word. Once inside, the door clicked closed, and she locked it before turning around to face him. Those blue eyes were filled with heat, shooting an arrow of desire directly to his groin.

A region of his body not in need of any further encouragement.

He stepped toward Mac as she stepped toward him. A beat passed, and then they both moved, eliminating the distance between them, arms wrapped around each other, mouths devouring. Raw passion and primal need fueled the kiss, spurred on further by the taste and texture of her. Sweat and suntan lotion filled the air, but Cole was still overcome by the subtle floral scent of Mackenzie. "You smell good," he muttered when he got his mouth free for a second.

She clung back to his lips. "I've been sweating in the sun most of the day. You lie."

"Maybe I like your sweat and want to create more."

He dove back into the kiss, and she met his intensity. She moved them further into the room. Her palms collided with his chest until he fell backward onto her bed. She climbed on top before he could react, her hot body covering his, her lips on his neck. She sat on his erection, and there were too many layers of clothing between them, because all he wanted to do was worship this holy goddess on top of him.

He took the green light with a greed he didn't often unleash and ran his hands up her sides, down, and grasped her lush rear. He rocked her further into him, and they both groaned at the contact.

Oh yeah, it was time to unleash. He pulled off her tank top. Her hands skimmed under his shirt, roaming over him with an abandonment he wanted to encourage, before his shirt joined hers.

She leaned back and sat up, rubbing the very center of her over the part of him desperate for an introduction. She glanced down at her bathing suit top and stopped. "This is snug. There's nothing graceful about how this comes off."

He sat up, keeping her in his lap. "As long as it comes off." He found her mouth again, the heat swamping him, and pulled back. "Are we moving too fast?" His dick twitched in a "what the hell are you saying, man?" move the rest of him agreed with. But his moral center stayed firm.

"We only have a week, and right now, I want this."

On that he couldn't argue.

She pulled at the top strap, pushing her elbow into the material, before sliding her arm down and shimmying the material up. She was right; it wasn't graceful, but he didn't care. Certainly not when one breast popped free. As she continued to struggle, he ran a hand up her stomach, over the round underside, before brushing over her pink nipple.

Body contorted and stuck in the top, she gasped and leaned into his hand, pressing all the warm flesh against him. Her nipple hardened against his thumb before he pulled back. Mac took a deep breath and wrestled her way out of the bathing suit, freeing a second breast just as glorious as the first.

Before her top hit the floor, he had her breasts in his hands, and all rational thought fell away. Not with her there, with him. Nothing else mattered, not tomorrow or next week or last year. He flipped her onto her back and trailed kisses down her neck, learning the taste and texture of her, loving her up. Her smooth skin was, perhaps, his new favorite flavor.

Her hands roamed over him. Little arousing murmurs escaped her lips as her hands played with the top of his trunks. She pulled the stretchy fabric away from his skin, and a rush of air breezed over the hottest part of him. He picked his head up and caught her hands.

"Not until you scream." He held her wrists and pinned them above her head, holding her eyes captive in his.

"You're going to be disappointed, Cole," she said with a rare show of confidence.

He grasped both her wrists in one hand and trailed the other hand down her body, over an erect nipple, and under her shorts and bathing suit bottoms. She gasped, and her body arched for him. "You lie," he said.

"I don't lie, you—"

He stopped her with a kiss and waited until she went limp before releasing her wrists and pulling down her shorts and bathing suit in one tug. His heart nearly thudded out of his chest at the site of her naked before him. And no doubt, she was a natural redhead.

She stirred, so he crushed his mouth to hers, tasting her, tangling tongues to the rhythm of his pounding veins. He slid a hand up her thigh, between her legs, and coaxed the very center of her. She whimpered and squirmed beneath him. Desire pounded through him, and he almost pulled off his trunks and dove into her wet warmth. Until logic stopped him.

His condoms were in his room.

Mac squirmed, shifting her position, claiming her pleasure. There was no way he was leaving until he got her to vocalize. He slipped one long finger into her wet heat. She gasped, digging her nails into his back. Oh no, she wasn't going to be quiet. He was sure of it. He added a second finger. She moaned a little louder, and her eyes fluttered closed, those nails embedded in his flesh.

He leaned forward to kiss a nipple, then used his tongue to mimic the motion of his fingers. Her moan turned into a throaty whimper at the back of her throat. He knew her sounds would stir him on, and he wasn't wrong. Those little noises, growing louder, filled him with such a sense of accomplishment. A little louder and he'd consider it mission complete. But what a mission. Tongue on her nipple, fingers between her thighs, he'd happily remain here all day.

Her hands left his back and fisted into the sheets at her side. "Oh God, Cole. I need to—" Her voice trailed off, her body squirming, her hands tugging on the sheets. He shifted his fingers inside her, hitting something good, because her hands released the fabric and she let out a high-pitched moan louder than her speaking voice.

He covered her mouth with his own. Mission accomplished. Her body shuddered underneath him. "Oh,

Mackenzie-Mac, you are a treasure."

Her breathing slowed and a smile graced her lips. He moved his fingers to petting her lightly as her blue eyes opened. "Why are you still dressed?"

"You got kinda loud there."

"That's a first. Let's make it a second. Undress." She propped herself up on her elbows, and his dick twitched in agreement.

He patted his pocket. "No condom."

She shook her head and laughed. "Men really don't know how to stop and ask for directions." She rolled over, pulled out a bag from under the bed, and tossed a shiny package his way.

"Still wouldn't have missed that for the world."

A contented smile plastered on her face. "Yeah, yeah, now strip." Without waiting for him to respond, she pulled off his trunks. She moved in a careful manner, cautious of his prosthesis. On her way back up his body, she ran her tongue up his good leg, up his shaft, and wrapped her lips around the part of him now openly begging for an introduction.

His heart tried to break free of his chest, and if it succeeded, he would have died a very happy man. She sucked him into her mouth, and his head fell back in pleasure. His balls pulled up tight, tingling, and wanting her to continue conflicted with getting inside her. He grabbed her shoulders to yank her up. "You keep that up and you would have grabbed the condom for nothing."

She wrapped herself around him and kissed his mouth with the same ferocity she had been kissing his other region. Sweat made their bodies glide together with ease. Everywhere they touched smoked. He rolled her to her back, slid the condom on, and pushed home.

They both gasped at the contact, at the fit. He was a goner. There was no coming back from this, no topping it, nothing. He couldn't say a damn word even if he wanted to, so he showed her the best he could with his actions. He guessed she felt it, because this time he did get her to scream.

...

Mac lay on her back, spent and sated, with Cole nuzzling into her neck. His fast breaths matched hers. She had never done more than soft moans during sex before, never had the urge. Cole first teased out volume with his fingers, but once connected he drove her right out of her mind. Her second orgasm hit with such intensity she couldn't help the scream that left her lips.

She should be mortified but felt too damn good to be embarrassed. Especially when Cole still hadn't moved. He remained connected with her, and all she cared about was how they felt together. Unable to help herself, her hand stroked up and down his toned back and squeezed his butt.

His head jerked up. "Can I help you? You want me to move? Park somewhere else?"

She shook her head even as her mind raced. He said "park" with no *R*, sounded more like "pahk," more Boston than anything else. A reminder he was, in fact, local. Her fling with a stranger had turned into sex with a local boy.

She focused on his green eyes, the feel of his body. Pass on Cole? No way. Certainly not the first screaming sex of her life.

He moved off her and brushed some hair from her forehead before planting a kiss there. "Be right back," he said before heading to the bathroom.

He wore nothing but his prosthesis, and she took in the slight halt to his gait, a view so different from normal and just as enjoyable. Limbs too sated to move, she stayed where she was. She could have a fling back home. And this one could easily stay on the ship.

Cole returned from the bathroom and pulled her into his arms. Rolling into him, she snuggled up, placing her head on his chest, the soft thump of his heart beneath her ear. Neither of them said anything. Her finger drifted over his skin, making a lazy path down to his left hip and back. On her return trip, she reached the top of the silky upper band around his leg. "What happened?"

He laughed in contrast to the way his body stiffened. "Never play pirates in bed when souvenir swords are lying around."

Mac let her gaze drift down his body. Damn, he was hot. "Any other scars from that incident?"

"I managed to get the scoundrel apprehended."

Another fake story. Why would he lie about the leg? He hadn't relaxed, and she was torn between asking more questions and finding some way to relax him. Not thoughts for a fling. Why did the real story matter? And why did she care so much about the leg?

She peeled her body off of his. "Can I see?" she asked and gestured to his left leg.

He sat up. "Really? Most people are a little put off."

For reasons she couldn't fathom, she wasn't. "Really."

His green eyes held hers for a beat before he crossed the prosthesis over his other leg. He pressed a button above where his ankle should have been. The sound of air being released filled the cabin. Then he slid the main part of the leg off, leaving the silky cover. He rolled down the band, past his knee. Several inches later, it left his body.

This leg had different muscular definition, a faint scar lining the stump. And now he was completely naked.

She reached out her hand. "May I?"

"Yeah." His eyes followed her as she ran her fingers lightly over his knee, down the stump, and back up again.

"Does it hurt?"

He finally relaxed. "Not for a long time. I do get phantom pains, though. Not fun." He stretched his legs out, much like anyone would.

With a shocking need, she wanted the truth. There was a story here, and it had nothing to do with swords or sharks. She also had the sudden urge to run her tongue up his mangled leg. Not fling thoughts. Those new emotions deserved to be shoved into a box, and locked. "I'm hungry, you?" Where were her clothes? She needed some distance and perspective, stat.

"A workout deserves some replenishing, I think."

If he sensed her discomfort, he didn't say anything. Which was good, because she had no answers.

• • •

Three hours and a large ice cream later, Mac and Cole went their separate ways for dinner. At least she was doing a good job eating her way through the cruise. Point one for the cruise goal list. And she'd gotten laid, so wasn't it really point two?

She'd go with two points. Not bad for day four.

"Mac, Mac," Quinn exclaimed as Mac made her way to their dinner table. "Did you hear about the aqua park?"

Mac sat down, thanked the waiter for the menu, and fixed the napkin draped across her lap. "What about the aqua park?"

"This girl has been thrilled about other people's misfortune." Rob rolled his eyes.

"Hush." Quinn slapped his shoulder. "One of the large inflatable structures sprung a leak or something and they had to shut it down."

Mac almost dropped her water glass. "What?" No way this was real.

"First instinct, dead on."

Rob raised a glass of wine in Mac's direction. "Always trust your first instinct."

Her brain stuttered over this information. "So if we hadn't chosen the zip line...?"

"You wouldn't have been able to do the aqua park."

Mac leaned back and rubbed her neck. "Wow. This has never happened. Never." She always ended up on the wrong path. How did she manage to get the right one? It twisted awkwardly deep inside, hinting at something she needed to focus on, but she brushed it away. Coincidence, that was all. Her track record proved it.

"So...first instinct. Cole. Go." Rob prodded a finger in her direction.

She gulped some water. Instincts and her didn't mesh, they'd learn soon enough. But she did know a thing or two about Cole. "He's...I don't know, fun to be around."

"Ooohhhh, are we using 'fun' in air quotes?" Quinn squirmed in her seat. "Tell me you did him, please tell me!"

Mac's cheeks burned. She was sure she still had some Greatest Sex of Her Life afterglow.

"Damn, look at that smile. Good for you," Rob said. And one of the other ladies at the table nodded.

Mac laughed. "I did not come here for a fling, even if my friends wanted me to have one. My life is too much of a mess back home."

"I suspect your friends were right," Quinn said.

"What do you want out of this cruise?" Rob asked.

Mac brushed at her napkin. "A fun time. A chance to recharge and put my life back on track."

"And Cole doesn't help you feel recharged?"

Mac couldn't stop the grin if she tried.

Rob leaned back and picked up his water. "Enjoy him. Great sex has a way of setting one's life back on track."

Mac raised her eyebrows. "I highly doubt that."

Rob took a sip of his drink. "I know, but wouldn't it be great if that was true?"

To that Mac could only lift her glass and tap it to his.

· · ·

Before dinner, Cole wandered down one of the many long corridors. He passed door after door. Some had Do Not Disturb signs out, and others had room service on the floor. Carts for the cabin stewards lined the sides, with several working at prepping rooms. He moved to the wall as groups and families traveled in the opposite direction. For the first time, ever, on vacation, he felt alone. Since leaving Mac.

When had sex ever left him out of sorts? As if he stood on the bow of the ship, one foot raised, a slight wind able to topple him over into the murky blue water.

Since Mac.

His leg intrigued her. Never before had he been with someone with such open curiosity. Open acceptance. Heck, he'd never even taken off the prosthesis with a date before. Went hand in hand with not being the type of guy to spend the night, no need to risk a reaction. And no one had asked him to. Until Mac.

No, he wasn't going there. He rounded a corner to the center of the ship, opened the glass door of one of the computer lounges. Quasi cubicles lined the sides, each housing a computer. He picked one, typed in his information, and sat there, staring at the revolving working indicator as he waited for the log in to complete.

He had nothing better to do than be lost in his own thoughts. He'd done his best to keep his mind off what was happening between Mac and him. This particular woman, randomly picked from a cruise ship, made a dent into him like no one else had. Didn't matter he wasn't prepared, and had no plans to be prepared, because something deep inside had latched and—

Oh, thank God, the page loaded. He scanned through his emails, focusing only on the important messages, and started with the update from Dani.

He clicked and tapped his fingers on the desk as he read.

From: Dani Martin
To: Cole Matterhorn
Subject: RE: Update

I booked a lovely three-week Australian trip to an older couple, and if I could join them on this trip I would!

If I have any say in it, you will never discover the true meaning behind my mystery booking.

Oh, and have fun. Knowing you, you've had a little extra fun and will be able to confirm that the size of the cabin does not make a difference.

~Dani

Yeah, yeah, he did have some fun. So much fun it had morphed into something he had no familiarity with.

From: Cole Matterhorn
To: Dani Martin
Subject: RE: Update

Great job on the Australian trip! Cannot confirm, found someone with water views.

Cole

P.S. What do you want for a souvenir this time? More rum cake?

He handled a few more emails, noting his top clients had yet to respond. No easy answers in his future, but he knew that. He loaded the emails filled with information and used the printer to make his research smoother before a hand on his shoulder stopped him. Trent perched on the edge of the empty seat next to him.

"How's business?"

Cole gestured to the small pile of papers waiting for him in the printer. Trent reached over and grabbed it, but not before shuffling through.

"Advertising?" Trent handed the papers over.

"Advertising. I need to figure out if I can make remote cost effective or drum up more business for staying with the rent increase."

"Do you really need an office?"

"My top clients book in person, and I get walk-ins. I'll lose both."

"But no rent."

"There are other expenses with remote. If I lose both, I might not be able to pay Dani." Cole scrubbed a hand down his face. It really was a lose-lose situation. He disconnected from the internet, not able to meet his friend's scrutiny. Not that keeping his head down made any difference to Trent. They'd been through far too much for Cole to slip one past him. Between his lease situation and all these new emotions with Mac, he felt untethered, and he didn't like that sensation.

"You look like you want to drown yourself in about ten beers."

Cole stretched and placed his hands behind his head, trying for casual when he felt more formal than his green dress shirt and black pants. "Maybe five."

Trent's gaze took in everything, and Cole stopped trying to fool him. "We're not talking about the business anymore, are we?"

He ran his hand through his hair. "I don't know. You started this."

Trent choked down a laugh. "Oh man. Not for nothing, but I think she's good for you."

"She doesn't help me figure out the lease situation."

"Not what I'm talking about." Trent shook his head. "Anyway, did you get to the aqua park before it closed down?"

Cole stilled. "What?"

"We had an issue with one of the inflatables. Something nicked it good and it deflated. I wondered if the metal on your leg took down the inflatable as well as my knee."

"Fuck you, you fell, and you know it. You serious about the inflatables?" He couldn't stop the grin from spreading. Mac's bad luck would have held true if he'd let her change her mind.

Trent squashed his eyebrows together. "You didn't go to the aqua park?"

"We went to the zip line instead. I made Mac stick with her first choice."

Trent stared at him as if he spoke a foreign language. Well, it wasn't the first, or the last, time that happened. "Anyways, glad you weren't affected." He patted Cole's shoulder and rose.

Cole scrubbed a hand over his cheek and headed off to dinner.

...

Two hours and a full belly later, Cole waited by a central staircase for Mac. Around him people passed by on their way to do whatever activity their evening held, and unless they wore bathing suits he couldn't begin to guess their intentions. He wished he could go into a guessing game, even with himself, or that crowds no longer bothered him. But along with losing his leg, he also lost his comfort in crowds. Especially when he spotted a random bag abandoned on the ground. He'd been close to an abandoned bag before, one that held a bomb inside. Close enough that the flying shrapnel had severed his leg beyond repair.

Cole stared at the bag as panic gripped him by the balls. Bags, crowds, commotions, a shift in the wind, all had been known to bring back those memories, fresh enough to taste the blood. Nine years had passed, nine years without so much as a scratch, and yet the fear remained.

Because terrorist shit still happened and could happen anywhere.

Only now he had a separate fear: what if that bag really did hold a bomb, and it went off as Mac strode past? She'd be close enough that a missing limb would be nothing. She'd lose her life.

The fear dug down deep, gripped his balls, and played a very real "what if" video montage in his mind.

Cole forced himself to breathe and look up and away from the gruesome images filling him. Only they morphed from fiction to fact. He didn't see the bag anymore. He saw that awful day much too long ago for these panic attacks to continue. Above him a high chandelier cascaded drops of light below, and all Cole could envision was the damn thing shattering into people. He closed his eyes, focused on his breathing, on the rumbling of the ship as it headed toward their next destination. On the soft music and voices overlapping. No screaming, no explosions, no reason to panic except if one lived in his PTSD brain.

When the images behind his eyelids faded and his breathing resembled a light jog rather than a sprint, he opened his eyes. The bag had been removed.

He didn't know if that made him feel safer or not.

The panic threatened to return, and he searched the area for something to ground him away from this hell. He found it. Orange and yellow, his personal marigold. Mac. A long red dress adorned her body, a slit up one side teasing him with a glimpse of her knee as she moved. The lingering memories and fears fled, her presence a beacon in his storm, shifting his thoughts to this afternoon, with her under him. His body stirred and images of how he could remove that dress, and what she'd be wearing underneath, were fast making him dizzy from loss of blood.

Not the kind that escaped his body.

He finally found something able to calm him faster than the lackluster breathing exercises. Maybe her image would help him long after they parted ways.

Her hair was swept up off her face, a shine picked up by the chandelier. His mouth went dry. She was beautiful, and he bet she didn't even know it.

"How was dinner?" he said when she got close, then cleared his throat. Had he really been having a panic attack moments ago? He might need to revisit that to cut down the wood in his pants.

The light caught her ruby lips. "Not bad."

"What's the plan for tonight? We could grab some drinks and see where the night takes us." He leaned in and kissed her cheek, needing her in a way that contradicted their afternoon activity.

Her cheeks rose in a tempting grin. "Sounds good to me." She paused, hesitating for a moment. "But can we find a quieter bar, so I don't have to guess what you're saying?"

"The lady's request shall be granted."

They headed back to the bar where they first played trivia with Trent, grabbing a seat by the window. The moon cast a glow on the water, choppy with the ship traveling to the next port. Mac leaned back, eyes trained out the window, and sighed. "It doesn't get much better than this."

Considering the way he watched her, he had to agree.

"Vacation, bar, or the cruise itself?" Cole asked.

Mac faced him, tucking her bottom lip under her teeth, and he nearly leaned across the table to kiss her. "A little bit of all three?"

He scooted forward, unable to resist her pull. "But not me?"

She grinned, lip freed, eyes shining. He'd follow her over the edge of the ship if she asked. "But would that be you, specifically, or the many wonders of a fling?"

Cole laughed and forced himself upright. "I'd say the many wonders of a fling, but then I'd have to share. So I'd go with the many wonders of Cole instead."

Mac guffawed. "Makes you sound like an amusement park ride."

He shifted until he was close enough their noses could touch. "I can promise you a good time, though decidedly not meant for those under eighteen."

The waiter chose that moment to stop by their table. Mac's cheeks sported a nice red tint, but she managed to place her order, as did Cole.

"You are a menace," Mac said once the waiter left. Her eyes held his, and desire shined there.

"I think you like me that way."

"I'm afraid I do."

"Good, because I'm not done with you yet."

Mac licked her lips, and Cole had half a mind to screw the drinks and bring her back to one of their cabins. Until loud voices stole his attention.

"I said I was sorry!" a woman half screamed, half cried, and when Cole followed the sounds, he found the drunk karaoke girl and the guy he presumed was her boyfriend.

"You didn't want me here. Why did you invite me?"

"Because I love you," she sobbed.

The guy knocked back a short drink. "You wanted to flirt and pretend to be single with your friends. You can't have both." He slid his empty glass across the bar and got up.

"Wait, no, that's not true!" The woman scrambled after him, and their heated voices faded into the hall.

Mac touched Cole's shoulder. "What was that?"

He studied her blank expression. "You couldn't hear?"

She shook her head, so he quickly updated her.

"Oh boy, that's not good. Is this cruise cursed? That's two couples fighting."

He took her hand, running his thumb over her knuckles. "Not cursed, not when I get to meet you."

"That sounds a little too sweet and our drinks haven't arrived yet."

"Then I'm doing something right." He brought her hand to his lips, placing a lingering kiss there. Their drinks arrived, but neither moved, not when his own fast heart rate matched the pulse in her wrist.

Mac swallowed. "Want to take this back to my room?"

Cole released her hand. "Whatever the lady wishes."

• • •

Mac unlocked her cabin, very aware of the man pressed against her backside, her body tingling with anticipation. The door opened and she got them both inside before meshing her mouth to his. Her drink trickled over her fingers, and she nearly let the alcohol fall to the floor to get her hands on Cole.

Instead she broke the kiss, bringing her wet fingers to her lips and sucking.

Cole growled and put his drink on a table. "You're killing

me."

Mac laughed and lapped up the rest of her spilled drink before throwing an arm around Cole. He tasted like the bourbon he drank, and she relished the sting on her tongue, soothed by the texture of him.

"I've been wondering something since I saw you dressed up tonight," he murmured.

"What's that?"

"What you have on under this dress."

Mac sucked in a breath and thanked her lucky stars she had packed her fun undergarments. She swallowed some of her drink and placed it next to his. "Why don't you find out?" She stepped away from him, holding out her arms, offering herself up to him.

Cole ran a finger over her shoulder, shifting her strap but not removing it, doing the same with the other side. Desire surged from that little touch, her panties going damp.

He leaned into her, pressing an open-mouthed kiss to her shoulder. She shuddered. "Where should I start?" His fingers trailed down her back, brushing over her bra strap.

"Wh-wherever you want." She could barely speak with the want consuming her. If he didn't move soon, she'd need to make him.

"I see," he said, voice controlled and calm, the outline of him through his pants the only indication she got to him like he got to her.

His fingers moved to her knee, trailing up the slit in her dress, bunching the fabric higher until he hit the lacey band of her underwear. Mac struggled not to move, not to grab him and pull him down to the bed.

Then his other hand bunched up the other side of her dress, until both his hands toyed with the edge of her underwear. He tugged it down, off her legs, her dress covering her.

Mac stepped out of the garment, feeling undeniably sexy

standing there in her evening clothes and no underwear.

Cole lifted her undies. "Red lace." He sniffed it; she pressed her thighs together. "You smell good, Mackenzie-Mac."

"Cole, I'm about to rip your clothes off."

His lips curved. "Patience." His wandering hands went back to her shoulders, this time pushing the straps down her arms. He coaxed the fabric over her breasts, revealing her red strapless bra.

He opened his mouth, but no words came as he pulled her to him, lips on her neck. She ground against him, all that hardness she needed to touch and feel. He pushed her dress off. A moment later, her bra released. She tugged open his shirt, needing to touch him and unable to wait. "Cole," she whimpered as his fingers slid between her thighs.

"You want me," he said after coming in contact with her wetness.

"What was your first clue?"

Mac pulled him down to the bed, and they removed the rest of his clothes, taking the extra time to get his pants and underwear off his prosthesis. Her body nearly vibrated from want as she reached for a condom. But Cole wrapped his lips around her nipple, and her body lurched in pleasure. The moan left her, not a quiet one. This man got to her like none other, and she wanted more.

She ripped open the package and Cole moved, allowing her to roll the condom down his length. He was hot and hard, and she had so many things she wanted to do to him. But first, she needed this. Then she needed a bucket list, because this man deserved a little worshiping.

Mac settled on her back as Cole moved between her legs, sliding inside in one smooth stroke. She bit her lip, the scream building inside, and he crushed his mouth to hers as he moved, swallowing her sounds as he set her off again and again.

It had never been like this, and she feared she'd grow addicted to her strictly week-long fling. For now she planned to enjoy as much as she could.

She ran her hands up and down his body, squeezing his rear, and Cole picked up the pace, pulling her through the tidal wave one more time before catching his own release.

Best fling ever

They lay there, breathing heavy, bodies still meshed together. Her body still tingled with pleasure, little aftershocks working through her. The desire to hold on and never let go stirred. She ignored it. That was the sex talking, nothing else.

He shifted off her and reached over the side of the bed, picking up her lace panties. "You color coordinate quite nice, Mackenzie-Mac."

She grabbed the underwear from his hands. "If you want to make a joke about my hair, you can leave."

He covered her body with his, hers revving up again at the contact. "Red is my new favorite color. Especially the marigold shade on some of the best parts of your body."

Mac was still boneless from the multiple orgasms, but she melted. He kissed her, running a hand through her hair. "All right, fine. You can stay."

He grinned and rubbed a thumb over her cheek. "Until when?" He bent and nibbled her collarbone.

She squeaked, her sated body demanding more. "Keep that up and I may let you stay until morning."

"Is that a challenge?" he asked.

She ran her fingers into his hair. "Maybe."

Day 5: Puerto Rico

Mac woke up sprawled out on her bed. She breathed in deep and was met with a masculine scent. A scent her cabin hadn't had before. Her eyes popped open to the hard chest masquerading as her pillow.

Cole. She breathed him in. How did he manage to smell so good first thing in the morning? He remained fast asleep. During sex he was all encompassing, taking over her entire body and bed. Asleep, he took up only a sliver of space. For the first time, she became the hog, spread out over the bed and him. It warmed her insides, plucked at her tender heart.

She studied his messed-up sandy hair, the way half covered his forehead and the other half stuck up in multiple directions. His eyelashes brushed against his cheeks. And somehow, the man slept with a smile on his face.

She guessed she put it there.

Her phone lit up, and she collected her glasses to investigate. She plucked it off the nightstand and noticed she had cell connection on top of her cruise wifi.

From: Dani Martin
To: Mackenzie Laurels
Subject: Flings

If he's a good kisser, then you better find out if he's good in other departments! I won't take no for an answer!

Mac held in a laugh.

From: Mackenzie Laurels
To: Dani Martin
Subject: My Fling

Other departments still have my toes curled. I give him a solid score of a 9. I fully plan to enjoy him for the rest of the trip, should help me feel quite refreshed when I arrive home. All the better for putting my life back together.

She clicked send and held the phone to her chest. Why had she ever doubted this fling idea? Before she could ponder that further, her phone rang. "Before He Cheats" filled the room. *Crap.* Sliding off the bed, she grabbed her bathrobe, tying the sash before stepping out onto the balcony.

"What do you want, Chad?" she barked into the phone.

"Where the hell are you, Mackenzie?" he retorted without any good humor. At least he was loud enough she managed to find the right position to hear without her hearing aids on.

"You fired me, as I keep reminding you."

"I'm done playing games. You need to come back."

She scoffed and once again contemplated throwing her phone off the balcony. Of course, she'd probably hit someone on the pier below with her luck.

"Look, with how we left things, what do you really expect?"

She heard what sounded like a wind tunnel and knew it had nothing to do with the glorious weather surrounding her or what would usually be wind against her hearing aids. "I want you back."

This time she nearly dropped her phone instead of throwing it. "What?"

"I want you back. I made a mistake, and I want you back."

As she struggled to process this, a soft thud and movement caught her attention. She turned and saw Cole standing in the doorway. He leaned against the slider on his right leg, stump unadorned. She didn't focus on the stump, not when the morning light hit the hard planes of his naked body; any shadows only increased the drool-worthy image. His brow wrinkled in concern. Leave Cole for Chad? Never in a million years. She held up a finger to him and turned back around.

"You don't tell me you cheated, move my stuff out, and fire me and seriously expect me back. You don't. I was a mistake all along. Not your fault, that one's on me for even agreeing to date you in the first place. But right now I'm hundreds of miles away, and after today you won't be able to reach me until next week. Stop calling, stop emailing, and move on. Oh, and Chad? Stop dating people you work with."

"But Mac, you were damn good at your job. I need you back."

"You're right, I was damn good at my job. And you'll find someone else. But do me and everyone else a favor? Keep your dick out of this one and maybe you'll keep her. Goodbye, Chad."

She disconnected the call and stared out at the island before her. Half of her wanted to crumble; the other half felt as alive as the blue sky dotting the horizon. Cole reached out and pulled her back into his sturdy figure.

"The ex?" he asked.

She nodded, and dammit, tears filled her eyes. She blinked them back.

"You worked for him?"

She turned in his arms, and the sincerity on his face did her in. "Yeah, I worked for him." She managed a small smile. "I lived with him, too. I've got no job, no home, and am on a cruise ship. See, Cole, bad decisions."

He pulled her close, and she placed her head on his shoulder. "This may have been the best decision you've had. It allowed me to meet you."

"Don't go there," she whispered, "please." She couldn't have her fling be better for her than her ex, and nothing in this moment felt like a fling.

He angled his back to the wall and held her close, one hand running a lazy path up and down her spine. He cleared his throat. "As you wish."

It was too much, all too much. She brushed her lips to his once, twice, before sinking in with everything she had, everything tumbling around inside and making her feel completely unhinged.

He ran his hands down to her behind and squeezed. "Once upon a time, I could pick you up. Sadly, chivalry doesn't work with the stump. Even if my intentions are nowhere near chivalrous."

That made her smile. She didn't know what it was about the man and the moment. She took his hand as he grasped onto the furniture and hopped toward the bed. Once there he sat, pulling her into the *V* of his legs. His hands slid into her bathrobe, against her flesh, before nudging her closer. She settled in, dipping her head until their lips met. The heat flared as his mouth devastated her with kisses that turned her legs to jelly.

One hand slid up her stomach, palming the weight of her breast. The other pushed her bathrobe away from her neck, exposing her shoulder. Her body positively hummed, yearning for more. She untangled herself to step back and tugged on the rope around her waist. The robe puddled at her feet, Cole's gaze soaking her up. He made her feel sexy and alive, especially as he reached for her. It had been so long since she'd been made to feel this way. She wanted to keep it, and she knew better than to allow herself to want. That behavior awarded her assholes like Chad.

"No, don't go there. Stay here, with me," Cole said, brushing a hand over her cheek. She closed her eyes at his touch, following the sensations. His other hand skimmed alongside her breast until he found her nipple, connecting with a firestorm of nerve endings. Much better sensation than thinking about…about… She couldn't remember his name and didn't want to.

She pushed Cole on his back and climbed on top of him. She wanted the mindlessness, needed it, now. She kissed him with everything she had, rocking against the most interesting part of him.

His hands did something wonderful and amazing to her breasts, and thoughts of anything but him faded away. Her blood heated and body raced toward that cliff, yearning to dive over, to release, into oblivion. Mindful of only herself, and her need, she grasped onto him and stroked until his eyes closed, until his hands stilled on her, until she felt him throb just as she throbbed.

Then she sank down onto him, onto all that hardness, and every nerve ending she had pooled in her groin and reveled in the sensation. Cole gasped and said, "Mackenzie," but she was too far into him, too far gone. She raised herself up and dropped herself down, knocking the rest of the words right out of him, replacing it with a moan that only heated her further.

She continued to ride him in mindless pleasure, her body

revved. When she started to whimper, started to get loud, Cole pulled her to him, covering her mouth with his own, and swallowed her cries. The shift halted her action, and before she could resume, he flipped her and drove her over the edge in one hard thrust she felt everywhere.

His own need fueled, he rode her through her orgasm before building her up again to follow him over the cliff a second time.

His breath heavy, he placed his forehead on hers. "Shit, that was stupid."

She couldn't think, could only concentrate on her breathing, but forced her eyes open to look at him. Paused at the concern on his face. And then reality sunk in, namely the realization of flesh against flesh. Everywhere.

"Shit," she agreed before pushing him off and racing to the bathroom. That was, without a doubt, the stupidest decision of her life. *Another famous Mackenzie decision, what are you going to do about it now?* Her brother's voice, of course, always his unsupportive voice. The what-ifs began rolling around in her head, and she clamped firmly against them. Too late for ifs, the past couldn't be changed.

She did her best to pee out all his little swimmers, but even if that was possible, the damage had been done. She washed her hands and stared at her face in the mirror. Her hair resembled a rat's nest, and her face looked sufficiently fucked.

She couldn't hide out in the bathroom forever. After a few calming breaths, she made her way back to Cole. He sat up in her bed, now wearing his boxers and his prosthesis. Knees bent, his head was in his hands.

"See," Mac said with a shaky breath. "Never let me make decisions."

His head shot up and his green eyes pierced into her. "No, Mac, don't go there." He patted the bed next to him.

She grabbed her robe, pulled it on, and joined him.

"About what just happened—" He stopped short when his cell phone rang. He turned toward the sound. "Sorry, everyone knows they can reach me today." He got up, rummaged for his pants, and pulled out his phone. Eyes on the screen, he held up a hand and answered the phone. "Danny, what's up?"

Mac knew they had to have this conversation, but the delay really worked for her.

• • •

Cole paced in the small open area of Mac's stateroom. His gait more off than normal since the tight suction fit continued to set, air released as each step settled the stump in more securely. Now was not the time to take a phone call, but he couldn't ignore business.

"Sorry to bother you, but there's a problem with the heater, and while I'm sure the weather is perfect where you are, it's damn near frigid here, and I'd like my hands not to freeze while I work."

He tugged on his hair. Not his biggest concern at the moment. "Call the building manager. The number's on the information board in the back."

"You know, this is one more issue we won't have if we switch to remote. I could be home, in my pajamas, sipping coffee right now."

He scrubbed a hand across his rough cheek. "Dani, not the time."

"You barely have a week left to make this decision. I know you didn't know that before you booked this trip, but you've had plenty of time. Toss a coin if you have to."

"Because all the best business decisions are achieved by a coin toss?" He didn't dare mention he'd thought the same thing.

"At this point, pulling a piece of paper from a hat at least gets us a decision. Or you can listen to your employee for a change."

Jesus, she was a pain in his ass. "Get to work. Let me know if you have any problems restoring the heat." He hung up the phone and turned back to Mac.

"Problems at work?" she asked in a small voice.

He joined her on the bed and held her close. "Heater isn't working." Among other issues.

Mac nodded. "I'm sorry about…you know, *that*."

He put a hand under her chin and tipped it upward. Her large blue eyes shone in the morning light. "Don't be."

He leaned back and pulled her to him. She didn't stiffen, didn't fight him, just curled right in. "About that risk we took, it was both of us. Either one of us could have gained enough brainpower, or control, to prevent being careless. We can't change it. And odds are everything will be fine."

Mac scoffed. "You really haven't been paying attention to my odds."

He kissed the top of her head. "You really haven't been paying attention to yourself. Was that your first instinct, to ride me without a condom?"

She pulled her head up. "Ride you…" She shook her head. "There was no decision. I just did."

"And I have a feeling your first instincts are spot on." He brushed her hair behind her ear. "Unless you have any diseases I should be aware of?"

Mac dropped her forehead to his. "No, I've never done this before."

"Same. And the last testing I had came back negative." He always used protection. Except for this morning. More meaning lay below that decision, but he had no desire to go there yet.

He rubbed Mac's shoulders, her muscles tight and unrelenting.

"Mackenzie-Mac, relax. Don't ruin excellent sex with questions of what may be."

A small laugh escaped her lips, and her shoulders eased. "Still, not something to do with a fling I've known four days."

He wanted to say they didn't have to be a fling but kept his mouth shut. He wasn't sure what he wanted or if he could be more. Instead, he shifted back and held out his hand. "Give me your phone."

"Cole..."

"Phone."

She sighed and grabbed her phone from the pocket of her bathrobe.

Cole woke it up and saw a picture of a lemon. He raised both his eyebrows. "This lemon thing goes far for you, doesn't it?"

Mac shrugged. "Kind of. It's really a long story."

A story he wanted to know. He opened up a new contact and plugged in all his information before handing it back to her. "There, now you have my contact information. Should you ever need to contact me, you can. I hope it's for a celebratory shag."

She scoffed. "Shag?"

"Sorry, sounds better than fuck."

She put her phone in her pocket and put her head on his shoulder. He held her close and let one dangerous thought roll in: maybe it wouldn't be so bad if Mac got pregnant. Maybe it wouldn't be so bad to have a reason to stay in touch, to continue their relationship.

Maybe it would be okay to have a reason to live. A reason he was still alive and didn't die the day he lost his leg.

• • •

Mac walked hand in hand with Cole along the streets of Puerto Rico. Locals and visitors alike crowded the narrow sidewalks. Bright storefronts welcomed shoppers, boasting common and unique items. The sun beat down on them, and Mac rubbed her nose.

"Getting a little red there," Cole said, grinning at her.

She pointed to her hair. "Do we have to have this conversation again? Red hair equals red face."

"You sure you put on enough suntan lotion?"

She stopped walking and had to jerk him back from their entwined hands. He turned to her, his ball cap shadowing the top part of his face. A Red Sox cap, no less. "You know damn well I put enough suntan lotion on." Mainly because he helped.

He took the cap off and pulled it down over her head. "You look cute."

She took in his flattened hair. "You've got hat hair."

He finger combed his hair a few times and held out his hands. "Better?"

"It'll do."

Cole draped an arm around her shoulders and pulled her along. "I make it a point to try out different restaurants on each island. Let me know when something looks interesting."

Mac wrapped an arm around his waist and continued walking. Something felt so good, so right, about being with him. Even after a morning dabbling with the dangerous side of sex.

From her back pocket, "Pocket Full of Sunshine" started playing. Cole leaned back and looked at her rear as she grabbed her phone. "Funny, I haven't heard your ass play music before."

She laughed and answered her phone. "Hey, Susie."

"Mac! How's your vacation? How's the hunk? And why is Dani demanding I get details on said hunk?"

Mac bit her lip and slid her gaze to Cole. They had stopped walking, and he leaned against a brightly colored bench, watching her.

"Vacation's going good. I'm with the other part of that string of questions right now."

Susie squealed. "Is he a rotten lemon or lemonade?"

Mac held Cole's green eyes with her own. "Lemon quality still to be determined."

"It's been how many days?"

"Day five, over halfway." Where did that twinge in her gut come from?

"You should have an idea of the lemon quality, then."

"When do I ever have an idea of the lemon quality?"

"Does it taste rotten or sweet?"

Mac swallowed at the first thought that came to mind. "Sweet," she said softly.

Susie squealed again. "Mackenzie's got some lemonade, Mackenzie's got some lemonade."

"How old are you?"

Susie's bubbly laughter rang in Mac's ear. "Twenty-eight, one year older than you, but I refuse to grow up. I'll let Dani know all is well with the cruise fling."

"I'll call her before I lose cell reception."

"Relax. Enjoy your vacation. And your fling."

Mac disconnected, shook her head, and made her way back over to Cole.

"Are your friends out to get me?" he asked, lounging against the bench, prosthesis crossed wide over his other leg.

"Not yet. I have to check on one later. She might be one to worry about."

Cole stood up. "Need me to talk to her, smooth the waters over?"

Mac wrapped an arm around his waist again. "Only if you mess this up."

. . .

Cole learned quickly that Mac's decision-making problems extended in every direction of her life. Including shopping. She took her time, browsing different shops, while he tended to get in and get out. Her inability to choose a souvenir for her friends turned into a never-ending saga.

Merchandise packed the narrow floor space, with racks of clothing in the middle, shelves along the side, full of kitschy little artifacts and souvenirs. Mac held two liquid-filled paperweights in her hands.

"It's silly, but we always give each other lame souvenirs. I can't decide between these two." She held them up. They were identical except for the color of the liquid and the type of fake fish floating inside.

He took them from her and examined them, then put them behind his back. "Close your eyes, and count to ten. When you open them, I'll have these in front you. Pick your first instinct."

She stared at him for a moment but obeyed. No sound left her mouth. He watched the slow movement of the words form on her plump lips. Seduced the hell out of him, whether she intended it to or not. He almost moved in and kissed her but held his ground.

When she opened her eyes, he moved the two paperweights in front of her. She hesitated. "First choice, Mackenzie."

She grabbed the one with green water. "This one. I hope Dani likes it."

Cole put the other paperweight down. Her friend's name had to be a coincidence. And yet the item he put back on the shelf looked a hell of a lot like the ones he'd seen at work. But no, that would be a real needle in a haystack. "Must be a thing. My employee has a desk filled with little items like these."

"Yeah?" Mac asked as she moved to the cashier.

"Yup. She told me the same thing about bad souvenirs, said it was some sort of contest. And her name's Dani as well. What are the odds?"

Mac stopped in her tracks, and Cole bumped into her. She turned and stared at him with wide eyes. "What is it that you do?"

Something on her face caused his pulse to kick. *This isn't a small world, this isn't a small world, this isn't a damn Disney ride.* "Travel agent."

Mac put the paperweight down on a stack of T-shirts and walked straight out of the store. Cole followed. Outside the air turned from cool air conditioning to humid heat. Cars drove past on the street, bumper to bumper down a narrow road. Mac stood near the edge of the sidewalk, pacing on two feet of empty cement, hands on her hips. She paused when he entered her space. "Dani Martin works for you."

The ball dropped. He grabbed her elbow and spun her to face him. "Yeah. She sold you your trip?"

Mac laughed without humor. "She's sold me all my trips. She's my BFF. Most of those items on her desk are from me."

Dani's desk was a shrine to bad souvenirs. He had no idea where she kept all her paperwork. He let go of Mac's arm and plowed a hand through his hair. "She all but threatened me to stay away from you."

Mac rubbed below her throat, a tension to her he hadn't seen before. "Why?"

"I don't commit."

"I'm not looking for commitment."

"She's protective of you."

"Yeah, yeah, she is." Mac stared at him as they both let this new piece of information sink in. Then her eyes slid down to his leg. She didn't say anything but clamped a hand over her mouth as she met his gaze head on.

Well, there went his secret.

Mac turned in a circle. "This just got real. Not that this morning was any different."

He pulled her close, sinking his lips into hers, not giving a damn who saw them. She pushed him back, gasping in a breath. "This got real the moment you knocked on my door with my luggage." He'd been fighting it, but he couldn't deny the statement held truth.

She stared up at him, her blue eyes swirling with so much emotion. He couldn't name a damn one but felt them just the same.

"Mac! It's Mac! She really is my compass." Quinn's voice broke through the haze. "Hey, don't you have two staterooms to do that in?"

Cole kept his eyes on Mac. All the emotions on her face transitioned to one strong one: distress. He watched her step back, break eye contact, and turn to Quinn and Rob. Quinn's smile faded.

"You two okay?"

"Fine," Mac said in a voice that shook. "Turns out Cole's local and my BFF works for him."

"Small world," Rob said, glancing back and forth between the two of them.

"Fucking small ride," Cole muttered.

"I need some less congested air," Mac said. Her hand gripped her throat as she headed down the street, clutching her oversize bag.

Quinn had a two-second silent conversation with Rob and ran after Mac.

Rob put an arm around Cole's shoulder. "Come on, let's go for a walk."

• • •

Mac placed one foot in front of the other, needing more fresh air than the current outdoors provided. Quinn followed, heels clinking on the pavement, but Mac couldn't stop. Cole was Dani's boss. The good-looking guy that Dani always said, "Under no circumstances will I set him up with any of my friends." Not that Cole wasn't nice, Dani always said he was. But she was adamant to not let anyone get involved.

Well, Mac had gotten involved. And after that morning, the involvement could be lifelong.

She reached a clearing and bent over at the waist, sucking air into her lungs. She let her bag fall to the ground and propped her hands on her knees. Quinn rubbed her back.

"Total freakout. Care to share?"

Mac remained huddled over. She turned her head in Quinn's direction. "He was supposed to be a fling. Not my best friend's boss."

"Would it be so bad if he's not a fling?"

Mac blinked back tears and straightened. "This is ridiculous. We've known each other five days. This should be a funny coincidence."

"Well, why isn't it?"

Mac opened her mouth. No words came out. She shook her head. The whole scenario was too much, too complex, and she couldn't get a handle on it. "I'm sorry, I really need to make a phone call." She pulled out her phone, clicked on Dani's contact, and pressed "call."

"Mac! Susie just texted me and—"

"—I'm sleeping with your boss."

The line all but went dead. Mac checked the connection, wondering if Dani was silent or if her ears were failing her again. "…Shit. I told him to stay away from you, but of course didn't give him, or you, any details to actually stay away from each other. There are three thousand people on that ship. How the hell did you find each other?"

"His luggage somehow got delivered to my room, and then he helped me find mine. Why did you warn him to stay away from me?"

"Because he's my boss. He doesn't even commit to leftovers. And you've had your fair share of shit men. I don't want to see you hurt."

Mac let a strangled laugh out. "It's weird, Dani. I thought I was meeting a random stranger, not my best friend's boss. And if you really wanted me to stay away, you could have at least mentioned his name. Or that we would be on the same ship."

"Huh, I never mentioned his name?"

"If you did, I didn't catch it."

"I figured the leg would help identify him."

"I'm supposed to assume every amputee is your boss?"

"Fair enough. You okay with this little development?"

Mac managed a deep breath. "I'm not the one who tried to prevent this meeting. Susie thought you wanted him all to yourself."

"Cole and me? Hell no. He's drop-dead gorgeous, but there's no spark. Answer the question, Mac."

Mac looked up at the blue sky, searched her feelings, and ignored the relief that Dani was in fact not crushing on her boss. "I'm okay. Weirded the hell out. What do I do with this information?"

"Continue your fling?"

A small smile broke through. "I guess I don't have a choice, do I?"

Dani laughed. "Well, there's a silver lining here. I can finally ask someone a question I've been dying to have answered: is he as good in bed as he looks?"

This laugh came loose and easy. "Ohmigod yes."

"Well, that's something. At the very least Cole makes up for Chad."

"Chad who?"

"Wow. Okay, have fun. You deserve it. Let me know if I need to kick Cole's ass when you two get back."

Mac disconnected the call and put her phone back in her pocket. She took another deep breath of sea air and reminded herself she was on vacation. No longer in freak-out mode, her chat with Dani had her calm and ready for the second half of her much needed vacation. With a certain man she wasn't ready to give up.

"Feel any better?" Quinn asked.

"I think so."

· · ·

"You had to get out of the inside cabin, didn't you, Matterhorn?" Dani's voice blasted in his ear.

"Well, hello, Dani. Nice to speak to you again today. How's business?"

Rob snickered as he rummaged through T-shirts in a small souvenir shop. Cole stood out of the way, a finger in his free ear to block the heavy beat of the music.

"Slow right now, which is good, because it gives me the chance to ask, 'What the hell?'"

"I didn't know Mac was your friend. I didn't even know she was local until she noticed Trent was from New Hampshire."

"Don't bullshit me. Your luggage ended up in her room."

"I'm not bullshitting you. The luggage situation here was a mess. That was pure random luck. Aren't you glad you can speak to your *boss* this way?"

Rob laughed and almost dropped a shirt.

"Right now, I'll speak to you as the guy fucking my best friend. You better not fuck her over."

"I'm not an asshole."

"Mac deserves happiness."

Cole expected bitching from Dani. The sudden shift to serious threw him. "Look, I know she deserves happiness. Anyone who spends five minutes with her knows she deserves it!"

"Not everyone."

He swallowed. Damn heat made his mouth dry. "You point me to that Chad and I'll kick his ass. Or I'll hold him down and you can kick his ass."

"And if you hurt her?"

"I'll kick my own ass."

"For someone who doesn't commit, you're sounding pretty whipped."

Rob no longer pretended to look at shirts and openly eavesdropped. Cole didn't want to go here, not in a shop on an island, but he knew things with Mac were different. If he wanted to get Dani off his back, he had to share.

"Mac's special."

"Wow." Dani was silent. "Wow. Okay. You're dating my friend. She's in a really rough place right now and—"

"I'm working on getting her out of it. She doesn't trust herself. She's got killer instincts, but she ignores them every time."

"You've known her five days. How the hell do you know that?"

"We played trivia, and I watched her get right answer after right answer, only to change it."

"Okay, who are you and what have you done with my womanizing boss?"

"Womanizing?" Would his lack of commitment be seen that way?

"Whatever." She took a breath. "It's more than just the rough place and the instincts, Cole. Much more. You could really hurt her. Even if you don't intend to, you could. I sent her on this trip to recover from Chad. Don't fuck that up."

"I have no intentions of 'fucking that up.'"

"Good. If your ass needs kicking, I request to be present and videoing."

"Request will be granted."

Cole ended the call with Dani and shoved his phone into his back pocket. This vacation wasn't feeling like much of a vacation right now. Instead, it felt like something epic and messed up. He didn't know whether to grab popcorn or run like hell.

"You okay?"

Cole focused on his new friend. He had to deal with the best friend/evil employee, and now he had to deal with Rob's scrutiny. "I just got the third degree from the woman running my office."

"Mac's freaked out. Do we go for a reunion or get her drunk and onto someone new?"

Cole stood, hip-shot, and tried to control the boiling blood at the thought of Mac moving on. Or being with someone else. Jealousy reared its ugly head at the hypothetical situation. "You heard me talk to Dani. You know I want Mac."

"Just checking." Rob glanced at the window. "Mac's outside."

Cole turned and caught Mac standing out on the sidewalk with Quinn, still wearing his baseball cap. His legs moved before he even told them to, and in two seconds he was outside on the street. A heartbeat later, Mac was in his arms. He rested his head on the top of his cap, warmth from her and the sun on his cheek.

"I want a better discount on my next vacation," Mac said into his chest.

He laughed like he hadn't laughed in a year. "I'll do one better: your next vacation is free. With me."

She pulled her head up slowly, her eyes large behind her

glasses. Cole sunk his lips into hers. She responded beat for beat, wrapping her arms around him and holding tight.

"That's so not a fling," Quinn said from somewhere outside their personal bubble.

Mac broke the kiss and rested her head on his shoulder. "I want to see Quinn and Trent together again and see if her cocky attitude fades."

"I'd bet money on that."

Mac looked into his eyes. "Never bet money on me. You'll lose every time."

A plan formulated in his head to put that theory to the test.

. . .

"I should probably warn you: Dani likes to talk about your romantic exploits," Mac said as she closed her stateroom door behind her.

Cole pushed aside the slight tinge of worry that crawled up his balls. Dani couldn't do any worse than Trent would. And Trent would enjoy it more. "Is that so?" he asked, stepping into her now that they were alone.

"Uh-huh. You don't have the best track record."

He slid an arm around her waist and pulled her body flush with his. "Dani doesn't know everything." He pushed the "yet" out of his mind. He'd heard Dani chat on the phone; no way in hell she wouldn't want to gossip about him.

Mac's smile faded, replaced by a serious tone, as her hand slid down his side to his left thigh. "You ran the Boston Marathon?"

He'd rather go back to discussing what Dani knew of him and relationships. "No. Trent and I were watching. I had hoped to run one day but..." He didn't think he could go back to that spot. The joy of running taken from him along with the leg.

She sucked in a breath, her eyes huge on his. "I remember hearing about the attack and following the aftermath. Time stopped for so many people."

He swallowed against his dry throat. He didn't like to think of the bombing. At all. Not the pain, not the chaos. Not the image of his mangled leg covered in blood. Not Trent only having a few scratches, or the very real possibility both of them could have been on a different victim list.

He let go of Mac and hobbled into the room. He'd been twenty-two years old, his whole life ahead of him, and that life had banked on the privilege of having two legs. His world changed in an instant, like it had for so many, proving to him that life was fleeting and could be taken at a moment's notice. Sure, his prosthesis allowed him to walk, but far from normal. More like walking on a stick.

"You really didn't want me to know how you lost the leg?" Her soft voice echoed into the silent cabin.

He propped his hands on his hips, flexing out the joints on his prosthetic foot as he rocked his left knee. "Not something I like talking about."

"Sorry." Her soft voice caused him to turn around. Her eyes were just as soft, shining truth to the single spoken word.

"I'm going to use your bathroom."

Mac put her bag down on her bed. "Suit yourself."

Cole let the heavy bathroom door latch close, giving him a moment alone. He propped his hands against the sink, trying to push away the images of the bombing. They lingered. Always had, always would. He looked down at his feet, imagining both sides being flesh and bone, two sets of real limbs like he used to have.

He hadn't a clue what life would be like if he hadn't been injured. He caught his reflection, knowing if a different timeline Cole stared back at him, they wouldn't know each other.

That also meant that different timeline Cole wouldn't be on a ship, with Mac in the other room. He wasn't the person he used to be, didn't know who that Cole would have grown into at thirty-one. He wouldn't have had the same baggage, but he'd have created something new, better or worse.

He'd played this game too often. The what-if game that could be summed up as, "What if I still had two legs?" The reality was that Cole ceased to exist that moment the first bomb went off. His continued comparisons were reaching for a ghost. It was time to stop comparing and make the most of whatever time he had left.

Back in the main part of the cabin, the harsh lighting had been dimmed low. Mac stood in the center, a soft glow illuminating her and the lacey itty-bitty lingerie in black with white stars she wore. His early thoughts vanished as his gaze ate her up.

"It wasn't my place to pry, but I think I can make it up to you."

He would have responded if his breath hadn't been knocked out of him. Acting on instinct alone, he crossed to her, collected two fists full of the back of her slinky outfit in order to devour her mouth.

Her hands reached around his neck, the air around them heating. He shimmied the fabric in his hands up and found—

Nothing. Jesus, she was going to kill him. He put his forehead against hers as his fingers roamed over her smooth round rear, before yanking her into his straining erection.

She moaned. Loudly. He swiped a finger over her sweet folds to find her wet and ready. He should have lost her with the whole Dani thing. Yet here she was, with him, wanting him as much as he wanted her.

He lost track of things as the heat encompassed him, consumed him. She popped the button on his pants, the only sound in the room metal against metal as she slid the zipper down. Then one hot little hand reached in and—

He grabbed her wrist before he lost his cool like an overeager teenager. His pants fell, snagging on the prosthesis. Epic mood killer. He expected Mac to walk away. Instead, she detangled his pants. One strap slid off her shoulder as the bottom hem rose to her hip. He couldn't remember any sight more erotic. He shucked the rest of his clothes, leaving the leg. With her in his arms, the earlier mood killer dissolved into a distant memory.

She gripped at his shoulder, and he pushed her tiny little outfit up, touching as much of her silky skin as possible. His control teetered on the edge, threatening to snap. Only this woman brought out this response in him, this insatiable need to have her. The need so strong he didn't know if the week they had together would be enough.

Mac settled onto the bed as he grabbed and rolled on the condom. His pulse raged in his ears, drowning everything out but this experience. He climbed on the bed, angling himself and sliding home in one move.

Too fast, all sense of control lost around her. He went to apologize, but she claimed his mouth, yanking his body down to hers. Those sweet moans vibrated through her. Not too fast after all.

She moved with him as he set a pace to drive them both into bliss. He couldn't get enough of her. Not her feel. Not her smell. And as she moaned again, certainly not her sounds. He covered her mouth with his own, tangling tongues, tangling just about every body part except his prosthesis. Her legs wrapped around him, urging him faster. He gave until her sounds could not be muffled, until she relaxed, until her smile set him off like a rocket.

Head buried in her shoulder, he struggled to catch his breath. "You kill me, Mackenzie-Mac."

Her body shook as she laughed, clenching around a very sensitive part of him. He pulled his head up and brushed some hair off her face. "I'm real glad Dani gave you this stateroom instead of me."

"Because you're angling for another night here?"

Well, yeah. "Because you deserve it. And it allowed me to meet you."

She tapped his butt. "Well, then, you can thank her for this fling." She forced him off of her and headed to the bathroom.

He rolled onto his back, stared at the smooth ceiling. His heart rammed against his rib cage. Not a fling. He hadn't a clue what to do about that, if he could be someone more, someone she needed.

Day 6: St. Maarten

Mac snuggled into her empty bed after Cole left to join Trent at the gym. She tried to feel bad about not exercising, but her sated body didn't care. She was relaxed and happy and couldn't remember the last time she felt this good. She ignored the strange twinge in her heart, the same twinge that acted up whenever Cole was around, and reached for her phone.

She scrolled through her email, pleased to find no messages from Chad. She did find a string of emails back and forth between Dani and Susie.

She clicked open the oldest unread one and rested on the pillow Cole had used as she waited for it to load.

> From: Susie Patel
> To: Mackenzie Laurel, Dani Martin
> Subject: Dani's Boss
>
> Holy crap, Mac, you snagged the hottie I thought Dani was keeping to herself.

From: Dani Martin
To: Susie Patel, Mackenzie Laurel
Subject: RE: Dani's Boss

Bite your tongue, Susie! I've seen Cole in one too many flings to even contemplate testing that water.

From: Susie Patel
To: Dani Martin, Mackenzie Laurel
Subject: RE: Dani's Boss

Well, then, it's a good thing Mac's looking for a hot fling.

From: Dani Martin
To: Susie Patel, Mackenzie Laurel
Subject: RE: Dani's Boss

I've talked to them both. I don't think this is ending when the cruise does.

From: Susie Patel
To: Dani Martin, Mackenzie Laurel
Subject: RE: Dani's Boss

Mackenzie's got a boyfriend, love it! Have fun, Mac! Enjoy a little lemonade for a change.

Mac closed her eyes and buried her head in the pillow. Her friends were going to drive her to drink. Why did she check her emails?

To: Susie Patel, Dani Martin

From: Mackenzie Laurel
Subject: Fling

My plans have not changed. It doesn't matter if Cole is local or not. I'm here for nothing more than a fling. So lemonade or rotten lemon doesn't even matter.

She sent the email and put her phone away before she wrote anything else. The turmoil of her life meant she needed this vacation to recharge, and once she returned home, it was time to make lemonade out of her own life. She didn't have time for a man. Though since he happened to be local, maybe she could revisit all this after she found a job and a home. Until then, she had a fling to enjoy and a few memories to create.

...

"Should we find Quinn, let you take your break with her?" Cole asked as he walked along the streets of St. Maarten with Trent. The area screamed quintessential vacation. To his left, restaurants and shops dotted the landscape, with a few buildings under construction. To his right, pure sand and water, with beach chairs and sunbathers already set up.

"Fuck off," Trent mumbled, hands in his khaki shorts, nametag still glistening in the sun. The warm breeze ruffled his shirt, changing the angle of the nametag.

Cole examined the buildings with second and third floors not in use by businesses. "I'm sure there's someplace you two could sneak off to."

"I said, fuck off," Trent said a little louder.

Cole stopped walking. "You said you've snuck a few trysts in here and there." He studied his friend and the refusal to make eye contact. He grinned and stuck his own hands in his pockets. "Well, well, well. Not looking for a fling, huh?"

Trent shook his head and stopped walking. "I wasn't expecting her."

Cole kicked some sand off the sidewalk. "So get her number and follow her home."

Trent turned down a narrow alley toward more stores. "Not that easy, man. At least your fling lives locally."

Cole followed after, eyes on the ground. If he wasn't prepared for unsteady surfaces, he ran the risk of meeting said surface with his face. "Mac's not a fling. I don't know what it is or what to even do about that."

"What a good little puppy," Trent snickered.

"Takes one to know one." They passed by a shop with a metal dog and cat in the window. "Perhaps they have a leash for you in there?"

"Fuck you," Trent muttered, his off-duty potty mouth alive and well.

Cole ignored his buddy as they continued walking in the hot sun. On a whim he turned into a jewelry store and browsed the items in the glass casing. He passed by diamonds, rubies, and sapphires; rings, necklaces, and earrings. And stopped when something yellow caught his eye.

"Damn puppy," Trent said. "You never buy jewelry. I've watched you avoid everything serious after the attack."

Soft island music pumped into the air-conditioned store. Cole tapped the glass above the necklace he planned to purchase. "That's right." He enjoyed a date, or a few, with the same person. Anything more than that had been off-limits, until now.

"You've never wanted anything with permanence."

He signaled to one of the staff. "Mac might already be permanent."

A man in a crisp dress shirt and dress pants came over, but Trent waved him away. "What the fuck? 'Mac might already be permanent'?"

Cole braced two hands on the glass and let out a laugh. "We skipped protection, so there's a chance…"

Trent shook his head. "Dude, there are condoms in the gift shop."

"There were condoms next to the bed. We didn't think. We just acted. And considering Mac's thing with decisions…" He shrugged. A year ago—heck, a month ago—the possibility would have scared him more than an unattended backpack in a crowded area. Something about Mac had him calm. She calmed him. And even if he couldn't fathom a year into the future, he knew he wanted more time with her.

"You've already bought the collar and given her the leash. Do I need to remind you it's been SIX DAYS?"

He didn't need to be reminded. She'd made a mark on him in six days. A mark he needed. "Six long cruise days. And you're stumbling over your feet at Quinn."

"I've only flirted with Quinn."

"So flirt more." Cole gestured to the staff watching them with eager eyes. He pointed to the casing. "I want the necklace shaped like a lemon."

· · ·

Mac lay on the beach with Quinn, sipping cocktails with tiny umbrellas and fruit.

"I haven't had breakfast yet. This counts as breakfast, right?" Quinn asked as she bit the strawberry off the stick.

"Probably not," Mac said and studied the area. No food vendors on the beach, but with shops nearby there had to be some options. "We'll need to grab you some food before I have to carry your drunk ass back to the ship."

Quinn laughed and popped a cherry in her mouth. "I'll be fine. Let's relax and enjoy the sun." She pulled her sunglasses down from the top of her head and settled into her seat.

"Last day in your twenties. If you keep drinking you won't remember it."

"Then I'm doing something right."

Mac switched out her glasses with her sunglasses. "Maybe you've got the right idea. I could book a cruise for my thirtieth, get drunk, have a few flings, before returning home older and wiser."

Quinn scoffed. "Number one, I have no intentions of being older and wiser. Number two, how old are you?"

"Twenty-seven."

"Three years. You'll be married to Cole by then."

Mac nearly choked on her drink. She gagged as the liquid went down the wrong pipe. "He's a—"

"Drop the fling thing, sweetie. I'll admit what happens next is anyone's guess. But I've got a feeling on you two, and this is not a relationship that ends just because the ship docks back in Florida."

Mac bit a cherry off the plastic stick with enough force the stick almost cracked. Her new friend meant well, but relationship potential or not, she had plans to stick to, and Dani's hot boss didn't factor in. "And what about you and Trent?"

Quinn tipped back her drink and brought the colorful liquid below the line of fruit. "A potential that will never get off the ground. He's being a good employee, and I'm looking for someone with sticking power."

Mac shook her head and concentrated on the water brushing up against the shore. In the distance, their cruise ship sat, dividing the blue background.

"My life is a mess back home. I never make good decisions. The absolute last thing I need is to start a relationship."

"Never say never. You have to have made some right decisions. You are on this trip, you have amazing hair, your bag is to die for, and your tankini is adorable. And you have a hunk hanging on your every word. Not everything is a rotten decision."

Mac pulled the pineapple off her drink and sank her teeth into the sweet juice. Quinn's words went against everything she had been told since she was about five years old.

"Fancy meeting you in a place like this," Cole's voice filtered in from behind.

Mac turned around and saw Cole and Trent making their way over. A grin spread over her face before she could stop herself.

"Oh good," Quinn said, waving her now half-empty drink. "Help me explain to Miss Mackenzie that not all her decisions are bad, otherwise she wouldn't be here."

Cole squatted down next to Mac and pushed his sunglasses up. "Not all your decisions are bad, especially if they're your first instinct."

Mac's heart ached in her chest, physically ached. "You haven't known me long enough. Bennett's been calling my decisions crap for years, and he has quite a heavy lead."

"Who's Bennett? I'll kick his ass when I kick Chad's ass. Any other ex-boyfriends I should add to the list?"

Mac couldn't help laughing, even as she caught the awkward standoff between Trent and Quinn. "Bennett's my brother. He first pinpointed my aptitude toward bad decision making twenty-something years ago."

"Older brother?" Trent asked.

"Of course."

"I have one of those. They're shits—no offense, Cole. Don't listen to older brothers. They live to mess with your head."

"I don't have an older brother, but I suspect this brother shouldn't be taken so seriously." Quinn finished her fruit and was three quarters of the way through her drink. Her head swayed a bit as she talked.

"How long are you guys staying on the island?" Mac asked, eyes on her friend.

"We were on our way back now," Cole said.

"Quinn, you need food or you're going back with Trent."

Quinn shook her head. "I'm fine." She raised her glass to the clear blue sky. "Happy last day of twenty-nine. Tomorrow I'll be an old lady." She knocked back the rest of the drink.

"Okay, that's enough," Trent said and took the empty glass away from her. "You done having a pity party for no reason?"

Quinn brushed him away and adjusted her bikini top, a strip of pale skin revealed. Trent went very still.

"Tell me something, Mr. Trent," she leaned forward and squinted at his nametag, "Decker, am I going home in a few days any different than when I arrived?"

Trent looked around him, then squatted low next to Quinn. "A vacation is what one makes of it. Having expectations just leads to failure. Oftentimes what one finds is not what one intended to find. So you can sit here and drink yourself into oblivion, or you can enjoy the trip, enjoy the people, and find out what may be."

"Right." Disbelief hung in the word as she turned her head away from him.

He grasped her chin and pulled her to face him. "Right." He held her there, close enough their noses almost touched. "Either get some food or I'm bringing you back to your room to sober up before the rest of this goes to your head."

She yanked away from his grasp. "You're not the boss of me."

Trent stood up, hands on his hips, radiating pissed-off male.

"See you back on the ship?" Cole asked, half laughing.

Trent mumbled something unintelligible and grabbed

Quinn's bag before looping an arm around her waist and forcing her to stand. "Come on, princess, we're going."

"Give me one good reason…" Her voice trailed off as he stepped close to her, nose to nose, eyes locked on hers. Without a word, Quinn slipped her feet into her shoes, pulled on her cover-up, and followed him back to the ship.

"Is he about to get into trouble?" Mac asked.

Cole shook his head. "I don't think so. Quinn's tipsy, and he's not going to do anything onboard. He cares for her too much."

He moved into Quinn's discarded chair, the metal of his prosthesis catching the sharp sunlight. "So, Bennett, tell me about this brother."

Mac shrugged. "He noticed my ability to make the wrong decisions as a kid, always picked on me, made me second guess myself."

Cole pulled his sunglasses off his head. "Your second guesses are wrong, Mac."

"What I decide to do is wrong."

"Mac." Cole shook his head. "The bad decisions I've seen you make have been your second choice. The good decisions are your first. Bennett was picking on you, teasing you. He just didn't realize how much he affected you."

Her memories warped, tilting off center, cracking the foundation. The images of her brother picking on her for making bad decisions, his voice echoing in her head for most of her life, altered to her brother creating her bad decisions. He reinforced her troubles, and she put too much stock in the things he said. Her childhood shattered and her memories lost the innocence. She looked back with adult eyes, the filter of youth lost.

She reached for her drink and chugged down a decent amount.

Cole raised an eyebrow. "You okay?"

She stared out at the white tips of the waves. How could she have allowed him that much control over such an important part of her? She didn't know if her brother truly didn't get it or if he enjoyed making her life hell or even how to finish unpacking it all. "Not really." Now she had no job, no home, no money, and no idea who she was. She needed therapy, but good luck finding that without income or insurance.

"I'm sorry," Cole said and grabbed her hand.

"Not your fault." She turned to face him, pushing her new thoughts aside. She'd work on them when she worked on everything else. "Thank you for what you said, really. I just need time to let it process."

He leaned forward and kissed her, gentle brushes of his lips to hers. Her heart broke and mended, an impossible combination.

Cole leaned back and fumbled with something in his pocket. "You look like you could use a gift."

Her mouth dropped open. "Cole, no, I—"

He held up a hand. "I don't normally do this. Ask Trent or Dani for verification. But I saw this and knew I had to get it for you."

He dropped a jewelry box in her hand, and her pulse kicked into marathon speed. She opened the smooth black case with shaking hands and found a necklace with a yellow gemstone pendant. A laugh escaped her lips. "A lemon? You got me a lemon?"

A smile spread across his lips. "I'm hoping it's not rotten."

Mac laughed again. It was so her. She held her hair out of the way, and he latched the necklace around her neck. The pendant hung down to the top of her cleavage.

"Damn, that's hot," Cole whispered, eyes on the pendant.

"Thank you." She placed a hand on his cheek and pressed her lips against his. She thought about turning thirty and wondered if Quinn was right. Then she shook those thoughts away. She'd deal with that later, much later, after she found a new job.

・・・

After soaking up some sun, Mac wanted to explore, and Cole agreed to join her. Walking next to him made her realize how fast she normally walked. She blamed the New England speed thing. They crossed across brick paths, the type of uneven surface Mac wouldn't have thought twice on, unless the soles of her shoes were too thin. She checked out scenery and shops and caught Cole looking down more than up, which she could only assume had to do with his gait.

Slowing down didn't bother her, not when she had him and the warm air and island smells to revel in. Bonus, it forced her to enjoy her surroundings more, including finding things she might have missed if she moved at her normal rate. Like the clock in the store window all but screaming for attention. She stopped dead in her tracks. Since she held Cole's hand, she almost tripped him in the process.

"What?" he asked.

She turned to him, his eyebrows creased in amusement. She tugged on his hand, careful this time not to mess with his balance. "Come on," she said and pulled him into the store.

From outside the clock had caught her attention. Inside it reeled her in, denying her gaze shift to any other objects. Mac approached the table topped with a variety of different items, only registering one: a large lemon with second, minute, and hour hands sticking out of it. Green leaves sprouted from the top, and a wooden base kept it upright.

"This is fantastic," she said on a laugh, picking up the clock.

"At what time does it turn rotten?" Cole's deep voice whispered into her ear.

Mac kept her eyes on the clock. "Hush. I need this."

Cole took it from her, examining all sides. He pointed to the second hand. "This is the time it takes you to come up with a good decision." He pointed to the minute hand. "When this moves, you've entered rotten lemon territory." And the hour hand. "Don't even bother if this moves."

She grabbed the clock back. "You think you're so smart."

He stepped behind her, pressing his body against hers. Hands on her arms, bare legs brushing. Or rather, her legs brushed against one bare and one metal one. She leaned back into him, all his warmth welcome even with the hot island air circling the store.

"You think you're not," he said.

She whipped her head around to face him. "My brother is a lawyer, my sister a doctor. I'm unemployed."

He didn't back away from her. "Intelligence and profession are two different things."

"Lawyers and doctors are smart."

"People from every walk of life are smart. It's about ambition, luck, choices."

She scoffed. "Choices." She held up the clock. "Rotten lemon."

He shoved his hands in his pockets, eyes on his legs. "You think I went to college to be a travel agent?" His gaze rose to hers. "I've got a business degree. Had ambitions of becoming a CEO of some Fortune 500 company someday, after working my way up the ladder. Then this happened," he kicked out his prosthesis, "and none of that mattered. And me as a travel agent or CEO is the same level of smarts."

She didn't know what to say to that. One didn't go through what Cole had and come out the same person. She wished he hadn't had to go through it in the first place, but she couldn't deny she liked the person he became.

"My point is, unemployed or becoming your ex's boss,

you're smart, Mackenzie-Mac."

"You've known me five days, Cole."

His green eyes studied her as he brushed back her hair. "I'll say the same when I've known you five years." His voice was soft, though loud enough she understood, spoken with a note of wonder.

Her heart leaped into her throat as he kissed her, quick and sweet. Her hands fumbled with the clock, and he grabbed it before she dropped it and completed the rotten lemon clock analogy.

She backed away from him and tried to regain her breath. Hand on her hip, she couldn't believe they were this wrapped up in each other so quickly. No way could this be lemonade. Life didn't work that way, not for her.

As she continued to wrestle with her emotions, her eyes landed on another clock, this one with a martini glass base. "Oh my God," she exclaimed as she grabbed it off the shelf. The hands stuck out from the olive, off-balance but somehow still sturdy. "Hello, souvenir for Dani," she purred.

"Dani doesn't drink martinis," Cole said beside her.

"You drink with your employees?" She couldn't stop the sinister curve to her lips.

"You've never had a drink with your boss after work?"

"I've had sex with my boss. Of course, alcohol was involved." She flipped the martini clock upside down and winced at the price.

Cole put a hand on her elbow. "That doesn't sound good."

"What? You've never had sex while inebriated?" She pulled her arm free, grabbed the lemon clock, winced again at the price, and headed to the register anyway.

"Mac."

She turned, and Cole stared at her with concern in his eyes.

"Relax, I started the relationship of my own free will.

Sober." She stared him down, telling him to drop it.

"Martini, for Dani?" He got the hint. *Thank God.*

"Yup. Dani Martin, who hates martinis. We tease her about it all the time, order her a martini each birthday, and make her drink it." Mac didn't know why Dani complained; they ordered Mac sour lemonade with something like 80 proof. She'd take the martini any day.

After she paid, Cole took the bag from her. His other hand pressed into the small of her back, directing her out of the store. "So, you buy souvenirs. What's mine going to be?"

She wanted to offer herself but clamped her mouth shut. "Souvenirs are for people not on the trip. I still need to find something for Susie. She's got a thing for magnets."

He leaned in close to her, his warm breath tickling her neck. "And if I wasn't here..." His voice trailed off, and he snuck his tongue out, swiping behind her ear.

She shuddered. A bead of sweat trickled down her back from the eighty-degree temperature, and he caused her to shudder. She turned to him. "Then I wouldn't have met you, would I?"

His eyes smoldered as he studied her face for a beat too long and a beat too close. When he moved back, she let out a breath. "Fair enough. You going to the show tonight?"

"Dani booked this two days prior to departure. What do you think?"

His soft laughter rustled her hair. "Trent mentioned the show wasn't sold out. You want to meet up for the second show, or should we go to the first, then grab dinner together?"

She turned to him. Because of the nature of the cruise, they hadn't had dinner together yet. Breakfast and lunch, but not dinner. It felt like a real date, the kind where he'd pick her up, wine and dine her, then drive her back home. The kind where she'd invite him in for a cup of coffee. The kind where he'd stay until morning.

Who was she kidding? He was staying until morning anyways. "Why don't we see the early show and grab dinner."

...

After dinner, Cole brought Mac to one of the bars. He'd never imagined this feeling he had when with her, this rightness to his life. He'd been off-kilter for far too long, and when in her orbit, it fixed itself. Unexpected and unplanned. He'd have to enjoy it and see how to continue things back on land.

"Thank you. This really has been a wonderful evening," Mac said, swirling the contents of her drink. Her silky blue top dipped low in front and hugged her curves. He enjoyed the view all the more since he'd already stripped it off her once and had plans to do so again, if she wanted him.

Cole leaned forward. "You saying you're done with me?"

Mac put her drink down. A grin rose over her face, her eyes heating. "Not at all. It's been a long time since I've had a night like this, and I wanted to show my appreciation."

He collected her hand and brought it to his lips. "Give me a chance and I'll give you many nights like this."

"Oh, but then it wouldn't be as special now, would it?"

He wanted to respond, but Quinn's voice interrupted. "Look, my compass."

Quinn and Rob approached them. Cole and Mac shifted to allow their friends to join, Mac reaching for her drink.

"See a show, he says," Quinn began by way of greeting. "It'll be fun, he says. Didn't mention anything about technical difficulties stopping the show."

Mac did a spit take and started coughing. "What?" she asked with half a voice. Cole rubbed her back.

Rob leaned forward, elbows on the table. "One scene change took longer than normal, then an automated message about technical difficulties came on. Ten minutes later—"

"It felt like hours. People were already leaving." Quinn flailed her hands.

"Ten minutes later," Rob reiterated, chin raised as he stared Quinn down, "they put up the lights and stopped the show."

Cole didn't even have to do the math. Their show had been fine. Which meant Mac went with her first choice for their dinner plans.

"That sucks," Mac said, voice back to normal. "The show was really good, too."

"You saw it?" Quinn picked up her drink and did not take a light sip, her shoulders relaxing.

Cole nodded. "We caught the early show. Mac chose."

Mac's drink was poised in front of her lips. At Cole's words, she put her drink down without taking a sip. He swallowed his smirk. She'd trusted him, and that trust turned into trusting herself. It felt good, and a sense of pride welled up for her.

"Well, damn," Rob said. "Thanks for warning us about a Mackenzie first choice."

Cole leaned back and shrugged, no longer able to swallow the grin.

Mac pointed at Cole. "You've possessed me."

He grabbed her pointer finger and kissed the tip of her pink nail. "One can only hope." She locked eyes with him, a warm glow to her face. He hoped she'd remember this feeling.

They broke apart when another visitor approached their table.

"Well, well, well," Trent said. "If it isn't the four troublemakers."

He squatted down in between Rob and Quinn, and Cole didn't miss when he made arm contact with Quinn.

"What happened in the theater?" Rob asked.

Trent shook his head. "One of the hydraulics has been

acting up. Every few weeks we do emergency work to repair it. There's talk we'll need a funeral this time. Sorry you missed the rest of the show. It's a good one."

Mac's wide eyes stared at Cole. "It can't be."

"I believe the facts suggest otherwise," he said.

"That my odd luck caused machinery to break down for good? I need to come with a warning label."

No, she didn't. The hydraulic was going to break down regardless. She didn't cause the bad luck. She simply had good instincts on how to avoid it. If only he could get her to see this, too.

Quinn sighed. "Those poor performers. How awful to not get their final applause and appreciation."

Trent grinned. "I'll pass those sentiments along." He stood up. "So, you coming to be tortured by the adult scavenger hunt? Most times the rating is firmly in the R category. Once or twice we've migrated into NC-17." He cocked an eyebrow, a mischievous glint to his eyes.

"Can we pick on you?" Cole called out.

"You can. But during this game, I can pick back. Drink up, folks, and come join the fun." He trailed a hand over Quinn's shoulder and grabbed her drink, knocked back the third remaining, and headed through the bar.

Quinn stared at her empty glass, her mouth gaped open. Cole smothered a laugh. "How dare he? He's not supposed to be drinking."

Mac grinned. "He's got two days left. I don't think he cares."

"He's not getting away with that." Quinn stood. "We're going to harass him." She grabbed her purse and stalked after Trent.

"How's the husband hunt going, Quinn?" Cole called after her.

She didn't acknowledge if she heard him or not.

Rob shook his head. "All things considered, very well."

"Shall we follow her?" Mac asked.

"Oh, most definitely."

Cole stood and, after he got his balance, reached out a hand for Mac. "I've heard stories about this scavenger hunt. We should at least be watching. And find out what Quinn's about to do."

"She's had one too many drinks today to stay out of trouble." Rob smiled, though, so even if Cole did wonder about Quinn's alcohol intake, she had her friend with her, and he appeared sober.

They exited the bar, trailing after Quinn's fast pace. "Is she going to harm him?" Cole asked.

Rob chuckled. "No clue. This isn't normal Quinn behavior. He's got her off her game."

Cole mulled that one over. He often cruised to follow Trent. He'd caught his friend lightly flirting, but nothing like how he acted around Quinn. "She's not the only one."

Rob paused, eyebrows raised. "Really?"

Cole nodded.

"This should be interesting, then."

They caught up to Quinn outside a lounge where she stood very close to Trent and he seemed to enjoy the proximity, making Cole wonder if he created it.

"You owe me a drink," Quinn said.

"They won't let me get one." Trent shook his head. "But I'll see what I can do." He took a step back from her, nodded over her shoulder to Cole and the others, and walked away.

Rob placed a hand on Quinn's shoulder. "You are in over your head."

Quinn faced Cole. "Is your buddy always such a prick?"

"Only when he wants something."

They entered the lounge. Down in front, Trent stood talking with two other cruise staff. He looked up at them, or rather, at Quinn. He smiled, wide and easy, until the female beside him whacked his shoulder.

Cole laughed and claimed a lounge chair, pulling Mac next to him. Mac settled in, her bare leg brushing his covered right leg. He liked this, being close with her, enjoying a vacation with her. This didn't feel like a run-of-the-mill vacation, though he'd known that due to the potential of it being Trent's last as staff. Between Trent and Mac, and their new friends, this felt like the kind of vacation he wanted to repeat. Or bottle up and make it real life.

Real life never matched vacation life, though. He'd do good to remember that. For both himself and Trent.

He shook those thoughts aside as a waiter stopped by their small round table, putting a drink in front of Quinn. He winked, a big grin not customary, and kept walking.

Point for Trent, Cole thought.

Mac laughed. "Love it," she squealed.

"Quinn, love," Rob said as he leaned in close. "You've met your match."

Quinn picked up her drink and took a sip.

"Did he get it right?" Cole asked.

She wiped her lips and swallowed. "Yes."

"Well, he drank enough of it. He should have figured it out," Mac said.

"Right, because he wanted to."

Up front, the loud speaker clicked on and a deep voice with a Spanish accent filtered over the system. The cruise director, Carlos, addressed the crowd.

Mac leaned into Cole. "I can't understand him."

Cole frowned. He didn't know how fun this would be for her if she couldn't hear. "He's introducing the staff, pointing out that it's Trent's last week and he's been a pain in his side."

Mac chuckled.

"Oh, Trent's going to be in charge. Will you hear him

better?"

Mac shrugged. "I guess we'll find out."

Carlos had a hand on Trent's back, saying something that had Trent smiling. The microphone was handed to Trent.

"Good evening, ladies and gentlemen," came Trent's voice. Cole checked on Mac.

She gave him a thumbs-up. *Good job, Trent.*

"As Carlos has said, it's my last week aboard this beautiful ship and working with this fantastic staff. I've been with Carlos for the last four months and," he spun around to his director, "no offense, have watched him absolutely butcher this game."

Carlos held up three fingers and pointed to the tallest. The audience laughed, eating right out of their hands.

"See the kind of abuse I've put up with? But not tonight, tonight I'm in charge, and since it's my last week, I'm willing to let things get a little wild. Who's with me?"

The audience cheered. Trent was in his element with this game, and Cole knew it would be one not to miss.

Trent went over the rules and the room broke into teams. Their group of four ended up as team number five and had a card with their number on it. Trent would call out something they needed to bring up to him, and one member of the team would grab the item and the number and run up.

"All right, ladies and gentlemen, let's get this party started," Trent called out as music started playing and he and the other staff danced to the beat. "Enough of that. We'll start off real simple. I want one member of your team to bring me two cruise cards," he held up a hand, "one with an even room number, one with an odd."

"We've got this." Cole pulled his card out of his pocket and held his hand out to Mac. She dug hers out of her oversize purse. Then he held them both to Quinn.

"What?"

"You're our runner," Rob said before pushing her out of the seat.

"I'm wearing heels, you moron," she called over her shoulder as she raced up to the stage with the rest of the contestants.

"Are we sure about this?" Mac asked.

Cole faced her. "For who? Quinn or Trent?"

"Both."

He shrugged. Either way, it spelled out good fun, and that matched the game. On the stage, three staff checked the cards, but Trent checked on Quinn, leaning in close to whisper something to her.

Cole pointed. "That looks like a very good idea."

Quinn returned and threw the cards at Mac and Cole. "Someone else runs next time."

"What did he say?" Mac shoved her card in her purse without checking which of theirs she grabbed.

"He pouted that it wasn't mine. But he walked me back to my damn room earlier today. He knows where I'm staying."

Rob wrapped an arm around Quinn and gave her a side hug. "He's flirting, love. Enjoy it."

Quinn grumbled.

"Next, I need to see something in an animal print." Trent twirled the microphone around.

Cole bumped Mac's shoulder, visions of earlier and her animal print underwear dancing through his mind. She shook her head and looked inside her bag.

"No time," Cole said.

Mac scowled, grabbed their number, and headed up. "You're going to regret this," she called over her shoulder.

He grinned, not likely. Quinn shared a look with Rob. Cole crossed his prosthesis over his leg, not saying a word.

Down on the main stage, Mac whispered something in Trent's ear. Trent glanced back at Cole, then gestured. Mac pulled her shirt collar to the side, revealing her bra strap.

Trent pulled the microphone up. "Ladies and gentlemen," he put an arm around a red-faced Mac, "we have animal-print underwear. Normally we have to wait until this game is much, much further along before the underwear comes out."

The crowd hooted as Mac made her way back to their group. "You happy?" she asked Cole.

He pulled her in for a kiss. "Your quirky underwear got us a point. I'm loving it."

"Let's see if we can top animal-print underwear," Trent said. "I need one member of your team...with...a tattoo."

Cole has seen all of Mac's body and knew she didn't have one. He had scars, no ink. They shook their heads and glanced at Rob and Quinn. Or, rather, where Rob stared at Quinn.

"Dammit," Quinn muttered as she grabbed the number.

Cole leaned forward. "Where is it?" he asked Rob.

"A butterfly low on her back."

"Ohh, nice," Mac said.

They turned their attention to the stage where a female had an ankle flower, a guy had a full back filled with a landscape, and another guy had some writing on his arm.

Trent came up to Quinn and said something but not into the microphone.

"He's standing very close to her, isn't he?" Mac asked.

Rob nodded. "That he is. He's playing with fire. I approve."

They watched as Quinn separated her shirt and skirt on her back for Trent. He placed an arm around her shoulders. "So the same team that just flashed me a bra has now showed off a lovely little butterfly."

Quinn blushed as the crowd went wild again.

Trent let go of her, and she made it back to her seat and finished off her drink before she even fully sat down. Mac laughed and hugged her shoulders.

"Your friend is enjoying himself too much," Quinn said.

Cole leaned forward. "Can you blame him?"

Quinn bit her lip, and Cole had to admit, he liked her with Trent. Trent might not have been as closed off as him post bombing, but his new connections remained surface level at best. Even on board, the setup meant after his contract he'd go his separate ways from the staff he worked with. Quinn shook the foundation Trent had built. More, she reminded Cole of the parts of Trent he'd hidden in the past decade. If given the chance, she'd be very good for him.

A bit like what Cole felt about Mac, which only proved how deep his thoughts went and how unwarrantedly close they were after such a short amount of time.

Trent's voice brought him back to the present. "Men, listen up. I need one of you up here, wearing…lipstick."

Quinn and Mac both rummaged in their bags.

"Oh, for crying out loud, you just re-applied," Cole said before grabbing Mac and sinking a deep, satisfying kiss to her lips.

"Pro-active and self-beneficial," Rob joked.

Cole pulled back and gestured to the group. At their nods, he grabbed the number and raced up. A man with a beard and red lips had already made it to the stage, and even with a closer seat, the lipstick had to have been on already. It went with the skirted attire.

Cole caught Trent's gaze the minute he hit the stage and knew he had teasing coming. Bring it. Trent let all the others leave the stage but held onto Cole. "Here's a little tidbit that most of you probably missed, and seeing as this man here has been my friend for over a decade, I'm not letting him get away with this."

Cole glanced at Mac, who scrunched down in her seat.

"He got his lipstick by planting a big wet one on a lady

he met day one on this cruise." Trent grinned as the audience reacted. Cole did not have to play nice like Trent did and sent his buddy the finger.

Trent's smile said, "Right back at ya, buddy."

Cole returned to the group and patted a still-embarrassed Mac's knee. "You did that on purpose," she grumbled.

"I play to win." He held her eyes, not intending a deeper meaning to filter through, that he wanted to win her. Her trust, her heart.

"It's just a game," Mac said, caution seeping into her voice.

He swallowed his emotions. "And we're having fun with that game."

Mac relaxed, and Cole did his best to go with the flow. It didn't matter if he felt more things than he had in years, no use diving off the deep end when his partner clearly didn't want to.

It stung, but he'd deal with that later.

The game continued and the questions and requests grew more and more bizarre. At one point, Rob wore Quinn's shoes to the stage, doing a good job at it, too. Though not as good as the person wearing what appeared to be kids' shoes, not that Cole could find a single child in the audience.

Near the end, Carlos took control back from Trent. "In honor of Trent's last week, one member of each team needs to give him a kiss."

Cole couldn't stop the grin. He stared at Quinn and knew the others were, too.

"Uh-uh, make Cole go and kiss his buddy."

Cole leaned back. "No way."

"Rob, you can get some action."

"Not the action Trent, or you, want, darling."

Quinn slid a pleading glance to Mac.

"Just tap him on the cheek or pull him down to the floor."

Mac grinned, and Cole held up his hand for a high five.

Quinn grumbled, grabbed the number, and made her way to the front.

"Oh, this is going to be good," Cole said.

"You enjoy tormenting your friend?" Rob asked.

"That I do."

On the stage, the team runners swarmed around Trent, most pecking his cheek. Trent's cheeks turned pink, and that made Cole hoot. No doubt about it, he picked the right week to vacation.

"What's Quinn going to do?" Mac asked.

"She should go for the cheek," Rob said, eyes trained up front. "But I think she's feeling bold."

"What does that mean?" Cole asked.

Rob grinned. "I wouldn't discount her going for more."

Cole turned to Mac. "What do you think?"

"I think I agree with Rob."

Only Quinn remained, and she stepped up to Trent, pressing her lips to his and lingering longer than any of the cheek kisses. Their entire table cheered, as did many of the others. Quinn broke the kiss and took a large step back.

Trent looked dazed. A hand by his side was fisted. Cole had never seen him this far off his game. Trent might not have claimed to be as detached as Cole had been, but neither of them welcomed commitment. Or letting people in. And Trent's face, heck, his entire body language, screamed that Quinn had gotten to him.

"Oh my God, Quinn," Mac squealed when Quinn sat down. "You planted one on him."

Quinn picked up her drink, only to find it still empty. "That was foolish."

Rob laughed and kissed the top of her head. "You knocked him on his ass."

"What?" She jerked her head up.

On the stage, Trent stood with Carlos, talking with the mic pointing down and stealing glances in their direction. His smooth attitude was gone. "Huh, I did, didn't I?"

"Yup," Cole said. "Nice work."

Rob leaned forward, eyes on Cole. "Seems to be a theme between you two."

Cole wrapped a hand around Mac. "To be fair, I'm easy to knock over."

"That's not the stories I've heard," Mac said.

He stared into her eyes, getting lost in the blue tones. "Physically easy to knock over. The rest is all about you."

Mac's breathing hitched. "A little deep there, Cole."

He forced a casual smile. Too deep, definitely too deep. Didn't matter that he felt it and wanted to keep it. The only thing that mattered was that somehow, his emotions were alone. She wanted a fling. He needed to enjoy a fling. Not like he couldn't track her down back home. If only he didn't want more.

Day 7: At Sea

Mac's flip flops slapped against the tiled floor as she walked toward the small lounge with Cole. "Hard to believe there's just one day left," she said. Around her lights bounced off shiny surfaces and passengers milled about. Up ahead a kid ran, followed by a parent in pursuit. Mac was used to parents dragging their kids back for running off. This father grabbed the kid and swung her around in the air, little feet kicking as the girl giggled. The father then propped the girl on his shoulders and waited for the mother to catch up.

Mac glanced at Cole, wondering if that would be them some day. And where did that thought come from? She'd never contemplated the future to that extent, and here she was, wondering about marriage and children with a guy she'd known less than a week. Her heart squeezed at the thought, and she realized how dangerously close she was to falling for him.

No. Bad Mackenzie. No falling. New job first. She needed to stick to her plan. Job and housing were her priorities. Romance came after she got settled. A lot after.

In the lounge they found Trent with papers spread out over the top of a piano.

"That was some kiss last night with Quinn," Mac said as they got close.

Cole put an arm around him. "Why don't you give her a real birthday gift later on…?" Cole's eyebrows shot upward twice.

Trent pushed his arm off. "Give it up. After Quinn's kiss, I'm being watched like a hawk for inappropriate behavior."

"You've got two days and no plans to come back. What are they going to do?"

"I'm a firm believer in not burning any bridges. Getting caught with Quinn would burn a bridge."

"So don't get caught," Mac suggested.

"As I've said, I'm being watched." Trent pushed some papers forward and crossed his arms on the piano top. "You two gonna play clean this time?"

Mac shrugged. "Haven't decided yet." She fingered the papers. "These the answers?"

Cole laughed.

Trent shook his head. "Don't encourage him. I'm trying to figure out which pile matches the crowd."

Mac looked at the dozen or so people chatting and waiting for the game to start. One family with preteen kids, a few couples her age, and some older groups. She turned back to Trent and gestured to his papers. "May I?"

He fanned a hand over the pages.

Mac turned them around and skimmed over the types of questions. One had a more general facts theme, another with current events, another with pop culture, and a final with more nautical themes. She faced the crowd again.

"The pop culture will probably give the family a lead. Current events will go to the older group by the window. Nautical might stump them all. This group is mixed; I think the general facts will be the most even playing field."

Cole blinked at her, and Trent golf clapped.

"Where have you been? That's where I was leaning, but you explained it better than I could. I'd kiss you if Matterhorn here wouldn't kick me."

Mac beamed, soaking up the rare praise like a wet sponge. Where she ended up next, she needed more praise in her life. Ego stroked, she headed to find a table. It took Cole a few moments, and a few whispers with Trent, but he joined her.

"You have a real knack for reading people," he said.

Mac brushed her skirt, fixing a small section that had folded up. "It's not that hard when you really look at people."

"Bullshit."

She looked up, not expecting the harsh word.

"Most people don't see all of that. You take the time to figure them out. You're a people person, Mac."

"So?"

"So you should be in a career that interacts with people. You probably pegged this group better than they could themselves."

Mac rubbed her temple. This felt way too serious, and she wasn't sure she wanted to know where Cole headed with this. "Are you done?"

Cole opened his mouth, then clamped it shut. He waved an imaginary board clean. "Fine. I'm done." Elbows on his knees, he studied Mac's face. She somehow knew he had something else up his sleeves and wasn't sure she'd like it any better. "New topic: I like to book my next trip onboard whenever possible, take advantage of those onboard credits."

"Of course," she said, heart rate already proving she knew where the conversation headed.

His eyes appeared darker in the low light, intensity radiating within. He gripped her knees. "Want to go somewhere else with me?"

"Cole—"

He dropped his hands. "You know as well as I do that booking now is not permanent. I just like spending time with you."

She liked spending time with him, too, more than she should, but that didn't change the facts. "My life is too much of a mess to make any plans."

He lowered his head but kept his intense eyes on hers. "Of course you'd say that. Think about it. No strings attached, an option for the future."

Mac rubbed her neck. "You know, I'm starting to believe all of Dani's complaints about her boss."

Cole replaced her hand with his own, and her tension fled. Whoosh, out the window from one touch of his strong hand. "Dani could find another job if I was really that bad." He kissed her, right there, in the middle of a busy area of the ship.

She needed to leave this vacation refreshed and with a plan for her future, not a future trip planned with her fling. Which meant she had one day left to make a decision. And say goodbye to Cole.

•••

Cole sat in the game room, waiting for the onboard internet to kick in. His mind wandered to Mac and how she'd read the room with ease. That skill would put her in high demand for most jobs. Heck, that's the type of quality he looked for in his employees, someone who could meet a person and figure out what type of trips they'd want to go on. Someone who'd listen with compassion and help as they could.

His email loaded, and he took care of a few business issues, forwarded some off to Dani to mediate until he got back. He read the updates from Dani, pleased as always to find things running smoothly. More pleased to find the heat had been fixed without issue.

Mind still on Mac, he had one more thing he had to do for her, and he knew she'd balk. So he turned to her BFF.

From: Cole Matterhorn
To: Dani Martin
Subject: Lemonade for Mac

I think Mac would be a great asset to our office. Thoughts? She could use it as a stepping stone, or maybe she'd enjoy the gig.

He checked a few other emails and prayed Dani was free and able to respond. His prayer got answered.

From: Dani Martin
To: Cole Matterhorn
Subject: RE: Lemonade for Mac

Who are you and what have you done with my boss???! You're scaring me, Cole. Next you're going to tell me you've bought jewelry for Mac and are planning on Happily Ever After. Don't hurt her.

But in answer to your question, Mac's a natural at vacations and customer service. She'd do great. HOWEVER, that's not going to work for three reasons: 1) Chad was her boss. She needs to not work for you. 2) She really did enjoy architecture, though Chad might have destroyed that as well. And 3) You still don't know whether we're going remote or not and weren't you worried about being able to afford

ME, NEVER MIND A NEW EMPLOYEE?

Dammit. She had to throw the lease situation at him. Though he should have expected it. Cole leaned back and tapped his fingers to the side of the desk. How much to tell his employee? How much to tell Mac's BFF?

FROM: COLE MATTERHORN
TO: DANI MARTIN
SUBJECT: RE: LEMONADE FOR MAC

JEWELRY: CHECK. HAPPY EVER AFTER: SHE MAKES ME HAPPY, DOES THAT COUNT? SHE'S REFUSING TO LET ME BOOK ANOTHER TRIP FOR US. ANOTHER REASON WHY I NEED TO KICK CHAD'S ASS.

ABOUT REMOTE VS. NOT, I'LL FIGURE SOMETHING OUT.

He sent the message and leaned back, steepling his fingers and resting his chin on top. Mac wouldn't want his involvement, and he really couldn't blame her for that. Didn't change the fact he had this gut-deep urge to help her, to give her whatever time she needed to figure out what she really wanted out of life. And Chad might have destroyed both Cole's ability to help and a career Mac might have reveled in. He'd figure something else out, some other way to be supportive.

As he prepared to log off, another email arrived from Dani.

FROM: DANI MARTIN
TO: COLE MATTERHORN
SUBJECT: RE: LEMONADE FOR MAC

AT THIS POINT YOU MIGHT BE THE ONE TO LOOK OUT FOR. MAC HAS A BAD TRACK RECORD. DON'T LET HER

HURT YOU.

If Dani was worried about him, then he'd already shared too much. He wanted to say Mac wouldn't hurt him. He knew better. Mac had been hurt too much to believe. Meanwhile he'd wrapped himself around Mac's finger and didn't care to find a way out.

In other words: he'd be screwed on his own volition.

He had his own decisions to make, and falling for Mac didn't help. The coin-toss idea still held merit, and if that held merit, he'd do good to at least consider Dani's request. Beyond the increase in advertising and need to be more visible without his physical location, he had to explore the costs of getting all the equipment set up and whether he wanted to convert a section of his home to a quasi-office, which led to pondering if he'd even want clients in his home.

He stuck to the costs, adding things up to compare apples to apples with staying with a lease. Either option had a lot to ponder. And his heart threw in a new wrench: which option would allow him to hire someone new?

Reality said neither. He needed to settle in and see how things went once he made a decision. Which sucked because he'd been planning on expanding before receiving the letter on the rent increase. Although remote would benefit from someone to manage the social media, even if he and Dani were good at juggling that.

Too much. He should have made this decision months ago, then he wouldn't be tempted to do something his business degree would choke him for.

Cole disconnected and pushed back from the computer, shoving his hands in his hair. He shouldn't have even contemplated offering Mac a job, beyond the valid points Dani had against the idea. Mac didn't need a hero. She needed support. She needed to believe in herself. That he could do easier than decide on the lease.

He ventured up to the pool deck and found Rob and Quinn but no Mac. Quinn wore oversize sunglasses, and her ereader lay on her lap. Rob put down his own ereader when he saw Cole.

"Mac's nose started looking like Rudolph, so she headed in to get ready for dinner." Rob thumbed toward Quinn. "Birthday girl's getting her beauty sleep."

Cole laughed and ran a hand through his hair. "I'll go check on Mac."

"What's the story for after the cruise?" Rob leaned forward.

"Why do you ask?"

"You look like a man ready to jump or run."

He stood there, staring at Rob. "I don't think I'm going to run." But he'd never been the type to jump. And still he knew how his actions looked and how they felt. He was jumping.

There'd been nothing to jump at, no desire to jump into anything in so long. He'd gone from indestructible college student to expecting death at every corner in the blink of an eye. But Mac felt right. She felt like a missing part of him in a way that had nothing to do with the actual parts of him that were missing.

She felt like the reason he survived, and he'd be damned if he'd walk away from that.

• • •

Mac sat cross legged on her bed, her papers with her future life options spread out before her. Job and housing ideas, she'd removed Cole since—check—fling acquired. Anything else came after her life resembled something other than a broken wheel.

All job options held potential—well, almost all. Going

back to her old job, under Chad, dealing with his behaviors... No, she couldn't do it. She wouldn't do it. She'd rather spend a year on Dani's couch. She crossed that option out. That left finding a similar job, or something in architecture, a new administrative assistant position, or something entirely new.

New. Did she want something new? Mac glanced out the window at the blue water and sky. She could work on a cruise ship, live the tropical vacation life. And work practically nonstop. No, thank you. *Stick with what you know, Mac.*

She pulled out her phone and went to a job search website. She started in administrative assistant. The field she'd been in since college, all her experience landed here. The listings populated, and on a whim she did a quick scan, finding nothing in architecture. It made her sad, she realized, but she pushed it aside and clicked slower through her options. They all started looking the same. Not that they didn't have bonuses, namely that they wouldn't be with Chad, but it would be the same old same old.

Huh, she wanted something different, a challenge. She'd been doing more than her job description and she'd enjoyed that, far too much. She scrapped the search, switched to architecture, and instead of scrolling mindlessly through, each job had her clicking and reading more. Until she got to the degree requirements that she didn't have. Stuck back at ground zero.

"So I'll do more administrative stuff. It's what I know and what I can do." And yet, in the back of her mind, Cole's "first choice" comments lingered. Had she always wanted to do administrative work? No, of course not. She hadn't had a clear direction, though, so there hadn't been something she'd passed on. At least, not obviously.

She stared at the papers in front of her. First choice? First choice meant architecture. She lacked the qualifications for her first choice.

"Not everything is that simple, Cole." She wouldn't win the lottery by thinking of some magical first choice number. Just like she wouldn't get back on her feet with a job in architecture. Maybe after she got settled…

No, too many maybes. Job. Housing. If the job didn't pay well, she could beg Dani to move to a two-bedroom with her. And Cole…Cole she'd worry about later, after she used the remaining day of this cruise to revel in his touch and attention.

She collected her phone, set up an email to Dani.

From: Mackenzie Laurel
To: Dani Martin
Subject: Jobs, Housing, and Decisions, oh my!

Why didn't I get a degree in architecture? That would make my decision so much easier. Nothing pays well, it's all the same old crap that I'm qualified for. I might need a roommate in the future. If I need to wear out your couch, might you be my roomie? <bats eyelashes>

~Mac

She cleaned up her papers and found out Dani had responded.

From: Dani Martin
To: Mackenzie Laurel
Subject: RE: Jobs, Housing, and Decisions, oh my!

You didn't get a degree in architecture because you didn't know you were interested in architecture. Chad bewitched you, only I suspect the field might stick more than he had any ability to. And what is with the roommate talk? You're supposed to be enjoying my boss, not

WALLOWING YET!

Mac laughed and loaded a response.

FROM: MACKENZIE LAUREL
TO: DANI MARTIN
SUBJECT: RE: JOBS, HOUSING, AND DECISIONS, OH MY!

YOU'RE RIGHT. I HAVE A FLING TO ENJOY. JUST TRYING TO GET MY DUCKS IN A ROW. ONLY TWO OF THE DUCKS ARE DRUNK, ONE'S SINGING BAD KARAOKE, AND ANOTHER JUMPED OVERBOARD.

YOU STOCKED UP ON ICE CREAM, RIGHT? I'M GOING TO NEED SOME. SEE YOU IN A FEW DAYS!

The next few months back home were going to be rough. But she'd have her fun now and her friends to support her later. The future would look better than her past. She'd make sure of it.

...

Against Mac's grumbling, complaining, and attempts to sway their afternoon activities, Cole steered her into the casino. He held two hands firmly on her shoulders, should she get any ideas of escaping. He wanted ten minutes, on his dime, to hopefully prove something to her. Then she could take control of their agenda.

The dim lights coaxed out the array of flashing colors from the slot machines. A lush maroon carpet lined the floor. Tables in the center filled with blackjack, roulette, and poker groups. Dings and bleeps filled the air. "What's your poison?" Cole asked.

"I don't gamble, not with my luck." Mac bit her lip as she looked around with wide eyes. The type of eyes from a person who'd been denying themselves for far too long. If he accomplished nothing on this cruise, he wanted to at least crack that wall hard enough she'd be able to take the rest down.

"Never?"

"No, not never. Bennett took me when I turned twenty-one."

Cole didn't like her brother. At all. He'd kick his ass after Chad's. "Let me guess, he continued to reinforce you choosing your second choice and you lost all your money in the first hour?"

"Half hour." A small smile broke free, and a flicker of hope brewed in those blue eyes.

"Rule number one: unless you have a strategy, go for what looks fun. Good instincts or not, no one wins every time."

He followed as she walked around, taking in the sights. A small commotion drew his attention to the roulette table, where karaoke girl cheered, covering her mouth, as her boyfriend wrapped his arms around her. Cole nudged Mac and pointed.

"Wow, guess they made up."

The friends from karaoke also cheered, no longer a divided group. "Looks that way. You want to try?"

Mac shook her head. "Absolutely not. Too many decisions. Besides, that table already has a winner." She walked past the rest of the tables and focused on the machines. Cole left the cheering group to follow.

Mac continued browsing, and Cole nearly stumbled into her when she stopped dead in her tracks at a machine boasting fruit. A laugh escaped her lips. "Even if this one's a bust, I have to try it. Look, there are lemons." She sat down on the round stool.

As Mac reached into her bag, Cole pulled a twenty from his back pocket and fed it into the machine.

Her head shot to his. "Cole? I can handle this."

"You're here because of me. The first round is mine."

She fingered the lemon around her neck. "You're too much."

He leaned forward and kissed her until he had to gasp for air.

"All right, all right, I'll take your money." Her lips slid up on the sides. She set her preferences before pressing the button.

Five rows on the digital screen spun. Watermelon, cherries, lemons, and strawberries appeared. Nothing lit up. Mac adjusted her setting and spun again. Still nothing. She spun a third time.

"See, Cole? Rotten lemons."

The rows stopped one by one, boasting a magnitude of fruit. Lemons appeared on each row, forming a *V* when all rows finished.

Mac gasped and clasped her hands to her mouth.

"That looks like enough for lemonade," he said close to her ear.

The lines started to light up, flashing as the counter rose higher and higher with winnings, and the sound effect of coins dropping came from the speakers. When all fell silent, Mac had tripled her money.

Cole nudged her arm. "Keep going."

She looked up at him. "What? I can cash out now, give you your money back and—"

He kissed her. "This isn't about money, Mackenzie-Mac. This is about trusting your instincts. Did your instincts plan on just three spins on this machine?"

She returned to the machine and pressed for another spin. This time the rows filled with watermelons and she earned another five bucks. Twice more she spun, and twice more she earned more than her bet. The next round did nothing.

Her shoulders slumped forward.

Cole laughed. "Even the best can't win every time."

"I know. I was just enjoying the rush. One more." She pressed the button, and five fruit baskets appeared in a row. The screen turned black and opened up to a filled fruit stand. "What just happened?"

"Bonus round."

Mac read the screen. "Pick fruit to fill in the basket, but be careful. If you get a rotten one, the round is over." She stared at him. "Rotten fruit—did you plant this here?"

She turned before he could answer and began tapping at the screen. She picked a group of blueberries, then an orange, an apple, and a lemon. Each one she tapped revealed points, and her total winnings dinged as the numbers moved higher. When she finally hit the rotten fruit, it was a lemon, and they discovered the only rotten fruits were the ones she hadn't touched.

"Oh my God," Mac squeaked through her hands covering her mouth.

The fruit on the screen cheered, and Mac's winnings rang up. By the time the screen switched back to normal, she had over $200.

Mac remained still, staring at the machine. Cole kissed the top of her head, a sense of pride bursting against his rib cage. He knew her instincts were good, but never would he have imagined this. If Mac didn't start trusting herself, she needed her head checked.

"I'm quitting. I don't care if there are more winnings. I'm quitting." With shaking hands, she cashed out and received a slip of white paper tallying $347. She stood up, and he pulled her into his arms.

"Do you believe me now that your instinct is good?"

She stared at the paper in her hands. "Starting to." Her glossy eyes found his. "I've never won anything before. Ever.

For the first time in my life, finding the rotten lemon was a good thing." She put the paper in her purse and clasped his face within her hands. "Thank you. Thank you, thank you, thank you." She kissed him once, twice, then pressed her lips hard against his before pulling back.

"I have a few ways you can thank me properly," he said, voice gruff in ways he hadn't expected.

Mac jumped in place. "Oh, definitely, there are plans for you, mister." She kissed him again before heading off to the cashier.

...

In honor of Quinn's birthday, Rob had asked Mac and Cole to join them at one of the specialty restaurants, which they gladly did. Good food, good company, and a chance to celebrate with Quinn, of course Mac wanted to join.

Now they followed Cole through the promenade. He claimed he had a surprise for Quinn, and besides the delicious smirk on his face, he gave them no other clues. Mac held his hand, weaving through the crowd with him. Behind her trailed Rob and Quinn, Quinn holding her charcoal pumps in her hand. The outside area with shops along the side held a growing crowd. Clearly they had more of an idea what Cole searched for than the rest of the group.

Finally he looked up, checked their position from all angles, and stopped. "This should work. I have no idea what the sound system will be like, but the view should be worth it."

Mac was touched that he kept her hearing in mind and squeezed his hand in a silent thanks. Chad had never understood that Mac couldn't hear everything. Meanwhile Cole went out of his way to do the opposite.

She stopped those thoughts. She didn't need to be doing

any comparisons, not when she'd be devoid of both men in a matter of days.

She squeezed his hand a second time, just because she could.

"What, exactly, are we doing?" Rob asked.

Cole flashed a wide smile. "Something I missed the last cruise I was on with Trent and knew I wouldn't miss it again. And considering he's talking more and more about not signing another contract, I'm not missing my last chance."

"Come on, give us a clue." Mac bumped her hip into his.

Cole laughed and shook his head. "And ruin the surprise? I think not."

"I thought you said this was for Quinn?" Rob asked.

"It is, but the rest of us are in for a really good time."

Around them more and more people gathered and the noise level rose. Mac began to worry about pending boredom for whatever this surprise was, as she needed to lean forward and ask for more repetition than normal. She was about to ask Cole for more details so she could be prepared when the lights switched into party mode with flashing colors all around. Banners and streamers appeared, all giving off a bright, eighties vibe, as "Footloose" blasted from speakers out of view. Mac crossed her fingers this would be more music and less talking.

The vibe around them skyrocketed, and the party atmosphere filtered through the crowd.

The music faded, and two singers came out on a platform, dressed in bright multicolor eighties-era clothes, complete with leg warmers, off-the-shoulder sweaters, and big hair. They started singing "It's Raining Men," and Mac relaxed. Music after all. This would do.

Then five men entered to the side of the singers, wearing trench coats, hats, and red speedos. Cole turned to them and yelled something, pointing up at the dancers. Mac couldn't make him out, not over all the noise, but noted he talked more to Quinn than the rest of them. She followed where he pointed and discovered one of the five men was Trent.

She glanced back at Quinn, whose eyes had grown wide, a flush to her cheeks. Mac couldn't blame her. The guy she had a crush on was presently on stage showing off a well-toned body. Mac would be drooling, but she had her own hot guy next to her. Still, the view, beyond Trent, was quite enjoyable.

"This is great," Rob yelled toward Cole. Clearly, Mac wasn't alone in her enjoyment.

Cole had his phone in his hands, angled up at the platform. "I know," he yelled back.

Mac laughed and hooted as the men on stage pelvic thrust toward the audience. "Anyone else notice that Trent's found Quinn?" She didn't know if he searched for the group or not, but his eyes were locked on the birthday girl, a smile on his lips, even if Mac did notice a tint of embarrassment on his cheeks.

The music continued after the segment, and Trent and the rest of the staff received a loud round of applause and cheers. They left the stage area and were replaced by other performers, dancing and singing to the loud beat of "Karma Chameleon."

"You doing okay?" Cole asked, no longer filming now that Trent had left, though Mac noted he hadn't put his phone away.

Mac nodded. "Songs are easier than speech. Most people don't understand all the words to songs anyways."

"That is true." Cole kissed her cheek, and she ended up watching him instead of the show. How had this man entered her life a week ago and made such a difference? He felt like he belonged there next to her, and not just for this vacation.

None of that mattered. In twenty-four hours, she'd let him go.

The high of the party atmosphere warred with the pending end of a good vacation. She wanted to stop time and stay right there, on this ship, forever. Her shambles of a life waited for her, and this would be the last fun moment she had for a long time.

She refocused on the music as the song changed, pushing down her thoughts. She'd enjoy this night, and the next day. No sense spoiling her lemons too soon. "Hot, Hot, Hot" now played, and Quinn pointed as Trent, Carlos, and the others came down a side stairway.

"Yes," Cole exclaimed and set up his phone again. He looked up and called out, "What?" while shrugging his shoulders.

Trent pointed at him, the finger clearly promising a threat.

The music swelled, and Mac clutched onto Quinn as the guys moved out onto the floor, continuing their dancing. She let the music take her away, enjoying having friends with her and on stage.

Until synchronization grew haphazard and Mac lost her cheering partner when Trent grabbed Quinn's hand and pulled her to him.

Mac cheered, Rob joining her. Quinn stumbled into Trent and grasped onto his shoulder. Both looked so happy to be together, and Mac had a momentary ping of jealousy. Until she remembered that they had even more complications than she and Cole did. She needed to enjoy these moments, as Quinn clearly enjoyed hers, and let the future be whatever it would be.

The song died down, and Trent started laughing. He walked Quinn back to their group. Before letting her go, he brought her hand to his lips, kissing her. A kiss Mac would bet money on involving tongue.

Trent let her go and turned to Cole. "You're an asshole

for filming this."

Cole laughed. "Why? Because I got you with Quinn?"

Trent shook his head but didn't complain, not that he had much time to converse. He followed the staff away, glancing back once at them, or rather, glancing back at Quinn.

She turned to Cole. "You got that on video?"

"Oh yeah."

"I'm going to need a copy."

Cole nodded. "I'm sending it right now."

"You gonna dance like that for Mac?" Rob teased.

Mac's cheeks heated.

Cole gestured to his prosthesis, even though his long pants covered it. "People might not go for the amputee in a speedo."

"Mac would."

Both men, and Quinn, turned to her. She placed a hand on Cole's cheek. "He's right, I would."

Cole's eyes turned serious. "Anytime, all you have to do is ask."

How about right now because we only have tomorrow? But Mac swallowed those words. It had to be the vacation high, the away from home vibe, because she had the urge to keep her cruise fling. Keep this man who didn't commit that Dani would never have set her up with. Keep this happy bubble.

A bubble, one that could pop at any moment. Because a cruise fling couldn't be real. Mac and Cole, just like Trent and Quinn, a fun time. Nothing more.

Day 8: At Sea

Midnight trickled past, and Cole found himself in the hot tub. Mac refused to retire to her room, an urgency about her he hadn't experienced before. The end of the cruise fast approached. A part of him wanted to extend their vacation for another week or two. A stronger part wanted to see what would happen when they got back to Massachusetts.

The concept still felt foreign to him, this desire to try something real with someone. And in many ways, it also meant a dark cloud leaving him. Something beyond work or a vacation to look forward to for the first time in nearly ten years.

On the other hand, something more than his leg to lose. Already the thought of not being with Mac in a week tempted him to panic. If something happened to her, he hadn't a clue how he'd manage to cope.

They were the only ones in the tub, the rest of the pool deck empty under the dark skies. Made it easier for him to remove his prosthesis without so many curious stares. Low light illuminated Mac's hair, casting shadows across her face.

The steam from the warm water created a mist.

Around her neck his necklace nestled between her breasts. He let his gaze wander over her, mesmerized by everything she was. The bubbles distorted his gaze, but he still zoned in on her stomach.

There was something to Mac and her decisions. Otherwise her second choice wouldn't be horrendous and her first choice lucky enough to win at the casino. So how did that factor into unprotected sex?

The truth of the matter was, it took two of them to make that decision. He'd been ready to stop her and get the condom. But she had moved and knocked every brain cell straight out of his head. Pleasure trumped, and he wasn't the type to think twice about pleasure. He also hadn't been too worried about the outcome.

Just like he could bet money on Mac's instinct, his own instinct said she was pregnant. He'd known her a week, her life was not in a good place, and the timing sucked.

But if she was, it wasn't a rotten lemon. He knew it deep down inside. He could look at her forever, spend his time counting her freckles, kissing her lips.

Raise their child.

He needed to get a grip, let time pass, let the answers come when they would. It was more than just a potential pregnancy, though. If she was pregnant, they would be a family. Would that be so bad? Two new connections in his life, when for so long there'd been none. A chance at a forever with Mac.

He should be freaked out. For years he ran from anything intense, thanks to the damn bombing. That marathon changed everything. Ripped away all his dreams, all his ambitions. Leaving him an unadorned stump of a man.

Not anymore. The potential of new life, of a life with Mac, had something shifting deep inside. Purpose. For years he refused all commitment, kept his family at bay, kept new and old friends at a distance. He couldn't risk losing them or the thought of them losing him. He had one foot out of this world already, pun intentional. Love, commitment, hadn't been in his plans. Too much at stake. Too much to lose.

He loved Mac.

Love after seven days? It didn't match the man he'd been. But he couldn't deny he felt it, down to his bones. If she was pregnant, he was proposing.

He relaxed against the bubbles, arms outstretched on either side. He'd deal with those thoughts later. Mac sat stiff, chewing on her lip. If he didn't soothe her, he'd lose precious time with her. The only idea he had was to call attention to some of her problems. "It's officially the last day of the cruise."

She played with the bubbles. "Yeah."

"One last day to enjoy the hell out of the trip."

She didn't make eye contact. "Yeah."

"We could spend it in your stateroom, or mine. I hear room service is pretty good." He shifted closer to her, draping one arm around her shoulders.

A small laugh escaped. "Sorry. I just can't believe this vacation is almost over." She turned her head and leveled him with those blue eyes. An unspoken conversation filtered between them, about how they'd only known each other for this short trip, in vacation mode. What would change?

Potentially everything.

He kissed her chlorine-tinted shoulder. "Vacations always go by fast." He scooted even closer, until their thighs touched. "Sadly, I don't have a hot tub back home."

He caught her mouth with his and wrapped his arms around her. The stress in her body floated off into the steam, and she melted into him. Her soft fingers skated down his naked chest, ripping a groan from the back of his throat.

Good thing they were alone, because he was sporting a hard-on that would not be contained.

Which only reminded him he wasn't prepared for this. In his pocket he had his cruise card and nothing else. No protection. He pulled back and looked up to the inky dark sky. "We need a bucket list, everything we want to do today that we haven't done already."

"Then we definitely don't need to stay in the staterooms." Mac smirked.

"There's always something new to try." He kissed her shoulder, sucking at the tender skin. As she ran her hand down his stomach and gripped his erection, his eyes nearly rolled back into his skull. "Bucket list, Mackenzie-Mac."

She removed her hand, much to his disappointment, and leaned back. "Well, my original plan was to eat my way through the ship before I had to starve myself at home. Haven't managed that yet."

His heart squeezed, but he kept his mouth shut.

"Thanks to you, I still have some of my onboard credit left. Shopping will have to be done." Her face frowned instead of the smile he expected the statement to bring.

"What's wrong?"

She shook her head, those blue eyes threatening waterfalls. He moved to her, cupped the back of her head, and kissed her. He kept it sweet, since they couldn't go much further. She molded her body to his, testing his will.

"You're my bucket list," she said against his lips. "I don't care what we do, as long as it's together."

An alarm bell rang in his head. Against everything they had established during their week together, this sounded final. One last day before they went their separate ways. Before he could complain, she kissed him again, a pleading kiss requesting he follow her lead without question.

Normally he wouldn't have complied, but her tongue

in his mouth always made his judgment a little hazy. And considering his suspicions, she wasn't getting away from him.

• • •

Daylight sprinkled in through the half-open curtains by the time Mac closed her eyes. She spent the night in Cole's arms, memorizing his scent, his touch, his look. She had a day left to enjoy him.

After living with Chad for a year, after being his joke, his tease, she couldn't find herself back in another man's shadow. She wanted to go home, eat ice cream, and lounge on Dani's couch. She wanted to decompress and figure out where the hell she wanted to go with her life.

She couldn't do that with Cole.

With those thoughts rumbling around in her head, her heavy eyelids finally closed. Sometime later, with the sunlight now strong between the shades, she woke up with a racing heart and fast breaths. Her body hummed with pleasure. Through her haze of being half awake, half asleep, she slowly registered Cole's hand between her legs, caressing her, and his mouth on her nipple.

She let her head fall back on the pillow and closed her tired eyes, let her body continue to wake up into a fiery state of arousal. Her hips bucked as his fingers entered her, exploring her, driving her absolutely out of her mind.

Cole's teeth nipped her collarbone. "I can tell you're awake. I couldn't let you sleep our last day away."

"What time is it?" she managed to ask.

"Breakfast is almost over." He kissed his way down her stomach. "I was getting hungry and thought I'd help myself."

She gasped as his lips pressed into her pelvic bone and grabbed his hair to yank him upright. "Only do that if you know what you're doing. I've had one too many duds in this department." Although if he was a dud perhaps that would help with her plan?

She knew she was in trouble when Cole's smile turned wicked. "I've never had any complaints, but you can be the judge." Then he lowered his head and whispered against her, his breath doing something erotic to the tingles on her inside. By the time his tongue met her flesh, she was writhing beneath the sheets.

He wasn't a dud. She knew that long before his teeth nibbled gently, and then not so gently, before he sucked her into his mouth, before he brought her to climax so hard she screamed. And since his head was between her legs, no one muffled her cries.

"Well, I'll take that as I know what I'm doing," he said once he sat up. He scooted up the bed and pulled her to him. "With all your hesitation, I didn't think I had to worry about the noise."

She wanted to wipe that smirk right off his face. "Grab a condom and I'll show you my appreciation."

• • •

Cole carried a plate with two muffins and Mac held their coffees as they entered the small lounge. By the time they made it out of her room, there hadn't been much time, just enough to grab food to go and still make it to the last day of trivia. He wasn't complaining; he had phantom tingles in his missing foot from how well she showed her appreciation.

The room held a decent crowd for the final day, and Cole glanced around, trying to find their friends. Quinn and Rob waved from a small table. Cole nudged Mac, and they weaved through tables and chairs to join them. "Look who showed up," Rob teased.

Mac grabbed her muffin. Cole tried not to smile too

much at the color in her cheeks. "We made it." She glanced around. "Trent skipping?"

Quinn pointed to a table nearby. "Speaker issues. He's trying to get the problem fixed."

"Oh, for both our sakes, I hope it's fixable," Mac said.

"Trent's got an added reason to make it work." Rob winked at Quinn.

Quinn shook her head. "Just doing his job."

"Bullshit," Rob fake coughed.

Cole laughed and leaned back, grabbing his coffee as he did so.

A few minutes later, Trent came in, squatting between Quinn and Mac. "Looks like I'm stuck with the speaker system. We've tweaked a few levels, but I'm not sure if that'll make a difference. Sorry about that."

"We'll be fine," Quinn said.

"Would it be better if I skipped the sound system all together?"

Quinn looked at Mac and after her nod reached over and squeezed his arm. "Relax, Trent, we'll be fine. The guys will help."

Trent clenched his jaw, probably grinding his back teeth, before pushing himself up and returning to his notes.

Cole put his coffee down and grabbed his muffin. "Here's the plan: Mac's first instinct is right. Don't let her change her mind."

Mac lightly pushed his shoulder. "You put far too much faith in my instinct."

He took a bite. "Prove me wrong."

She shifted her gaze to her own muffin. Something shifted. He felt it deep in the pit of his stomach. He put down his food and drink and leaned in close to her, brushing her hair back with his breath. She jerked away from him.

"You hit my microphone."

Crap. "Sorry." He inched back. "Mackenzie-Mac, you know your instincts are good. Don't start doubting yourself now."

He moved out of her personal space, leaving her cheeks flushed. She looked at him, eyes wide behind her black frames. He didn't know if it was the lurking end of the cruise or something deeper, but a battle brewed deep inside her. Before he had a chance to question her or figure out what type of battle geared up, Trent's voice broke in, halting the advancement.

"Good morning, ladies and gentlemen," Trent began against a static background. "Another lovely day at sea. Sadly it's our last. You folks lucked out in the weather department. A few weeks ago we had rain almost every day." He leaned back against the wall and eyed the room. "My audience numbers did go up. I suspect we've lost a few participants to the sun."

He reviewed the rules, dangled the souvenir pens as the prizes. When Cole wasn't watching Mac out of the corner of his eye, he noticed Trent had an eye on Quinn. After the first question was given, and Mac refused to answer, Trent popped over.

"Sound system any better?" he asked.

"I caught enough," Mac said.

"I'll manage. Don't worry about me," Quinn replied, not looking him in the eyes.

He squatted down next to her. "But—"

"No buts." She poked him in the chest. "I know how to take care of myself. I'll be fine."

He grabbed her finger and searched for something in her eyes. Cole knew the feeling. "Fine," he said and stood. He shared a look with Cole, and Cole nodded. The women were off today.

Sad the notion didn't deter him at all.

Mac remained quiet on the second question as well. Rob held the paper, repeated the question for Mac and Quinn, but he and Cole were the ones coming up with the answers.

Cole finished off his coffee and leaned into Mac. "Forget what I said. This is a game. Right or wrong, let's have fun. Didn't we have fun the first time when we got every answer wrong?"

A smile crossed her lips. She reached over, squeezed his hand, and started participating in the game. A few rounds later, Trent came back over and glanced at their answers.

"Not bad. Where are all the right answers coming from? It can't be Cole."

"Blow me," Cole said.

Trent smiled his "fuck you" smile.

"Most of those come from our redheaded firecracker," Rob said.

Mac blushed.

"Nice." He pointed to the paper. "Got a different answer for the first two?"

Mac nodded.

Trent squatted down next to her. "What's your guess? Come on, tell me."

Mac cupped her hand over his ear and whispered.

Trent laughed. "Get them to change their answers." He stood. "Current answer: wrong. Mac's answer? Right."

Cole grinned like a proud parent until Mac jabbed at his shoulder. He didn't bother reiterating the obvious. Doubly so when her first instincts helped them tie for the win.

Mac held a hand over her mouth. "How is that possible?"

Cole pulled her close and kissed the top of her head. If he dared say anything, he'd ruin the moment, and right now, Mac believed in herself. He wanted her going home with this feeling.

Trent addressed the other team first before making his

way over to them. He shook his head, but his smile said he planned to enjoy this teasing. "Mac deserves the prize, not so sure about the rest of you."

Contrary to his words, he handed a pen to Quinn first, hand lingering, sparks damn near flying for everyone to see. He shook it off quicker than Cole would have before handing out pens to the others. Or rather, the others except for Cole.

"Still don't trust you," Trent said.

Cole laughed. "Sure, that's why you live with me on land."

Trent handed it over. "Haven't you stolen enough from me over the years?"

Cole tossed the pen in the air and caught it. "A few. I mark it down as a business expense."

Trent laughed. "A cruise is a hell of a business expense for a pen." He patted Cole's shoulder and headed back to the table where he had his stuff.

Quinn, meanwhile, was bent over a piece of paper, writing something down. Before anyone could question her, she jumped up and went after Trent.

"What's she doing?" Mac asked.

They all watched as Quinn handed the paper over to Trent.

"Giving Trent her contact information," Rob said.

They watched as Trent smiled at her, slipping the paper in his back pocket. Quinn nodded once and made her way back to them. She deflated into her chair.

"You okay?" Rob asked.

Quinn nodded. "Yes. This trip might not have gone like I wanted it to, but at least I've gotten some new friends out of it."

Rob pulled her to him in a side hug. "Never say never."

Mac cleared her throat. "Good thing I already have your cell number, otherwise I'd feel left out right now."

Quinn reached out, grasped Mac's hand. "You are going

to have so many texts from me you'll regret this."

Mac shook her head, laughing. "Not likely."

Cole liked that he wasn't the only one making a connection with Mac on this trip. A wayward thought entered his mind: maybe if Mac tried to blow him off, he could get their cruise friends to remind her of his potential.

. . .

Mac walked along the string of onboard stores, bag in hand, her last few indulgences complete prior to returning to a frugal life. She squeezed Cole's hand. Last few indulgences indeed.

Ahead, a crowd of people gathered around a central table, set up with T-shirts and signs boasting deep discounts. Another table had jewelry on display. Mac nudged Cole and gestured to a familiar couple. "Looks like they made up."

Shark Shirt placed a sparkling bracelet on Hat Lady's wrist.

"More like he groveled and she finally accepted," Cole said.

Mac ignored the couple to glance at all the shiny items and their supposedly marked-down prices.

Cole pressed in behind her. "See anything you like?" he asked.

She shook her head. "Nope, just looking." She moved their entwined hands to the stone around her neck. "You already got me something."

Cole laughed. "Make sure you show that to Dani."

"Why?"

He ran his free hand through his hair. "I've never bought a woman jewelry before."

Her blood ran cold. "Never?"

He shrugged. "No big deal."

Mac backed away from the crowd. "No, Cole, this is a big deal. You've never done this, and yet you bought a necklace for someone you've known a week. A fling." She couldn't breathe. This was all way too much too fast. It went against her plans, and she needed to keep to her goal: go home alone and put her life back together.

He grabbed her shoulders. "We're not a fling."

She closed her eyes and willed her breathing to stabilize. His words settled deep inside. They had to be a fling. Later, when her life resembled something she could be proud of, then she could think about her sandy-haired cruise fling. She needed to find a way to get him to see this, to understand.

All her life, things had blown up in her face. Nothing good lasted, certainly not something that existed entirely on a cruise ship. Vacations were always a departure from the norm. Whatever magic that had surely wouldn't last back on land. Not home where everything was in complete upheaval.

She didn't want to get into this now, not in the middle of the shopping area. She wanted the rest of the day with him. But the can of worms had been cracked, and she couldn't keep those slimy bastards inside. "I can't continue this after tomorrow." The words physically ached as she spoke them, but she held tight. She'd come on this ship with one goal and she wouldn't abandon it now.

He shook her shoulders and she opened her eyes. And wished she hadn't. The pain in his face made her want to kick herself.

"What are you saying?"

Don't back down, Mackenzie. That's how you let Chad in. "My life is shit right now, Cole. I need to find a job, find a new place to live. I need to pick up the pieces."

"And you can't do that and date me?" The pain flashed into anger.

"This isn't a can and can't situation; I'm not ready for this, for you. I need to put my life together first. I just got out of a bad relationship, with my boss of all people. I need to stand on my own without relying on someone else." She poked him. "And you can't honestly tell me after never being in a serious relationship that a single week with vacation goggles makes things different."

He bent, looking her directly in the eyes. "I've experienced moments that have changed my life forever. Yes, I can."

She looked around. They couldn't do this here. She grabbed his hand and pulled him along. His hand in hers felt different. Cracks in the foundation. A Mackenzie specialty.

His stateroom was the closest, and she brought them there. He unlocked the door and stepped inside. She prepared to continue their conversation, but he backed her against the wall. His mouth met hers, his anger bitter on his tongue, the kiss demanding, rough, and still every bit as arousing. He had one hand in her hair, the other pressed into the small of her back. She wrapped her arms around his shoulders, pulling him closer even as she knew she had to push him away.

"I'm sorry," she whispered when she freed her mouth.

"Bullshit. This is bullshit, Mac. You're going to toss me out of your life because a few things aren't going well?"

She pushed him back and paced into the room. "A few things? I don't call no job, no home, no money a few things. I have no idea where to go from where I am, and I need to figure that out."

He took deep breaths, and she really wished they had some place without thin walls to have it out. She stared at a picture away from him, not making any sense of the pixelated image before her.

"What if you're pregnant?"

What? She whipped her head around. Her stomach lurched. "What if I am?"

"You're not going to let me take care of you?"

Oh, for crying out loud. "Cole, this is the twenty-first century. I don't need to be taken care of. Don't you get it? I need to find myself, and I can't do that wrapped up in a man."

"Is that your first instinct, Mackenzie, to leave me?"

She stared at him as the crack in their foundation traveled to her heart. Her first instinct was to fling herself at him, curl up in his arms, and stay there for the rest of her life. "Yes." Her first instinct would only get her hurt.

He let out a huff of a humorless laugh. "Fine, have it your way. I thought this whole lemonade/rotten lemon thing was your friends teasing you. But I see it here. We're lemonade. But you're making us rotten lemons."

She closed her eyes but couldn't stop the tear from sliding down her cheek. "Give me your phone."

He stared at her, square jaw set, stiff and distant. Then he stomped to a drawer and tossed his phone her way. She clicked it on, added a new contact, and plugged in her limited information. Hand shaking, she handed his phone back to him.

"I don't want this to be the end, end. I just need to find myself first. Please, understand. I'm lost. As long as I stay with you, I won't find what I need."

He took his phone. "You're letting your past dictate your future." The green of his eyes dulled, the crack ripping through him.

She flung herself at him, hungry mouth searching hungry mouth. He responded beat for beat. She slipped her hands under his shirt, running over his muscular back. He pushed her until a foot of space separated them.

"Either you're with me or you're not. I don't do games."

She caught her breath and swallowed the lump in her throat. No doubt in her mind, she was the rotten lemon. She picked up her bags. "I'm sorry, Cole. You have no idea how sorry I am."

He stood there and watched her go, breaking her heart with every step she had to take.

...

Cole traveled alone often. He was no stranger to doing his own thing, meeting new people, and still having a blast. Especially on a cruise ship, how could one feel alone?

He found out how, by being trampled on by a woman who doubted her gut instincts. He'd tried to show her worth, to build her up and be a supportive person in her life. The only thanks he got was a broken heart.

How the hell had he gotten here? The past ten years he hadn't made any lasting connections, didn't let anyone in, didn't risk losing them. He'd let Mac in. He'd lost her.

This feeling was very different from the bombing, no physical pain to go along with the emotional scars. Back then, everyone had been impacted by the event, as national disasters dug deep, even to those unaffected. It shouldn't compare to a breakup after a measly seven days.

It did.

She'd become a part of him, someone to worry over. The reality of another attack always lingered in the back of his mind, and he didn't know if he could handle it if something happened to her. Not when the last words they shared would be how sorry she was. Sorry his ass. Life was too damn short to play games. She wanted to get her life together. He'd been failing at his for ten long years.

Cole tugged at the collar of his loose T-shirt, his small cabin walls closing on him more than usual. He couldn't stay here, couldn't remain at the scene of the crime, as goddamn messed up as that sounded in his head. No bloodshed, no crime. Only internal bleeding.

He left his room, wandering around the ship with no

intended direction. One foot in front of the other, the only thing he could focus on. The last day buzz filled the air but not him. Heck, he could have been on the damn *Titanic* and still walking around like a fool.

A hand on his shoulder stopped him. Trent.

"I called your name five times." Trent glanced around. "What happened?"

Cole shook his head, words clogged in his throat.

Trent stared, waiting for more information.

He forced his mouth into working order. "Mac ended 'the fling.'"

"What fling?"

He raised his hands. "Tell that to her."

"Fuck," Trent murmured low. "Sorry, man."

Cole kept walking with nowhere to go. "Fucking lemons, fucking ex-boyfriends." He kicked a trash can with his prosthesis as they passed, continuing to mutter swears.

"If she had waited a day, I could have drunk you under the table," Trent said.

Cole laughed in spite of himself. "You've always had a soft side for a drunk."

"You know it. Nine times out of ten they're fun. Pathetic but fun."

"I need a drink."

Trent shook his head. "Nope, wait until tomorrow. I don't want you killing yourself. We'll both get shitfaced."

"Not going to work this time." Because he loved Mac. This pain had been his goal to avoid, and now he had no place to go, nowhere to run.

Trent patted Cole's back. "Come on. I can sit with you for a bit."

. . .

Mac tried to placate her aching heart with a double scoop of butter pecan, to no avail. Hell of a way to end a vacation. She still went to the dining room for dinner, more so she could see Quinn and Rob.

"Okay, what's wrong?" Quinn asked as Mac pushed around a piece of chicken on her plate. "What did Cole do?"

Want more from her than she could give. "Nothing. I ended the fling."

Quinn and Rob gasped.

Mac stabbed a cucumber.

"But that wasn't a fling," Quinn said.

Mac sighed and pushed the remains of her chicken dinner away. "Regardless, my life back home is a mess, and I need to get myself in order before I start a relationship."

"Is this the infamous bad Mackenzie decision process?" Quinn asked.

Rob reached for a roll. "Looks like."

"I know what I'm doing. And now it's done. So if I've messed things up beyond repair, at least I did it early."

"Before you fell for him?" Rob swiped a thick glob of butter on his bread.

"Exactly."

He pointed the knife at her. "Liar."

She stared at him, his brown eyes forcing her to admit the truth clawing at her deep inside. "Fine, I'm lying. But that doesn't mean—"

"I wanted that," Quinn interrupted. "I wanted what you've got but are throwing away."

"You've got Trent."

"I've got sparks with a guy who's keeping me at arm's length."

"Both of you need to stop and listen up." Rob popped a piece of bread in his mouth. "Here's the honest truth: Mackenzie, darling, you found love. Hard, fast, pure. And not one sided. The kind of love there's no moving on from. If Cole wants to help you out of your current life mess, let him. Because that's what couples do, help each other through good times and bad. He's already there for you for the bad. What the hell are you running from?

"And you, Quinn, darling, platonic love of my life. So what if you haven't spent much time with Trent? He's not here on vacation, he's here for a job, and not only is he failing to keep you at bay, but he's risking things because of you. The two of you are in sync with one another and heat up the whole goddamn place. A spark doesn't burn panties."

Quinn picked up her wineglass. "We live across the country from each other."

"So visit him. Or have him visit you. It's going to happen."

Quinn turned away from Rob. "What do you say, Mac? You and me, we'll go dance the night away, drink the night away, and nurse hangovers on the plane ride tomorrow."

Mac smiled and reached out to grasp Quinn's hand. "I'm exhausted and about to sleep on a couch when I get back home. Let's get a drink, dance a little, then let me get a good night's sleep before I return to hell."

Quinn squeezed Mac's hand back. "Sounds like a plan."

...

Later that night, Mac stumbled back to her room. The ship rocked her weary head, her heart ached, and her intoxication level was high enough to take both edges off. Of course, it also left her stomach queasy and tumbling, insisting the rough seas were not acceptable.

It took two tries, but she got her cruise card in the slot and her door opened. Once again, her room felt lonely. Airy. Missing a certain sandy-haired amputee.

She pulled out her luggage from under the bed and began

piling her clothes up inside. Over a week ago she sat in Dani's office, crying her eyes out and being coaxed into a cruise. Now she prepared to go home, with the knowledge she felt something scarily close to love for Dani's boss.

Irony. No job, no home, no money, and a different ex.

She rubbed her aching heart and her stomach rolled over again, the kind of roll that forced bile up. Dammit, she shouldn't have drank so much. She swallowed it down and continued packing her belongings. Next stop: Dani Martin's place. All she wanted was a home to go to.

A tear slid down her cheek, and her stomach lurched again. Okay, so having a mixed fruit drink after a day of mostly ice cream wasn't her best idea. She drank some water to soothe her stomach.

She should really apologize to Cole. Spend one more night in his arms. She could find herself while dating him, right?

Her stomach rumbled, and this time the contents pressed down as well as up. Okay, so she couldn't keep seeing Cole. She knew that. And the thought made her woozy.

She curled up on the section of the bed her luggage wasn't taking up, her stomach now rumbling like a hot spring. The room spun even with her head on the pillow, her mouth dry and clammy. The pressure in her stomach built until she was forced to move, forced to brave the dizzying effects, and rush to the bathroom.

She'd once made a joke about cruise bathrooms being so small one could sit on the toilet and throw up at the same time. Lucky her, she got to verify the joke was legit.

Day 9: Florida

Cole threw the last of his belongings into his backpack and switched on his phone. The first thing he received was a text from Trent, asking if he'd had the chicken at dinner, since it had been linked to several cases of food poisoning. Wouldn't that be Cole's luck?

He glanced around his postage stamp–size room and checked for anything left behind. All he found was his trampled-on heart. At least he didn't need it anymore.

A loss like this hadn't been a part of his life since the bombing. He hadn't let it, knowing life to be fragile as fuck. A bomb could be on the ship. Or the plane home could crash. Or there could be a shooting at the mall. So many potential catastrophes and he'd already found himself in one, in a country where they became more common every day.

And yet his heart suffered, no large-scale catastrophe required. All because he'd let his guard down, let someone in. Proved his original life plans were correct. Something would take the rest of him one day; he didn't need any entanglements.

Of course that reminded him that something could happen to Mac, and even though she hurt him, he didn't want anything to happen to her.

He verified the safe was empty one last time and left his room to head to breakfast. The last-day vibe filled the air, a mixture of tired, refreshed, and upset about the end of a vacation. At the dining room, he bumped into Quinn and Rob.

"Hey, it's Cole," Quinn exclaimed and flung herself at him.

He looked around, but no sign of Mac.

Rob looked around as well. "We were meeting Mac here, but she's late."

Cole forced his concern down, not his problem. "I'll let you two go then."

Quinn grabbed Cole's arm. "We're worried. She's never been late for anything. I know she butchered things up with you two, but we were hoping she was late because you reunited."

Concern increased and grasped his broken heart. Many all-too-real scenarios ran through his head, even if the ship didn't show signs of any explosions. He shook his head.

"We called her, and she didn't answer," Rob said. "We walked by her room and the Do Not Disturb key was in, so we really did think you two got back together."

He glanced at his watch. "When did you two stop by?"

"Ten minutes ago."

And everyone was supposed to be out of the rooms already. *Fuck*. He scrubbed a hand over his cheek, trying to stay put. He couldn't. Then Trent's text clicked. "What did Mac have for dinner?"

Rob and Quinn looked at each other. "Chicken, I think. Why?" Quinn said.

Cole tried to bite back this new urgency strumming

through him and failed. "Dammit. It's been linked to food poisoning. I'll check on her."

As he walked away, he heard Rob say, "That'll teach her for throwing away what's good for her."

He took the steps two at a time as he raced to Mac's room. The backpack banged into his spine, but he paid it no mind. When he reached her door, he pounded. Sure enough, the Do Not Disturb key stuck out of the slot. He listened and heard nothing from inside. Panic gripped him by the balls. He pounded again. "Mackenzie, open the damn door."

"Good morning," came an Indian-accented voice from behind him. "She lock you out?"

He turned to see Mac's steward. Cole pretended to pat his pockets. "Yeah, can you give me a hand?"

The steward laughed and came over to help. Cole could have kissed him. The door opened, and Cole entered. On Mac's bed, her suitcase lay open and half packed. Clothes and items covered her bed and her table. However, there was no Mac.

Did she somehow fall overboard, or did someone enter from the balcony, or…

"Mac?" he called out, taking a step further into the room.

"Go away," came her worn-out voice from the bathroom.

The fear loosened his grip on his balls. He opened the door to find Mac, in her pajamas, curled up in front of the toilet, head resting on the seat. Her hair was pulled back into a messy ponytail and her glasses were off. "Oh, Mac," he said as he squatted down next to her.

She didn't move. "Go away, Cole. Please. This isn't pretty."

He didn't care. He kissed the top of her head. "You need to be out of your room."

She groaned and pulled her head up. She remained on the floor, her back against the sink. "I keep trying to move, but I can't. The room spins and I end up back here."

Bags hung under her eyes, a slight imprint on her cheek from where she had rested her head. And his heart ached for her. "I'll finish packing and help you out of here."

"You don't need to do this."

He looked back at her. He did need to do this. Because he loved her and he took care of those he loved. A sickness was a hell of a lot better than any of the scenarios rolling around in his head. "Where are your clothes for the day? I'll bring them to you and you can try and get yourself put together."

"On the shelf in the closet."

He left the bathroom door open and found her clothes, brought them to her. Then he went about throwing all her items into her luggage. She'd probably care about the wrinkles. He didn't. All he cared about was taking care of her.

Strange feeling. He'd only been taking care of himself, with no plans to do more. And yet flipping off this particular switch would be impossible.

After every last item was accounted for, he returned to the bathroom. Mac sat on the floor, dressed, and brushed her teeth. He knelt before her and felt her forehead. "Feeling any better?" Her skin felt clammy but not too warm.

"No. There's a good chance I'll throw up on your shoes." She put her toothbrush in the sink, and he used a cup to give her some water. Then he got her glasses and hearing aids.

He threw the rest of her belongings into her bag and made a quick three-pass inspection of the room.

"I've got everything, even triple checked for you. Let's go." In one hand, he held her luggage and carry-on; the other he held out for her. She looked up at him with emotions swimming in those blue eyes, questioning why he was even there.

"You don't have to—"

"Put a sock in it, Mackenzie. You able to move on your

own?"

A tear trickled down her cheek, and she shook her head. He pulled her up, held her against him, and breathed in the top of her head. He didn't care she hadn't showered. He didn't care she'd been throwing up. All he cared about was her safety.

Still, he gave her a moment before moving.

They made it to the elevators before she leaned against a wall and slid to the ground. "I can't move," she moaned.

He swallowed the fear and helped her up when the elevator arrived, trying to figure out what else he could do to help her feel better.

...

Mortification consumed Mac. She'd had the night from hell, spent mostly in her bathroom. No chance to enjoy a nice bed for the last time in who knew how long. Instead she got intermittent spurts of sleep while rolled into a tight ball in the corner of the bed, willing the evil to leave her. Or claim her.

Wish not granted. She had to be found by Cole with her head in the toilet. The least he could do was look at her with disgust, not with concern, and it nearly broke her the rest of the way.

Now she sat in one of the onboard lounges sipping a bottled water Cole had somehow found. Miraculously she no longer felt like she had to throw up, point in the plus column, but sleep wanted to claim her. She tried to stay awake; she did. But with Cole's shoulder next to her as they waited to debark, she lost the battle. He looked better than a king-size bed with one thousand thread count sheets, and she rested on his shoulder, closing her eyes for only a second.

...

Cole took Mac's glasses from her as her head against his shoulder had them squashed askew. He hadn't a clue if she would want him to do anything about her hearing aids; all he knew was that she took them off to sleep. She didn't flinch. He guessed she hadn't slept much the night before.

Without moving her, he managed to get his phone out of his pocket and sent Trent a text letting him know Mac was sick. Then he sent Quinn and Rob a text giving them an update. He didn't know when Mac's plane left or what her plans were for getting to the airport. But he knew who would have that information.

Phone in hand, he waited for the call to connect.

"Well, well, well," came Dani's sarcastic tone. "Couldn't even wait until normal business hours to check in, huh? I should've forced Mac to keep you entertained."

"Not now, Dani. Mac's sick. She's out cold next to me, and I have no idea about her flight or anything."

"What did you do to her?"

Jesus. "Nothing, she got food poisoning from some contaminated chicken. I found her this morning with her head in the toilet."

"Oh no, poor Mac! Four vacations throwing up. I'm banking on this one being your fault?"

"Yell at me later. I need her information."

"All right, I'll throw you a bone. When I get into the office, I'll forward her details. She should have a Hello Kitty pouch with all her papers."

"Hello Kitty?"

"Bad souvenir joke from when I went to Japan. You'd be surprised how useful bad gifts can be. My guess is the pouch is in her purse."

Cole looked down at Mac's oversize bag. "Everything's in there."

Dani laughed. "So you should be able to find her deets."

He prayed the pouch was on the large size. "How's she getting to the airport?"

"Taxi. Her flight's not until later; you'll be home first."

Mac hadn't stirred as he spoke on the phone. He hoped she started feeling better before his flight. Leaving her like this was not an option.

"Well, this explains why she hadn't responded to my emails or texts today."

"I think she spent the night in the bathroom."

"Think? Where were you?"

"My room. She pushed me away."

"Because she was sick?"

"Because she believes her life is a rotten lemon."

Dani was silent. "Well, I'll be damned, you *are* lemonade. I would've pegged you for a rotten lemon."

"Yeah, yeah. Remind her of this when she's back to her senses."

He disconnected with Dani and managed to grab Mac's bag without waking her. He rummaged through, looking for a Hello Kitty pouch. He found sunglasses, her wallet, a small umbrella, tissues, hand sanitizer, and a few other items he couldn't identify before he found it. He pulled it out.

Inside he found her passport, customs declaration, and flight information. Dani was right, Mac's flight left a few hours after his. Which meant he could keep her with him until they got to the airlines. And bonus, it was the same airline. If only it was the same flight.

He brushed her hair back off her face. Her mouth ajar, she slept deeper than he'd ever seen.

The worry tried to climb into him again, so he distracted himself with his phone, catching a response email from the Andersons, the ones he'd inquired about their feelings on going remote. A smile came over him as he read the words, *We're here for you, not your location. As long as you don't relocate to Mars, we're good.*

Coin toss no longer needed to make a decision. The dice settled into place, one option finally ahead of the other, with a safety net underneath. Either way he still had his top client. And top client plus remote equaled a potentially viable solution. He glanced at Mac. Maybe he could make remote work for her, too?

No. Wrong path. At least Dani would be happy.

"Damn, she's really in slumber land, huh?" Trent said as he walked over to them. He wore worn jeans and a Red Sox T-shirt, nothing of the preppy boy crap he wore on the job. Behind him he pulled a large suitcase.

"Yup. I was just talking to Dani and she didn't even stir. Officially unemployed?"

Trent laughed and sat down on the other side of Cole. "You know it. Dude, you're fucking surrounded."

"Not even off the ship and you're already swearing."

Trent held out his hands. "Do you see a name tag? Hell no. For the first time in six months, no one knows my name just because they picked up the goddamn ABCs."

Welcome back, Trent. "Mac's on a later flight. She can't fly like this."

They both looked at her. Mac flinched but didn't wake.

"Poor Mac. What ya gonna do about it?"

Cole focused on the freckles on Mac's red nose. He had no clue.

• • •

Mac woke and pulled her head up, realizing with horror she'd been drooling on Cole's shoulder. She wiped her mouth and his shirt.

"Oh good, you're awake," he said as he handed her glasses over. She put them on and fixed her hearing aid, whistling from its shifted position. His hand moved to sweep back her hair but froze at her look. "How are you feeling?"

On the other side of Cole, Trent leaned forward.

Sick, confused, in her own personal hell. What a loaded question from the guy she broke up with the night before. "Fine."

He raised an eyebrow. "Try the truth."

She slumped back into the seat. She no longer felt like throwing up, and the runs seemed to have stopped. Small miracles. Her head rocked on its own little ship, swaying at a rate not related to water. And if that wasn't enough, her heart ached, physically ached, looking at Cole. "I feel like shit." Close enough to the truth.

"We'll need to get moving soon. Are you going to be able to handle it?"

"Do I have a choice?"

"Between the two of us, we'll help," Trent said.

From the depths of her bag, "Single Ladies" began playing. She reached in and pulled out her phone. "Hey, Dani."

"Oh good, you're awake. I was testing Cole. Did he get my email?"

Mac eyed Cole, who had the decency to look sheepish. She pulled the phone away from her ear. "Dani wants to know if you got her email?" Well, this was weird. They knew of their connection, but this little interchange really hit home.

"Yeah." Cole held out his hand and took the phone. "I got the email and found Mac's information. She just woke up... You think I'm not aware of that? Uh-huh... That's what I thought."

Mac had no clue what was going on as she took the phone back. "Hi, Dani."

Dani had the audacity to laugh. "You sound so bewildered."

"I just woke up." And she wanted to go back to sleep.

"Cole called me earlier, totally freaked with you passed out and not knowing what flight you were on. Not sure why you pushed him away, he's the furthest thing from a rotten lemon. And I'm still shocked by that!"

Mac closed her eyes. She was the rotten lemon. "I'll talk to you later."

"Okay. Love you, travel safe."

"Bye." She put her phone back in her purse.

"Let's try this again," Cole said. "How are you feeling?"

"Why are you here?"

"I'm supposed to leave you fast asleep and alone? Or with your head in the toilet?"

"Ugh, don't remind me. I'm really sick and tired and throwing up on vacation. You didn't have to check on me, not after last night."

"I bumped into Rob and Quinn. They were worried as well. And if it wasn't for me, where would you be right now?"

"You would have been kicked out," Trent began. "Nicely, but you probably only had another half hour before someone made you move."

Mac groaned and turned back to Cole. She studied his green eyes. Without his help, she would've had a far more unpleasant experience. "Thank you."

Trent nudged Cole as a garbled announcement played overhead. "That's us. We should get moving. If our third member can handle it."

Cole stood up, grabbed a brown backpack from the floor between his feet, and put it on his shoulders. "Come on, let's see if you can move."

She grasped his outstretched hand and rose to a standing position. A wave of dizziness threatened to overwhelm her, but she planted her feet firmly. Before she could reach for her bags, he grabbed the handles with one large hand; his other hand left hers to support her back.

Both men moved at her painfully slow pace. They didn't seem upset or hurried. Trent chatted with people as they passed, stopping to harass a crewmember here and there. It gave Mac some time to rest up along the journey. And through it all, Cole stood beside her, as a partner would be. She pushed the jumbled thoughts from her head; it only succeeded at making her feel woozier.

Ten minutes later, while Trent chatted, Mac's head spun. Her legs dragged and she couldn't push herself any further. The world had a sudden chair famine, and she really needed one under her butt yesterday. Before her legs gave out, she moved over to the side and slid to the ground, as graceful as a drunk duck. It was either park her ass on the floor or fall.

"Mac?" Cole asked, squatting before her. She forced herself to look up into his eyes. The urge to burst into tears nearly consumed her, but she held back.

"I'm okay."

"Will you quit it with the bullshit?" he groaned. "You've had nothing to eat or drink, right? We need to get you something."

Her stomach made a definitive "no" motion, and she shook her head. "No food."

"You're weak."

"I've got food poisoning, and alcohol on top of the cursed chicken, though that certainly is not in my system now. Just give me a minute." She tried to take deep breaths, regain control over herself. Stop the damn room from swaying. Her head felt like a balloon filled with helium, and it wasn't fun.

A minute later, she didn't feel any better, but she managed to stand and keep walking. Trent took hold of the bulk of their bags, allowing Cole to give her more support. This time she made it into the taxi before the need to collapse overwhelmed her.

...

Mac fell asleep again in the taxi. Her skin remained clammy in contrast to her sunburned nose. Cole tapped his foot on the floor as he watched her sleep and debated what to do. One thing was clear: she couldn't be left alone. He fiddled with this phone as Trent turned around from the front seat.

"What are the chances there's room on our flight for Mac? Or her flight for me?" The tapping of his foot increased with the questions and lack of answers.

"Man, you are so fucking whipped. But the answer is we won't know until we check."

They got to the airport, and Mac remained asleep. He shook her awake and her eyes opened, only to close immediately again. This was bad. He'd dealt with food poisoning before, but something about Mac being in this state was giving him flashbacks to that awful day. The panic inside him spread, but he forced it aside. God, was this what it felt like for Trent the day of the bombing? Cole had been in and out of it, thanks to his injuries. Time stopped and sped in different ways. He glanced at his friend but didn't dare ask. He didn't want to know the answer.

"Need a wheelchair?" the taxi driver asked, pointing to a row of them over the side.

Cole was so relieved he clasped the older man's shoulder. "Genius." Trent went with the driver to get the wheelchair. Cole managed to wake Mac up long enough to get her into the chair, where she promptly fell back asleep. Trent grabbed their luggage as Cole wheeled Mac.

"Can't believe she fell back to sleep." Trent laughed as they readjusted the luggage.

"I can. Let's see what we can do about getting her on our flight. I can't have her fly alone like this. Look at her."

Mac slumped to the side in the wheelchair, her mouth

ajar.

"Poor Mac," Trent said, shaking his head.

Between the two of them, they managed to carry/wheel the luggage, and Mac, up to check in. A brunette with hair pulled into a tight ponytail tried to take their information, but Cole held fast.

"Look, we've got a situation here. The woman in the wheelchair's on a later flight. I need to see if there's room to switch her to ours."

The brunette wedged the ticket out of Cole's hand and tapped on her keyboard. "I'm sorry, sir, your flight is booked."

Dammit. Cole grabbed Mac's information. "What about her flight?"

Again, they waited. "Also booked." She offered no other suggestions.

Cole plowed a hand through his hair in pure frustration. He looked back and forth between Trent and Mac as an idea popped into his head. He took a step away from the counter. "Can you do me a huge favor?" He knew he was asking for a lot, but considering Trent stayed with him while on land, he figured he had a shot.

"What?"

"Switch tickets with Mac."

Trent let out a breath. "We have to see if the airline will accept the transfer."

"You willing?"

"Yeah, I'm willing."

He paused. "No jokes?"

"Between Mac and Quinn, let's put the jokes to rest."

"Why aren't you finding Quinn and dragging her off to a corner?"

Trent laughed. "She's probably already in the air. Let's get Mac taken care of."

Cole turned back to the clerk. "How about we switch his

ticket with hers?"

"I'm sorry, sir, I can't switch tickets."

Frustration oozed and simmered. Cole contemplated punching something, but that wouldn't help a damn thing. "What do you mean you can't switch tickets? She's in no condition to fly alone. She'll be a liability unless you let her fly with me. Don't you get it?"

The woman's expression softened. "I understand, but I have to follow protocols. And protocol says I can't switch tickets unless they are returned."

"So return them. I'll pay any rebooking fee."

"Well, that, sir, I can take care of." Fake smile in place, she took Trent and Mac's information. He managed to wake Mac up for a second, and she gave a verbal okay, though in her state she would have agreed to a ticket to Mars. The next thing he knew the tickets were returned, and he purchased new ones for both of them. At a much higher rate than even Mac's ticket was purchased a week ago. Then again, he knew Dani would search for a deal.

"That cost an arm and a leg," Trent muttered after everything was straightened out.

"I've already lost a leg. That was a tail."

Trent adjusted his bag on his shoulder. "So...what are you going to do when you get home?"

Cole stopped walking. "What do you mean?"

"You've just moved a pretty penny to get her on the same flight as you. What happens when you land at Logan airport?"

"She comes home with me."

Trent raised an eyebrow.

"I'm not leaving her like this."

Trent glanced around. Other passengers wandered the area, wheeling or carrying luggage. He leveled his gaze back on Cole. "Do I need to remind you she dumped your ass?"

Cole ground his teeth together. "I'm taking care of her." He'd forgotten how much of a pain in the ass his friend could be.

He reached into his pocket and pulled out his phone, partly to put an end to this conversation.

"How's Mac?" Dani asked once she picked up.

"Out like a light. I've got her on my flight. Trent's on hers. She's staying with you, right?"

"Yeah, Susie's picking her up at the airport."

He took a deep breath. "Call Susie. I'm taking Mac home with me."

Trent laughed nearby.

"Put Mac on the phone."

"She's fast asleep. I doubt she knows the flights have been switched."

"Cole, she's staying with me. I've already bought the ice cream for dinner; her stuff is at my place. I'll call Susie, but drop her off at my place."

"You'll be at work."

"For a few hours. She's a big girl. She can handle herself."

He glanced at Mac. "She's currently drooling on her shoulder."

"Ohh, Mackenzie." Dani's voice raised an octave. "Fine, take her home. But the minute she wakes up and kicks your ass, you bring her to my place. Got it?"

"She's too sick to kick my ass today."

"I take it back, Matterhorn. Maybe you are a rotten lemon."

He hung up before Dani could yell at him any further.

Trent grinned. "You've got two women pissed at you and you're only sleeping with one."

He grasped the handles of Mac's wheelchair. "You done?"

"For now. Let's get Sleeping Beauty through security."

· · ·

Mac woke up, expecting to find herself still in the taxi or on the ship the way her body swayed. Not in a wheelchair facing rows of blue cushioned chairs at the airport gate. She sat up with a start and put a hand to her still-woozy head.

"Mac?" Cole asked, lightly grasping her shoulder.

"The last I remember was the taxi. How long was I out?" She had fleeting images here and there, but nothing that resembled an actual memory.

Cole looked at his watch. "About an hour."

"You don't remember security?" Trent asked from across from Cole. "They had to do a strip search and everything."

She stared at him, blinking. "Now I see why you two are friends."

Trent and Cole laughed; she wanted to curl back up and sleep for another year.

"You need to eat, Mac."

"Don't start with me. Just let me get some rest and grab me something to drink before you two depart." She was about to close her eyes when she caught the two men giving each other a look. "What now?" She was dangerously close to sobbing, drained of every last thread of dignity. Misery was not a good look on her. Good thing she already broke them up.

"You're in no condition to fly alone. I switched your ticket with Trent's."

Her eyes widened, and a sudden burst of energy had her sitting up straight. "What? How?"

"Well, he—" Trent was stopped by Cole's hand on his chest.

"I pleaded with the airline, and they did the switch."

She knew there was more to the story, judging by how the two interacted, but that wasn't her priority right now. "You didn't have to do that. I'm fine."

Cole crossed his arms. "Really? Get up and walk."

She didn't even bother moving. "Fine. Let me call Susie and let her know I'm on a different flight."

"She knows."

Mac paused with her hand in her bag, reaching for her cell phone. "Explain."

"I spoke with Dani."

She took a deep breath, but the pressure on her chest remained. "Of course." She dropped her purse to her lap. A week ago, Cole was a stranger whose luggage appeared in her room. Now she was on the same plane with him heading back home. It was enough to make her already-woozy head woozier.

She slumped and rested her head on the back of the wheelchair.

Cole leaned into her. "You've got to eat, Mac. Name something you think you can stomach."

She closed her eyes against another wave of nausea. "Don't. Mention. Food." Well, at least she didn't care she could no longer afford to eat.

"Then I'll just grab you something." Cole stood and walked off, exuding pissed-off man.

Trent took Cole's vacated seat. "He really does care. You know that, right?"

She wanted sleep. Maybe she could close her eyes and wake up on Dani's couch? "I don't expect to be taken care of by the guy I dumped last night."

He laughed and crossed one leg over the other. "Cole doesn't give up easily. Not when he has a reason to care again."

Curiosity stirred. What insight did Trent have into Cole's behavior? But her heavy eyelids trumped. She found herself in the world between awake and asleep, where her eyes closed and she heard what was going on around her, unable to respond, until it all faded to quiet.

· · ·

As the plane flew high between the clouds, Cole looked out at the white fluffy stuffing against the blue backdrop. Hard to believe vacation was over. Harder to believe he'd found someone who changed all his self-preservation rules and then promptly demonstrated why he had said rules in the first place.

Mac curled into a tight ball beside him, head on his lap, fast asleep. He'd be lying if he told himself this little contact didn't do anything for him. One look at Mac, and he knew he'd break his rules ten times over for her. Having her in his life was worth the risk and fear.

They managed to get Mac to eat a few crackers and drink some water. All she wanted to do was sleep. He told himself sleep was what she needed, sleep off the sickness so she could get back to her vibrant self.

Didn't stop the worrying, not with everything he'd been through in the past nine years. The panic tried to grip him, tried to crawl up his spine and settle in. He refused to let them. Panic didn't solve a damn thing, and as long as he took care of her, she'd be fine.

The flight attendant made her way down the aisle, stopping at each row to offer drinks. When she got to him, he ordered a cola.

"Anything for you wife?" she asked with a smile.

He glanced down at Mac. One week and someone thought they were married. "Got any ginger ale?" Mac might need something soothing when she woke.

The flight attendant nodded and moved on, and he went back to watching Mac sleep. He had games on his phone to play, music to listen to, yet all he wanted to do was watch her.

I can't continue this after tomorrow. Less than twenty-four hours ago, she said those words to him. And here she was, asleep on his lap. Was he wrong or right to step in, help the woman who had annihilated him the day before?

My life is shit right now, Cole. I need to find a job, find a new place to live. I need to pick up the pieces. He wanted to help her with those pieces. Maybe after today, after he helped her get home safe and sound, maybe then she'd see he could help her without being a trap.

Of course, he still had to tell her he was bringing her home with him. As the plane prepared for descent over Boston, he nudged her awake. "Mac, love, you need to sit up."

She blinked, those blue eyes focusing on him. She stirred, pushing herself into a raised position. Hair a mess, face creased from his pants, yet still a beauty. She closed her eyes again for a moment before getting into her seat properly.

"I can't believe you're still exhausted," he said.

"I can." She leaned her head back and moaned. "This food poisoning has knocked me on my ass and didn't let me sleep last night." Her blue eyes met his. She may have broken them up, but her eyes drank him in.

"You need to rest up. I'm bringing you home with me."

Her mouth dropped open. "I'll be fine at Dani's."

"Dani's working." *Dani's not in love with you.*

"Cole, you've already done so much, too much. Have you forgotten last night?"

"Have you forgotten last week?"

She closed her eyes. He leaned forward and kissed her.

"I can't believe you did that. I've been throwing up."

"Not since you brushed."

She opened her mouth, then closed it. "Fair enough."

Luck was on his side; she stopped fighting him and rested her head on his shoulder. He knew the fight wasn't over, just delayed. He'd take the small victory.

• • •

After the plane landed, Mac managed to walk without the immediate need to plant her butt in a chair or on the ground. The lingering effects of the rocking ship and the food poisoning had her slow and wobbly. Cole was by her side, patient as ever, and messing with her head and her heart.

As they walked, she rubbed her bare arms. Florida's warmth had faded to Massachusetts' cool spring weather. She had a sweater and jacket for back home but hadn't been the one to do the packing thanks to the food poisoning from hell.

"Cold?" Cole asked.

"Yeah, wish I knew what you did with my sweater and jacket."

He moved over to the side and squatted down by her carry-on. "I saw your jacket as I was packing, figured you wouldn't need that until after you got your luggage back. Your sweater should be in here." He unzipped the bag and pulled out her red hoodie.

She took it from him. He zipped up her bag again and helped her tug it into position. Who was he? What guy knew to prepare like this?

They made it to the baggage carousel, Mac's feet refusing to go an inch further. She plopped down onto a bench, weary body sighing in relief. Cole put his bag beside her and pulled up her carry-on. "You okay?"

What a loaded question. She nodded. She felt better than before the flight and had managed a long walk. That counted, right? His jaw ticked, but he didn't call her on the lie. Instead, he settled next to her. He tugged her head down to his shoulder, and she closed her eyes out of sheer exhaustion. And maybe to breathe him in, just a little.

Cole stirred, and Mac sat up, the sounds of metal machinery filling the air. The carousel began rotating, and he moved to collect their items. Or, she assumed, to collect their items. She hadn't the energy to follow him, and with everything he'd already done for her, she figured that part a given. She caught others glancing at him and his awkward gait. He wore long pants, his prosthesis hidden. An urge built up to tell them to mind their own damn business. She didn't know where the urge came from or why it was so strong. Not the time to investigate feelings beyond surviving the day.

She focused, searching for her bags before remembering Cole didn't need her help. He'd already helped find her lemon bags before, and odds were there wouldn't be any others to confuse the issue.

After he collected their luggage, she followed him outside, where he grabbed a taxi for them. Once they were settled in and on the road, she returned to a previous conversation.

"You can drop me off at Dani's, you know. I'll be fine."

He leaned close to her, arm propped on the center seat in between them. "Figure it out. I'm taking care of you."

"Even after everything?"

"Especially after everything. Give it up, Mackenzie-Mac."

He was still the only one to use the odd mix of her full and nickname. Most people she didn't let use her full name at all, preferring Mac over Mackenzie. Somehow when he said it, the sound didn't grind her ears.

Too weak to fight and, she had to admit, a bit grateful to not return to an empty apartment, she stared out the window on the ride. Cole handed over her crackers and water, and her stomach had settled enough that she finished both. The taxi slowed and turned in to a residential area. Houses dotted the landscape, filled in by bare trees that would look lush in the warmer months. They stopped in front of a two-story colonial in a nice neighborhood.

Mac turned and eyed Cole. He shrugged. "I bought it a few years ago when the market was good. Better than paying rent to someone else's mortgage."

She couldn't argue with that, even if she never had the chance to build equity. Her eyelids drooped, and her head wanted to fall off her shoulders again. Should have napped instead of staring at the scenery. She exited the taxi and took in a deep breath of the cool air, hoping to spark some kind of energy into her system. With her eyes on her feet, she managed to get inside the house and remove her jacket.

Cole dropped their luggage by the front door and grabbed her hand, heading for the stairs.

"Cole," she protested but was too weak and tired to pull back.

He paused. "You're about to fall over. You've been sleeping in contorted positions all day and probably all night. Come on." He didn't immediately move, his face pleading with her.

"Okay."

He brought her upstairs, into a room with dark wood furniture. "This is my room," he said. She sat down on the bed, still taking in her scenery. Cole squatted before her and removed her shoes. "Trent uses my spare room when he's here. The other bedroom doesn't have a bed." He lifted the covers, revealing cream sheets on a rounded mattress that made her think of a cloud. She all but licked her lips as she climbed right in. "I'll sleep on the couch if you want."

He wrapped the covers around her shoulder and leaned forward to kiss her head. She removed her glasses and hearing aids, and he took them from her.

"You hungry?" he asked.

She shook her head.

"Okay, but you're eating later. Good night, Mac."

In a moment of weakness, she reached out and grasped onto his arm. "Stay." She didn't know what possessed her, but in that moment, she didn't want to be alone. Blame it on feeling crappy, but she wanted the comfort.

He didn't question her. He slipped off the prosthesis and liner in the same amount of time most people took off their shoes. His pant leg hung loose around his stump as he curled up behind her and held her close. She drifted off to sleep before her eyes closed.

...

Cole held Mac in his arms as she slept. Not the way he had hoped to get her into his bed. Nothing mattered until she was better.

He breathed her in. An ache remained deep in his chest, now mostly due to Mac's wellness. A thought floated to mind: this was how it should be. Mac in his arms, in his house, in his bed. They were home and his determination level through the roof. She was the one for him. End of story.

He needed to cool his jets before he took nine years of avoiding domestic behavior and jumped in too fast. Which, he could admit in his own head, he'd already done. She'd given him a reason to reevaluate his plans, and damned if he gave up easily.

Mac squirmed when his grip on her tightened. He let her go and slid out of bed. She rolled over, arms spread from side to side. He grinned. "Take the whole bed, Mac, anytime," he whispered.

He sat on the bench at the end of his bed and put his liner and prosthesis back on. His stump slid in, creating the suction needed to keep the prosthesis on. The noise didn't even cause Mac to stir.

He brought his luggage upstairs. Thought about leaving it

so Mac could sleep, then remembered how dead to the world the illness had her. So he unpacked without using the bed. At least he was able to watch her sleep.

He tossed the last dirty shirt into the laundry basket when his front door opened below.

"Lucy, I'm home!" called out Trent, followed by, "Damn, it's fucking cold."

Cole made his way downstairs, where Trent shucked off his jacket.

"Sleeping Beauty still here?"

"Yeah, she's asleep upstairs. Your flight okay?"

Trent grinned, the light catching on his teeth. "The delay worked out for me. I bumped into Quinn and Rob."

Cole took in the width of the smile, not a normal post-contract look for him. "You grabbed an airport quickie."

He laughed. "No. Thought about it, but no. Not fair to Rob."

"So what did you do?"

"Gave Quinn the kiss she deserved."

Cole moved to the kitchen. "When are you flying out to California to get busy with her?"

Trent followed and hopped up on the counter. "Haven't decided yet." He looked around. "So, what're you cooking for me?"

Cole checked the freezer. Two frozen dinners, an ice cube tray with dehydrated ice, and a lot of ice crystals. "I always clean out my supply before a trip, and with Mac sick, I haven't managed a food run."

"Takeout." Trent jumped down. "Pizza. I've been eating the same crappy pizza for six months." He went over to the folder of takeout menus and grabbed Domino's. "Hello, my old friend."

"Of course you'd go for the worst processed crap out there."

"I'm sorry, did you want McDonald's?"

Cole shook his head and laughed. Just-off-the-ship Trent was always a fun handful. He clasped a hand on his shoulder. "Knock yourself out."

"Excellent." Trent opened the menu. "Any idea what Mac will eat?"

Cole glanced up to the second floor. "I doubt she'll be hungry. Maybe we can get a slice of cheese in her."

"You got it." Trent seized the phone and placed an order for much more than three people. "You know," he said after he hung up the phone, "it's really shitty of me, but it was fun to order food from someone with an American accent."

Cole groaned. He grabbed a glass and filled it with water. "I'm bringing this up to Mac."

Trent followed him into the living room. "Oh. My. God. Unlimited streaming!" He jumped onto the couch with the remote.

Cole climbed the stairs to the sounds of the TV turning on. In his room, all was quiet. Mac was now on her back, sprawled out over his entire bed.

He put the water on the nightstand and climbed in next to her. "I've got water here for you."

"Okay," she whispered, her eyes remaining closed.

"We're ordering pizza, if you want any."

She shook her head, already drifting back to sleep.

He leaned forward, kissed the top of her head. "I love you, Mac." *Shit*. He remained perfectly still, breath held, waiting for a response from her. She didn't flinch, her only movement the gentle rise and fall of deep breathing. The words echoed in his head, his heart hammering against his rib cage. He'd spoken soft enough, she might have missed it with her hearing loss. Nothing about her body language suggested she had a clue.

Relief wanted to claim him, but he couldn't deny he

wanted those words shared.

What an odd feeling. He wanted to share deep, meaningful words with this new person in life. He wanted permanence, a commitment. Fear should have gripped him by the balls. It didn't.

He left the room in silence and made his way back downstairs. He nearly missed a step and tumbled. "Shit," he said at the bottom. She breaks up with him and then *he* tells *her* he loves her? "What a boneheaded move."

"What happened?" Trent called out from his position on the couch: lying down, shoes on the cushion.

Cole sat across from him. "I told her I love her."

Trent sat up. "Fuck. For real?"

He nodded.

"And you mean it?"

"Why would I say something like that if I didn't mean it?"

"Fuck. Damn shit." Trent held up a hand. "Sorry, sorry."

"I know, post-contract potty mouth, let it out."

"You fucking fool. You fell in love on a goddamn eight-night cruise. You've known her for eight days. She dumped your sorry ass last night. You've moved heaven and hell to get her back here, she's going to go ape shit on you tomorrow, and you told her you love her?"

"Pretty much."

Trent laughed.

"Laugh all you want. I'm going to marry her one day."

Trent stopped laughing. "You run from commitment."

Ran, past tense. "I don't run anywhere anymore. I was waiting for Mac."

"Damn. Hold something inside. I don't want her to fucking destroy you."

Too late. Far too late. Whether or not Mac heard him, he couldn't change the way he behaved. "Where's the pizza? I'm starving."

Home: Day 1

Mac opened her eyes to the morning light. Disorientation seized her as she tried to make sense of the blurred surroundings. This wasn't her cabin, nor Dani's couch. The dark furniture and green comforter were unfamiliar. The man beside her, on the other hand, she knew.

She wanted to sit up, but her head and stomach suggested she keep it easy. She took stock. Cole slept beside her. She had managed to change into sweatpants and a long-sleeve T-shirt yesterday, Cole's clothes, since her winter clothes were at Dani's place. Where she should be.

There was no footing, nothing stable to latch onto. Of course her life was as stable as a livewire at the moment. Cole shifted beside her, rolling over until he wrapped himself around her. He said nothing and judging by his own deep breaths he stayed asleep.

This wasn't good. All she had to do was get up, get dressed, and force Cole to take her home—err, to Dani's. No big deal. Except she didn't move. Her limbs sank into the bed like lead. The rest of her body agreed the bed was more comfortable than Dani's couch, especially with Cole still wrapped around her. Heck, it was more comfortable than the bed on the cruise. Her head threatened to revolt if she attempted any sort of movement.

Where was her phone? She could check the time, email, text. She could check the news, see what was happening in the world. She looked around. Her purse was probably around there somewhere, but who know what her battery life looked like?

The steady breathing in her ear lulled her into a state of tranquility. Her eyelids dropped down over her eyes. She'd lie there for a few minutes, gain some energy, then get moving.

When she opened her eyes again, the bright light enveloped the room. She no longer had an extra human blanket, and the other side of the bed had grown cold. She sat up, moving slow, expecting her head to force her right back down. It didn't. She still felt like shit, but functioning shit.

Her glasses and hearing aids sat on the nightstand next to her, and she put on the former to better take in the room. A dresser and armoire were the only furniture, with a pair of crutches leaning against the armoire. On the tan walls were two pictures of island views. She wasn't sure if this matched the man or not. Of course, how much did she really know about him after a week?

With her feet over the side of the bed, she contemplated whether to hunt down his shower or not. She pushed forward, letting her feet hit the hardwood floor. And stood. She wasn't sure how long her stability would last. The cold morning air sent shivers up her skin, and she wished she had her plush rose bathrobe.

At the foot of his bed, she noticed a green housecoat. He either left it there for her or himself. Well, she was cold. She pulled it on, grabbed her hearing aids, and made her way downstairs. She wanted to continue to inspect his home, but the wooziness had returned, and holding onto the walls became more important.

"Well, if it isn't Sleeping Beauty." The voice took a moment to identify and locate, but as she cleared the bottom of the stairs, she saw Trent in the living room.

She groaned and leaned against the railing. "I take it you made it back okay?"

With one hand around the couch, he grinned.

"He bumped into Quinn after we left," Cole said as he entered the room. "Rob says Trent nearly took Quinn on the floor."

Trent grinned. "Thought about it."

Mac let out a weak laugh as Cole stood in front of her.

"You feeling any better?" His green eyes seemed to soak her up, examining her face. Considering she hadn't even run her fingers through her hair, the sight couldn't have been pretty.

She looked at her feet. "I'm standing and the room isn't spinning...much."

He put a hand around her waist and brought her over to the couch. She curled up and leaned her head back against the brown leather.

"You want something to eat?" Cole asked.

"We've got leftover pizza," Trent said.

Mac lifted her head. "For breakfast?"

"I've eaten the same fucking food for the same fucking meals for six fucking months. Yes. Breakfast. Don't tell my mother."

Mac let out a laugh. "Wow, language, Trent."

"Blow me."

Cole sat next to Mac. "Down, boy." He turned to Mac. "He'll calm down in a few weeks."

She studied Cole's face and asked the only question in her head. "Why am I here?"

"Oops, that's my cue," Trent said and left the room.

Cole waited until they were alone before speaking. "Why do you think you're here? You were sick."

"I slept, that's all I did. I could have done that at Dani's."

"And you would have managed the plane ride home?"

He had her there. "No."

He said something, voice barely above a whisper, and she couldn't make it out. She shook her head, and without any prompting, he repeated. "Why is it so bad if I take care of you?"

She stared at him and asked herself the same question. Besides her rotten luck and bad decisions? Besides no one except her parents ever really taking care of her? And right there was the answer. No one else had gone to this extreme for her. Except her cruise fling.

He gave her the unconditional support she craved, the kind she only got from Dani and Susie. The kind she'd hoped Chad would offer. It clicked deep down, that internal need she'd long had unfilled and figured would remain unfulfilled. And yet here sat a person who barely knew her and gave her support when she needed it most.

No, too much. She needed to stand on her own two feet. She wouldn't let anyone become her crutch, certainly not someone she'd labelled a fling.

The doorbell rang, but neither of them moved. "I'll get it," Trent said as he walked back through and opened the door. "If it isn't trouble in the purest form. Miss Dani Martin."

"Trent Decker. Back on land. Where's the potty mouth?"

Mac turned and caught Dani giving Trent a hug.

"Don't be such a fucking wiseass, bitch."

Dani laughed, slapped his shoulder, and made her way into the house. She crossed her arms and eyed Mac and Cole. "I've had almost a week to get used to this and it's still strange. Mac, you look like crap."

Mac put her head back on the couch. "Thanks, Dani."

Dani came over and wrapped her arms around her friend. "You feeling any better?"

"From Chad or the food poisoning?"

"Food poisoning. I got my answer on Chad when you hooked up with my boss."

Mac groaned and avoided looking at Cole. "I still feel like crap, but slightly better."

"Need me to take you back to my place?"

Mac tried to speak, but Cole spoke first. "She's not going anywhere."

Mac spun around to look at Cole the same time Dani did. "Excuse me?" she asked.

Dani propped her hands on her hips. "What's your excuse today? Yesterday it was that I was working and you weren't, but today the office is closed."

"And tomorrow we'll both be at work, but Trent will still be here."

"You're making me babysit your girlfriend?" Trent asked.

"Hey," Mac called out.

"Right, sorry. You're making me babysit the girl who dumped your ass?"

Mac thought fondly of her empty stateroom, without all this commotion going on. Shame she had no place of her own.

Dani grasped Mac's shoulder. "Ignore both of them. This is about what you want."

Mac focused on Dani's face, the one that said she'd support whatever she came up with. "I want a shower and clean clothes."

Dani grinned. "I brought over some of your stuff, just in case fling boy convinced you to stay."

A shower sounded like heaven, especially if Cole's was larger than a stripper pole. She stood up, and the room swayed in a way that had nothing to do with the leftover effects of the ship.

Cole was next to her, supporting her arm. "You're not stable enough to shower."

She stared at him, ready to battle. "Come on, Dani, you can help me."

Dani supported Mac and tossed her keys to Cole. "Get her stuff out of my trunk."

"Mac, all you've had in twenty-four hours are crackers and some water. You should eat first."

She avoided the look of concern in his eyes and shook her head. "No. Shower first, then food."

Cole let out a huff of purely male frustration before stalking to the door with Dani's keys. Once he was gone, Dani spoke. "You really have him wrapped around your little finger, don't you?"

Mac didn't respond. The little she knew of Cole from Dani's stories did not match the man she'd met.

"Yeah, she does," Trent said.

Mac ignored them both and made her way upstairs. She couldn't handle everything that life had piled on her, not without at least a shower. In the bathroom, she sat down on the closed toilet seat, her woozy head already in need of a break. Out in the hall, she heard Cole's voice, and Dani's, not that she could decipher a word. Before she could contemplate eavesdropping, Dani entered, carrying towels and Mac's belongings.

She closed the door behind her and put the items down. "Can we talk about how much he's into you?"

Mac placed her head on her knees. "Can we not?"

Dani began setting up items. "If you insist. I've known Cole for four years. I've seen him date. I've seen him throw back." She paused and looked at Mac. "I've never seen him like this."

Dani started the shower, and Mac removed her hearing

aids and Cole's bathrobe.

Dani spoke, but Mac gestured to her empty ears. Dani spoke louder, over the running water. "So the question is, why are you still here?"

Mac paused with the bottom of Cole's shirt in her hands. "Excuse me?"

"I know you. If you didn't want to be here, you would have fought him tooth and nail."

"I could barely stay awake."

"And now?"

"And now I'm taking a shower."

"It's okay to like him and want to be here. You know that, right?"

Mac sighed. "I refuse to go from Chad's house to Cole's."

"I see that as moving up."

"I do, too, but still. I need to be on my own."

"Why?"

Mac's head started to spin again, and she hadn't even stepped into the shower. "Dani," she pleaded.

"Cole's not a controlling, manipulative asshole like Chad. Why can't you stay with him while you figure out what to do next?"

"Because I'm sick and miserable and have no clue what I want to do with my life."

Mac forced the nausea away, stripped, and got in the shower. She stepped around the shower chair, confused for a second before remembering Cole never showered at her cabin and never got his prosthesis wet. The handheld showerhead was easy to reach, so she plopped down and angled the warm water over her head, soothing her as it washed away the effects of the past day. She nearly moaned.

Dani started speaking, and Mac couldn't understand a word, so she stuck her head out to hear.

"I'm calling bullshit, Mackenzie. You're afraid to go for

what you want. Which is partly why you're here with me and not letting a hunk lather you up."

Against Mac's woozy state, her body perked up at that notion. She tugged the shower curtain closer to her. "I don't need a relationship. I need a job."

"And I'm talking about a job. You loved working for Chad. Not Chad himself, he's a selfish asshole, but the work you did there, you were talking about it all the time. So what if you don't have a degree? Get one."

Mac settled back into the chair. The water beat down on her, and she tried to clear her mind and think. She already knew she enjoyed the work, that a part of her wanted to find something new in architecture. Dani's comment only drove the point home. Still, there were limitations to how far Mac could go.

She pushed her head out of the shower, otherwise she'd never hear Dani's response. "I don't need double the school loans. I could possibly do some lower-level jobs, but that's it."

"You'd pay it off faster as an architect. And you'd enjoy those lower-level jobs more than some other administrative assistant one."

Mac yanked the curtain closed again. The thought tempted; it really did. She could see herself in that field. Heck, she could see herself doing Chad's job because she often stepped in for him in small ways. The thought brought a smile to her face, a content feeling through her. Maybe, just maybe, it would be the way to go.

Dani's voice pulled her out of her thoughts. "...work for him..."

What? Mac stuck her head out, again, giving the shower curtain a workout. "Repeat that?"

Dani appeared sheepish. "Sorry. I said that Cole had emailed me, suggesting you work for him. Can you believe it?"

Mac's good mood faded. "He did what?"

Dani grinned. Mac squinted. Surely she didn't see that right, but nope, the smile was right there on her friend's face. "He did. I told him off. But he saw your excellent interpersonal skills and thought you'd do well in travel agency."

"Why would I want to work as a travel agent? No offense, but it's not for me."

Dani wrapped her hand around Mac's holding the curtain. "Don't get upset. My point is that he had an idea, wanted to help, and he clearly didn't mention a word of it to you. Because he listened to me and what I said rather than plow forward with his own agenda like certain ex-assholes. Think of it as a safety net, even though I know you don't want to work for someone you've had sex with again."

"Damn straight I don't."

Dani squeezed her hand. "My point is that you have options and people that care for you. I'm still shocked that I'm liking Cole with someone, never mind one of my BFFs, but he's said things that shows he knows the real you."

"Dani, what do you want?" Her toes were going to start pruning before they finished this conversation.

"Stay here. He's right about Trent being around until you feel better. And sleeping with a hot guy in his bed is a lot better than my lumpy couch." She let the curtain fall back.

Mac grabbed her travel shampoo with more force than necessary. Too many deep thoughts while she recovered. Staying scared her. She wished she had never given up her apartment. Then she'd have a place to stay even if paying rent would grow questionable. She could have Dani over or even Cole, but it would be her place.

And those thoughts didn't matter. She didn't have her own place, and no thought process changed things. But if having Cole over worked, then being here had to work as well.

Cole's voice popped into her head. "First choice." He was

the only person to push her to stick to her instincts. What was her instinct? She reached for her soap. Her instinct was to feel better. End of story.

• • •

At the first creak of the stairs, Cole turned, wanting to jump over the couch and go to Mac. He forced himself to stay put and not do anything to cause Mac to yell at him again. She had some color back to her cheeks, wet strands of hair framing her face, and his heart stuttered. Instead of his old sweats, she wore jeans and a bulky pink sweater. She could wear a trash bag and he'd still find her beautiful. He followed her path into the living room and across the couch from him.

"Feeling any better?" he asked once she settled in. Dani stood nearby.

She raised a shoulder. "A little."

Trent entered from the kitchen. "We've got pizza." He spoke while eating a slice off a paper towel.

"Oh God," Dani said. "The great post-contract pig-out." She walked over and lifted Trent's shirt.

Trent pulled back. "What the hell?"

"I wanted to see your yummy abs before you pack on the pounds and bulk out."

"Bulk out? I can handle junk food."

"You're getting older, buddy."

Trent held out his hands to his side. "I'm thirty-fucking-one. And I want my fucking pizza."

Dani laughed.

Cole ignored them and continued to study Mac. "You want something to eat?"

She locked eyes with his and bit her lip. He prepared himself for the fight, for her to say she was going to Dani's. Instead, she said, "Yeah."

Since Dani was picking on Trent, Cole moved over to squat in front of Mac. He reached up and brushed a strand of her wet hair, just to touch her. During the night, he had kept to his side of the bed, trying to give her space. Only he failed. When he woke, his arms and leg were wrapped around her. "What do you want?"

"Just something light."

"Toast?"

She nodded.

He wanted to lean forward, taste her again. Feel her lips against his. Know she felt better. But the exhaustion was back in her eyes. He stood up. "Rest. I'll be back with food."

...

A few hours later, Dani had gone home and Cole had left to do a quick food shop. On top of the sickness, Mac felt the rocking and rolling of the ship. Hard to put her life together when lying her head on the back of the couch made the most sense.

Across from her, Trent lounged, scrolling through Netflix fast enough to make her woozy head spin.

"Do you realize Cole has two unemployed freeloaders on his couch?" she said to him, not focusing on the ever-changing images on the screen.

He stopped on a foreign film. "Freeloader?"

"You're not working."

He picked up his beer and brought it to his lips. "I worked for six goddamn months."

"And now what?"

"Now I wait until I stop swearing at the world before reintroducing myself to society."

"Fair enough."

Trent settled on a comedy, though Mac barely paid

attention to what occurred on screen. Something with lots of talking and she hadn't bothered to get the captioning working. Her mind wandered to Cole and his behavior. "You know Cole well, right?"

Trent put down his beer. "Over ten years."

"Tell me about the bombing."

Trent slowly picked up the remote and paused the show. His eyes locked on her, clearly debating whether or not to answer. And she caught something else lurking beneath the surface. She spoke before he could. "You were there."

Trent nodded. "I was there."

Mac glanced over him, but thanks to the eighties night, she knew damn well he wasn't missing a limb like Cole. "You weren't hurt."

Trent swallowed. "A few scrapes and bruises. I didn't get hit with the shrapnel like Cole."

Mac's heart clenched. She'd seen images of that day, of course, but never of someone she knew.

"We both liked running, had talked about one day running the marathon. Senior year, we didn't know if we'd be close to the city in the future, so we went to support the runners." Trent ran a hand through his hair. "One minute we're watching runners cross the finish line. The next, boom, smoke, pure panic. People screaming and running. I tried to navigate a way out but realized Cole wasn't with me." He shook his head. "It took some time, but I found him and tried to slow the bleeding, and you really don't want to hear about this."

"He lost the leg right away?"

Trent stared at her for so long she wasn't sure he'd respond. "Not right away. They tried to save it, but you know how that ended up. It was too badly damaged. And Cole shut down. No more marathon talks, or plans for after college, or getting serious about anyone…until you."

Mac swallowed the lump in her throat. *Until me.* "What does he want with a mess like me?"

"He doesn't care about that. He wasn't looking for you. You blindsided him. But he's not going to give up without a fight."

She was afraid of that.

Trent tossed the remote several times between his hands. "Look, the bombing, the leg, all of that shit killed a big part of him. He'll do some running on a treadmill but refuses to get a prosthesis made for running. A lot more than just his leg died that day. Since meeting you, he's more like the Cole I knew, but he's still got those scars, and they run deeper than his stump."

Mac clutched at her neck, balling the fabric. Music started playing from somewhere, but she couldn't identify what or where.

"I hear angry chick music?"

Mac listened and caught "Before He Cheats" playing. She groaned. "My ex's ringtone."

Trent stood and followed the noise to the kitchen, where her phone had been set up to charge. "You planning on messing up his car?"

Mac laughed. "Not until now. Wanna help?"

He returned and tossed her the now-silent phone. "We'll see how much of an asshole I turn into."

She looked at her phone to see if Chad left a message, only to have it start ringing again. "What do you want?" she barked after she answered.

"You back from your little impromptu vacation?"

"You care?"

"Yeah, I care. I want you back at work."

If her head wasn't unsteady, she would have banged it against the couch. "Are you for real? Because we've had this conversation before. I'm not working for you. You fired me.

That seals the deal." Even if she considered staying in the field, working for Chad was a no-cross zone.

"I made a mistake. Come back."

This time she did bang her head on the couch, but only once. "Chad. Let it go. How many times do I have to explain this to you? Fucking the manager while dating your assistant is not a good idea. Telling your assistant during a weekly meeting is downright scum."

"You tell him, Mac," Trent shouted.

Mac picked her head up and smiled.

"Who's that?" Chad asked.

"Nothing in my life is your business anymore," Mac seethed.

"You screwing someone else already?"

She looked at Trent and rolled her eyes. "Yes, I'm screwing someone else. Someone who doesn't find it fun to ask me to make all the decisions and laugh when they're bad. Someone who actually knows what he's doing when he goes down. Someone who isn't a flaming asshole."

Trent laughed his ass off in the background.

"Mackenzie, this isn't funny anymore."

"Really? Because this stopped being funny when you started fucking Kit. Give it up, Chad. Stop calling. I will never work for you again. I will never date you again. Get lost." She hung up the phone and threw it on the couch. Perhaps not her best idea if she would need a recommendation. But the odds of Chad giving her one were not that great to begin with. "What an asshole."

"I disagree. I find it quite amusing that Cole gives good tongue."

Mac groaned and lay down. "I'd try and point out women lie, but you'll just ignore me. So I'm saying this: don't harass your friend with that piece of supposed information."

Trent picked up his beer. "You're no fun." He finished

the beer off. "However, after dating that ass, who is nothing like Cole, I wonder why you keep pushing Cole away."

Mac rubbed her temples as the pressure behind them built. She knew Cole was nothing like Chad, part of the reason she hung out with him in the first place. But none of that changed her need to be independent and stand on her own two feet. And perhaps her desires would have more strength behind them if she had left with Dani, but she wasn't ready to transition to a lumpy couch. "When do you go back to work?"

"When I figure my shit out."

"I'm trying to figure my own shit out so you of all people should get why I want to do that on my own."

"What's your instinct here in regards to Cole?"

Ugh, she was so done with this conversation. "Why aren't you on a flight out to California to see Quinn?"

"Because I'm a swearing asshole at the moment and Quinn doesn't deserve that."

"And if she was local and you were the one on her couch?"

Trent grinned. "Then we wouldn't be talking."

Mac chuckled. "I like this not-talking thing."

Trent mimed clearing the air. "Silence will be granted. Don't blame me. Cole is my closest friend. I've seen him in his darkest moments, and I want him happy. But if you're not there yet, then I can respect that. And not for nothing, but Cole's an honest son of a bitch. He will, too."

Mac stared at her phone and scrolled through her listings. She brought up Cole's contact, thumbing through the details he had left her. All of them.

"And for the record," Trent continued, "I will gladly help you fuck up that asshole's car."

Mac smiled and opened up the ringtone section for Cole, setting his ringer to "Call Me Maybe."

• • •

Cole pulled into his driveway and cut the engine. Before vacation, the house in front of him would have been dark, empty. Now lights shone through the living room and kitchen windows. Two people were there, waiting for him. A lot had changed in a week. He'd already brought in the groceries, then decided takeout sounded better than cooking.

He got out of the car and walked up the side path to the kitchen entrance. "Always strange to have people here when I get home," he said as he brought food into the kitchen.

"Daddy, Daddy, what did you get?" Trent said with mock enthusiasm.

Cole turned to Mac. "He being a pest?"

She smiled. "He's fine." She sat at the kitchen table. Not lying on the couch with her head supported. Good. He hoped she'd actually eat.

He pulled himself together and unpacked the bags. "Baked ziti for Trent," he said, handing over the round metallic tub.

"Come to Papa." Trent sighed and dug in before Cole could get the next item out.

"Chicken with mashed potatoes." He grabbed the next metallic tub and passed it to Mac.

"Thanks. I must be brave to try chicken again." She smiled, a slight blush rising up to her glasses.

"What's wrong?" he asked as he gathered his own meatball sub.

"You don't have to do this for me."

"Bullshit," Trent said around a mouthful of pasta. "Just put out and call it a wash."

Mac choked on a piece of lettuce.

Cole rubbed her back. "Trent, knock it off."

"You don't care about the money, dude. She does. Work

it out in the bedroom."

Mac took in a deep breath. "I'll find a way to thank you. I appreciate it. I just feel bad. I'd feel bad if it was you or Dani."

"You'd sleep with Dani?" Trent asked.

"You're starting to get on my nerves, Trent. What happened to the nice guy I met on a cruise ship?"

He waggled a fork at her. "Six months of being nice to every whiney, mopey, bitchy passenger. I need another week before I start to balance out again." He shoved food in his mouth. "But don't worry, I'm heading out tonight."

"Bar?" Cole asked, taking a bite of his own food. He knew the Trent post-cruise drill.

"Yup, meeting up with some buddies for drinks."

"Need a designated driver?"

"We'll work it out."

Cole turned his attention back to Mac. "How are you feeling, Mackenzie-Mac?"

She looked up, and a smile crossed her pink lips. "A little more human. Thanks."

Her smile quenched his heart. The first time since they arrived back home that she looked happy to be here, with him.

They chatted about this and that throughout the meal, and when finished, Trent popped up and threw out the trash.

"I can't believe you ate that entire thing," Mac said to Trent. "That was probably a full box of pasta."

He patted his flat stomach. "You've never seen me eat until now. Muscles need fuel."

Cole laughed. "In a week, when the asshole fades, he starts moaning about his stomach killing him and his pants shrinking in my dryer. Then he gets back into the groove."

"Blow me, Matterhorn." Trent grabbed his jacket.

From the living room, music started playing. Mac groaned.

Trent paused with one arm through the sleeve. "Seriously, does that asshole not get the hint?"

Mac made her way into the living room and picked up her phone. "Before He Cheats" stopped playing. "No, he does not. He's a stubborn-ass mule, and I should really have my head examined for dating him, possibly for even working for him." She shuddered.

Cole had a very bad feeling brewing in his gut that had nothing to do with eating too much. "That was Chad?" he asked from the doorway.

"Yup, you should have heard it. Mac de-balled him earlier today."

Mac grinned at Trent.

Cole held out a hand. "Give me the phone. I'll make sure he never thinks about calling you again."

Mac shook her head and put her phone on the table. "Leave it alone." She left the room. A minute later, the bathroom door closed.

Cole eyed her phone.

Trent removed his coat. "Don't do it, man. She warned you."

He didn't give a damn about the warning. "Is he getting the hint?"

"Assholes generally don't."

"He's caused her enough trouble. The least he can do is stop—" Mac's phone rang again, giving Cole the only opening he needed. He swiped the cell, making contact before Trent could. "Mackenzie's phone."

Trent swore and stifled a laugh.

"Who's this?" came a male voice. A male voice filled with a pompous air and Cole hated him immediately, didn't matter he already disliked Chad. Time for a well-deserved ass kicking.

"The person who answered Mac's phone. Who's this?"

"Put Mackenzie on."

"No way in hell. She doesn't want to talk to you."

"I don't know who you think you are—"

"The guy erasing your memory. Not that hard to do, bud."

Chad growled. "Listen, you asshole. There's no way Mac's moved on."

Cole raised an eyebrow. "There's no way that Mac's moved on?"

Trent laughed.

"None. She's too much of a little mouse."

"Funny, she's more of a lioness with me."

He smiled at the sound of Chad stuttering.

"Let's get one thing straight. Mac's not yours. She doesn't date you. She doesn't live with you. She doesn't work for you. And she won't do any of those things ever again. So give it up and stop calling her before I call the police for harassment."

"She needs a job. You should be grateful I'm willing to help her out."

Cole fisted his free hand. Where did this a-hole live? He'd like to continue this conversation in person. "Fuck you. She has a job, with me."

He flung the phone to the couch. And noticed Trent had stopped laughing. He looked up. Mac stood in the doorway, face almost as red as her hair.

"You done?" she asked through clenched teeth.

"I think he'll stop calling you now."

"Not your problem, Cole." Her hair was about to set on fire. "You fucking asshole. I told you not to call him."

"He called you."

"Did I give you permission to answer my phone?"

"But—"

"Did. I. Give. You. Permission?"

"Well, no."

"That's right. I didn't. And why the fuck did you tell him

I was working for you? How am I going to get unemployment if he thinks I already have a new job? Or did you even think that maybe I'd need a good recommendation from my former boss, especially if I want to stay in the same field?"

Shit. He took a step forward. "Mac, I'm sorry. I'll fix this."

"How? How will you fix this? You gonna call Chad back and explain you were lying about the job thing? How do you think that's going to work out?" She ran her hands through her hair. "I'm going to Dani's." She turned and headed for the stairs.

Cole was rooted to the spot like a damn tree. How had he managed to mess this up so succinctly? "I'll drive you."

She looked past him. "Trent, would you mind?"

Trent looked back and forth between the two of them, face carefully blank. "Sure, no problem."

"Thanks." Mac leveled Cole with a blue stare full of steel before stomping up the stairs.

Trent golf clapped. "That was fucking brilliant."

"Shut up."

"First you tell off the ex, which was great. Then you don't stop when Mac's standing right there, epic. And you had to fuck over both her career and unemployment options."

"I said shut up," Cole barked.

Trent smiled. "You, my friend, are in the doghouse. Time to start groveling." A bang thudded upstairs. "I'd give her a day or two first. Wait for Dani to let you know she's calmed down." He patted Cole's shoulder and jogged up the stairs after Mac.

Cole sat down on the edge of the couch. *Fuck*.

• • •

Mac dug her spoon into a pint of Ben and Jerry's. Some flavor with a lot of ingredients, most of them revolving around chocolate, a must-have for her current predicament.

"Can I go to work and throw something at him?" Dani asked, eating her ice cream out of a bowl.

"I'll help." Susie licked her spoon. "What time does the asshole get to work?"

Mac groaned and leaned back against the couch, her new home for the interim. "He messed up everything I was trying to figure out. What am I going to do now?"

"The plan remains," Dani said. "We eat lots of ice cream. You stay here. Mi casa es su casa until you find a new job."

"But I'll have no money to contribute. You really shouldn't have sent me on that cruise."

"Wah," Susie said. "Regardless of the way it ended, he got you over Chad."

Mac rubbed her aching heart, pushing something hard into her skin. She reached into her shirt and pulled her necklace out.

"What's that?" Susie put her ice cream bowl on the table, pushed her very pregnant self out of a soft chair, and waddled over.

Mac sighed. "Gift from Cole. I should hock it and give Dani the money."

Dani choked on her ice cream. "That's what Cole gave you?" She sat down on Mac's other side. "Holy crap, Mac. The guy never buys his dates anything tangible, and he bought you this? A gemstone that looks like a lemon."

Susie reached for her bowl and Dani handed it to her. "He's lemonade."

Mac put her pint on her lap. "Are we forgetting his little chat with Chad?"

"If you're looking for a perfect man, you'll die lonely," Dani said.

"Not when I have my BFFs with me."

"I'll toast to that," Susie said, raising her bowl. "Ice

cream is so much better than alcohol, and I can participate." She settled her sweet treat on her round stomach.

"Hush, Susie, I think Mackenzie could really use a drink."

Mac groaned. "I had one the night I called things off on the cruise. Two hours later I returned it to the toilet. I think I'm okay without alcohol."

"I blame Chad." Susie raised her hands, her bowl perfectly safe on her stomach. "You were doing good before Chad. Then he comes in, beats up your self-confidence, enforces the rotten lemon decisions, and turns you into a Mackenzie that had lost her spark. Now, just a week after meeting Cole, you're stronger, vibrant, and starting to trust your decisions. I think his first choice versus second choice theory is dead on."

Mac moaned and curled into a ball. "Can we get back to yelling at Cole?"

"She's deflecting. I think you've hit something, Suz."

Mac put her pint down on the coffee table and left her friends alone. In the bathroom, she leaned on the counter, staring at herself. The bags under her eyes were hidden by her frames, but still unattractive. Her hair was all stringy and her color pale despite the length of time she'd spent in the sun. Her nose had started to peel, and little white specks pulled away from her red skin. She looked as bad as she felt.

Cole's voice rang in her head. "What's your first choice?" He put so much emphasis on her decisions, decisions she notoriously got wrong. Yet she won at slots, and she won at trivia. What was her first choice here?

Her reflection had no answers. Her heart hurt, and she felt like shit. She wanted the damn food poisoning effects to leave her alone. She wanted a home and a job. She needed to do those on her own.

No choice, only need. She'd finish her pint, maybe have another, and in the morning it would be time to pull on her big-girl panties and get her life back together.

Home: Day 2

Mac adjusted her laptop at Dani's small kitchen table. Her coffee cooled next to her, in a mug with the words "bite me" on it. Matched Dani's mood on a normal day. Today it matched Mac's as well.

A new chapter began. Regardless of if she was ready or wanted it. She was done letting others dictate her life for her. Time for her to take charge and make her own lemonade.

Somehow.

She filed for unemployment, crossing her fingers that it wouldn't be contested. Then she emailed a few coworkers. Or rather, former coworkers. Asking for favors wasn't her thing, but she needed recommendations if she had any chance of making this her ongoing career. Because architecture was her first choice. She didn't know what to make out of Cole being the one to see the power of her initial instincts, only that she saw it now and she deserved to be happy. A career in architecture would make her happy.

Which meant she needed to level up. The person she wanted to be would take charge and make magic happen. She started an email to an architect she'd had positive interactions with, often times due to Chad dropping the ball. Her fingers hovered over the keyboard. She'd only bother him or make things worse if she emailed. Right?

Mac shook her head. For the first time, she caught it. She had an idea—the email—and then talked herself out of it—in this case, expecting a problem. But what did she have to lose? Absolutely nothing.

And the email was her first instinct.

She wrote it and clicked send before she could second-guess herself any further, trusting her gut. If nothing else, Cole had changed her outlook on her decision making and instincts, and she really needed to thank him for that.

Her hand went to her neck, where she still wore his necklace. Her heart kicked hard at the thought of her cruise companion. But this was what she'd always wanted to do post-cruise: sit in Dani's kitchen and put her life back together.

After being manipulated by Chad, she couldn't let the phone thing go easily. Even if Cole hadn't managed to mess up her unemployment, he'd still thrown a wrench into her plans.

She'd fix herself, find out the real outcome of his chat with Chad before figuring out what she'd do about the lingering ache in her chest.

She glanced up and caught a piece of paper tacked to Dani's refrigerator that she'd missed before with her name on it. Mac rose and collected the paper, opening it up.

Mac,

Did you know there are some amazing architecture programs that are part time and fast tracked to get you back in the field? Think about it. I'm game for being your roommate, but there's also someone else happy to do that, no spare bed required.

You've got this!

Dani

Mac groaned and decided to ignore the alternate roommate option. Instead, she settled at her laptop and opened a fresh browser tab to see what these options were that Dani suggested.

• • •

Cole should have expected the flying notepad when Dani got to work. Hands on his keyboard, he turned to the floor where the offending office supply lay in a crumpled heap. "Feel better?"

Dani put her mitten-covered hands on her hips. "Nope. You promised me an ass kicking."

"Help me hunt down Chad and you've got it."

Dani shook her head. "Not Chad. You. You messed things up with Mac. Where's the ass kicking?"

His heart ached, had been since she shut him out. He'd been pacing, antsy, unused to this level of worry and guilt. He'd slept like crap and practically rivalled Trent in his assholery. "Let me talk to her."

"No. How could you give Chad that much fuel? She wants to work in that field and he's her only experience."

Cole shoved his hands into his hair. "The asshole was calling Mac, repeatedly. He was harassing her. And since I don't know where to track him down in person, I couldn't talk to him with my fist."

Dani put her bag down at her desk. "Damn you. Stop making me like you and Mac together."

Cole couldn't stop the grin. "Put in a good word for me?"

She leveled a finger at him. "You still owe me an ass kicking."

"Not if I fix this."

"Uh-uh. You messed up, even if not on a permanent scale, so you get your ass kicked. I sent her on that cruise to make her feel better."

"Is she really worse now that she knows me?" He needed this answer, deep down inside. "Have I not helped repair the harm that Chad and her brother caused? Because if you answer yes, I will back away, even if it doing it kills me." The thought alone cut straight through. He had no doubt it would send him back to the shell of a person he used to be. And that, he realized, was on him. He needed purpose in life and he wanted it to be her, but he couldn't pin that on her.

Dani fisted her hips, glaring at him, her gaze softening the longer she did so. "No. She's not worse. And yes, part of that is you." Dani wagged a finger at him. "But most of that is Mackenzie herself."

He raised his hands. "Of course, because she's amazing. Not for nothing, but forcing her on that cruise was a good idea."

Dani scoffed. "Because she met you?"

"No, because she needed a chance to recharge and find herself again."

A silence not normal for his office lingered. "Damn, you really do take the fun out of this. Give her time. Maybe the ass kicking can be avoided."

"I know another way to avoid that ass kicking."

Dani crossed her arms and glared at him.

"I made a decision regarding the lease."

"And...?"

Cole glanced around. The small office had been such a thrill to set up. He put his ideas into action here, created something for himself that matched his needs and goals. A lot of blood, sweat, and tears went into building his business. Bittersweet to let it go.

And yet, he wasn't the person he used to be, most of that due to meeting Mac. His goals no longer to remain unattached and live life like tomorrow might never happen. Now he wanted a future, and a life, with a certain specific someone. If she gave him another chance, he'd make this next stage in his life work to her benefit as well.

"I'm not renewing. We're going remote."

Dani hooted. "Excellent, working in my pajamas here I come!"

"Except I'm going to turn one of the rooms in my home into an office space. Can be used for client meetings and allow for an easier share of resources and materials."

Dani held up a hand. "I get that, I really do. But will I have the option to be remote in my home at least some of the time?"

He mulled that over. He still needed to solidify all the details. Business or not, Dani held a position of power at the moment due to Mac. "I think we can work something out."

"And do I thank Mackenzie for this sudden decision clarity?"

"Well, I've got the Andersons staying with us regardless of location."

Dani stared at him.

Cole scratched his cheek. Tried to think of the man he'd been before getting on that ship and opening his door to Mac holding his luggage. He'd started to gain some clarity on the decision on board, but he'd had to, anyways. She'd made an immediate impression on him, had him thinking of things differently, even if on a subconscious level.

"Probably," he finally admitted.

Dani studied him for a bit longer, then held out her hand. "Hi, I'm Dani Martin. You must be the Cole Matterhorn Trent told me about."

He shook her hand, even though he eyed her with a heavy

dose of doubt. "You have a point here?"

"You've been running from everything, holding everyone out away from you. Until now."

He glanced at his covered leg. "I don't run."

"You replaced actual running with figurative running."

"Are you my employee or therapist?"

Dani shrugged. "I thought I was a friend. You ever ask why I haven't considered another job?"

He flashed her a smile. "Because I'm charming and a good boss?"

"Because you needed me. You needed someone levelheaded as backup."

He studied her and thought back over the years. When he dropped the ball, Dani picked it up. She allowed him to leave on vacations, at a moment's notice, without any worries for his business. Without her, he'd be lost. "So I'm going to lose you if I get my shit together?"

Dani laughed and patted his shoulder. "Nah, you're a good boss, and I like the work. But it's nice seeing you grow. Don't regress while Mac figures her life out."

"You speak like you think I'll get another chance."

Dani went back to her computer. "You might."

Not a declaration he could bring to the bank, but Dani would be in Mac's court over his. He focused on his computer. Safer territory.

• • •

Mac spent the day researching jobs and, God help her, colleges. She felt in over her head and more than a little overwhelmed, but a new calm had enveloped her. For the first time in she didn't know how long, possibly ever, she was in the driver's seat of her own life. Whatever happened from here on out was her own making.

Her phone vibrated. She turned away from her browser, blinking the room into focus. Damn, her eyes needed a break. She fumbled with her phone, hoping for a response from one of her contacts, only to find two texts from Cole. The first was apologizing. The second could have been from an inspiration meme: you are stronger than you give yourself credit for.

She wanted to respond but didn't know what to type. *Give me time*, perhaps, but even that didn't feel right. So she left the messages read and set her phone and computer aside. She needed to stretch, finish unpacking, and find Dani's gift.

By the time Dani arrived home, Mac had the martini clock waiting on the kitchen table.

"What's that?" Dani asked as she took in the clock, laughing.

"Your souvenir, and my contribution to being a mooch."

Dani tilted it upside down, checked out all angles, a wide grin lighting up her face. "It's perfect."

"I found a lemon clock for myself."

"Ooohhh, I wanna see, I wanna see." Dani jumped up and down like a five-year-old being offered candy.

Mac reached into her now-organized luggage and pulled out her clock.

"Nice. Very Mackenzie." Dani picked up her martini clock again. "I love this. Much better than the two rum cakes Cole got me."

Mac laughed, remembering Cole's expression when he bought them. "He almost forgot. He got that the last day in the onboard shops."

"I think he was distracted."

Mac ignored the stirring of emotion that erupted. "Yeah."

Her phone started playing "Call Me Maybe," and Mac stared at it, forgetting she had even used the ringtone. When she saw Cole's name, she hit "ignore."

Dani smirked when Mac looked up. "Who was that?"

"Wrong number."

"Funny, you don't normally set a song to anyone you don't care about."

The song began again, and Dani snatched the phone. Mac bit her lip, but Dani didn't answer. At least one person in her life asked first. "Does he know you gave him a ringtone?"

"No."

"This is a heavy ringtone for a guy you're avoiding."

"I gave it to him before he talked to Chad."

"But you haven't deleted the song."

Mac snatched her phone back. No, she hadn't deleted the song. She might have to if he kept calling, though. And even that didn't feel right. Because the song still stood. She wanted him to call her. Maybe. And she had just met him and the whole thing was crazy.

She ran her finger over his listing.

"Just call him already," Dani said.

Mac dropped her phone to the couch. "Not yet."

"When? He's miserable, you know."

Mac frowned, not her intention. "I don't want him miserable. I just need to finish what I started before you pushed me on a cruise."

"And you fell for my boss."

Mac laughed. "Not intentional. Come on, let's get dinner and discuss which of my future options gets me off your couch quickest."

"I know a one-legged man that'll help."

Mac put her hands on her hips.

Dani raised hers in surrender. "Fine. I'm in a weird middle position, but I'll back off."

Mac bit her lip. "Tell him I'm okay. And I'll see him when I'm ready." If he was truly meant to be, he'd trust the truth in her request.

Home: Day 10

"I hereby call this meeting of the unemployed couch surfers club in session."

"Fuck you, I have a bed."

Mac shook her head at Trent, perched across from her at the coffee shop. They'd been meeting for a week for coffee and wifi and moral support. They'd both been sending out applications; in Mac's case that included colleges. Going back to school had grown into something she was looking forward to. She wanted to land a job in her field as well, but if she didn't, she'd take the long way there.

Her contacts had all responded favorably for recommendations, leaving her hopeful. Her unemployment was still in review; in a week or two she'd know the results there. She had her first interview tomorrow. Things were falling into place, slow but sure. One area left, or rather, one person left, but she wanted one more win, a sense of completing this journey by her own willpower, before she contacted Cole.

He'd continued to send inspirational messages, one a day.

He'd shifted over to actual memes, and yesterday's involved a person standing over a canal, encouraging her to make the jump. She nearly sent him a thumbs-up. His messages had turned into something she looked forward to, a pick-me-up on even the bad days. He'd given her unconditional support, let her know he was still there for her. If she fell, he'd catch her. Heck, even separated he still managed to catch her. Soon, she'd thank him, because she knew her current state had a lot to do with his support, even if she still needed this part of her journey to be separate.

Also, she missed him. Her heart was torn without him, the pain not diminishing at all as the days passed. He wasn't a footnote in her life, or an inspirational chapter. He meant much more to her than that. Powerful words tempted to be applied, but she kept her mind on her task. There would be time for him later, and she had plans to more than make up for needing her space.

Her phone lit up with an incoming message from Cole. She clicked to check, not caring that to Trent it probably looked like she lunged for it, curious what today's meme would be. Only she didn't find a meme.

I wanted you to know that you've inspired me. Trent and more recently Dani have been on my case about running. Trent wanted me to run again. Dani pointed out that I ran from everything else, especially relationships and commitments. (Trent, the bastard, agreed.) You changed all of that. You showed me that I needed something to live for, rather than living in fear and thus letting the terrorists win. I may have lost my leg, but that doesn't mean I can't run. I've started the process of getting a running prosthesis, and hopefully one day I'll cross the finish line, past the spot that took my leg.

He followed the message with a picture of a running prosthesis. Unlike the one he wore, this looked more like a curve or a large hook. Mac's heart beat fast, and she clutched a hand to her chest, where she still wore the necklace he gave her. This man who didn't volunteer the information of how he lost his leg, who denied he was a runner anymore, now took a big step toward his future.

A future he wanted her in. And he thanked her, Mackenzie Laurel, who did not have her life the least bit together. At least, not when they met. Like him starting the process, she'd started hers, and they'd both found a tiny pot of gold at the end of their paths.

Figuratively, unless Mac managed to land a really kickass job. Or Cole ran to the end of a rainbow.

"You okay?"

She glanced up at Trent and noted she still clutched her necklace. She showed him her phone. "Did you know about this?"

"Yeah. At least, I knew he was getting there, didn't realize he'd actually done it. Damn near took the bastard almost ten years. It's about time."

Mac nodded, taking her phone back. She itched to respond, struggled with the urge to run into his arms.

"You really were the catalyst."

She locked eyes with Trent.

"You broke him out of the bubble the bombing put him in, gave him what he needed. And even if you decide to never make up, you've given him a lot."

Mac mulled those words over. She'd helped Cole, and if she never saw him again, that help would continue. Just like his first-choice comments had changed her life. They could go their separate ways and each be better for it.

And now she really, really wanted her cruise fling back.

The café door opened, and Mac waved as Susie entered.

Susie wasn't unemployed, but she did have random days off and liked to join in on the moral support. Mac figured being eight months pregnant also had something to do with it. She wore sandals even in the thirty-degree weather, thanks to her swollen feet and belly.

"Want your usual?" Trent asked, already standing.

Susie practically swooned. "Yes, please." She reached into her purse, but by the time she pulled out her money, he'd already gone up front. She shoved the bills under his drink.

"How are you feeling?" Mac asked as she closed her laptop and addressed her friend.

Susie rubbed her stomach. "Good. I ache, I'm bloated, but this little guy keeps me happy." She glowed as she talked.

Mac leaned forward and rubbed the belly. "How are you doing, little guy?" She was awarded with a swift kick. "Football player, Susie, I'm telling you."

"I know."

Mac's email dinged, and she opened her laptop.

"Ready for your interview tomorrow?" Susie asked.

Mac nodded, distracted by the email from a former coworker, with FYI as the subject. She faced Susie. "Yes. Nervous but excited, too, if that makes sense?"

The interview was for a job similar to her previous one, and she liked how the listing made a point of there being room to grow.

"It does." Susie reached across the table and grabbed Mac's hand. "I'm so proud of you."

"Thanks." The wording in the email preview dragged Mac's attention back, and she held up a finger to Susie as Trent rejoined them, blocking everything else out as she read.

HEY MAC,

MISS SEEING YOU AT WORK! I'M NOT A GOSSIPER...OKAY, I'M TOTALLY A GOSSIPER, BUT I FIGURED YOU SHOULD know this one: Chad's been fired!!!! That's what that womanizing slime gets for getting involved with his staff. He knows better, and the whole "I didn't get caught before" thing is complete bullshit.

If he's gone, can you come back? We really do miss you here.

Mac covered her mouth with her hand, a gasp leaving her lips. She read the email three times, disbelieving the words, but each pass had them right there, staring back at her.

"What's wrong?" Susie asked, her worried voice breaking into Mac's stupor.

"I…" Mac glanced up at her two friends. "Chad's been fired."

Trent threw his head back and laughed. "Good."

"I agree. Looks like he got what he deserved," Susie said.

Mac read the email a fourth time. "I can't believe it." She paused. "No, I think I can. I'm surprised. Nothing seemed to touch that man."

"That's what he gets for messing with you." Trent raised his cup, pushing the money back toward Susie.

Mac and Susie raised theirs as well to clink them together, as much as someone could clink paper cups.

They all sipped.

"So things are going well for Mac. How about you, Trent?" Susie asked, pushing the money in his direction again. If this followed how things went last time, then the money would be left on the table as a tip.

"He's still taking the long way back to humanity," Mac said. Trent's swears were down to a normal level, but like her, he'd been needing time to decompress.

Trent grinned, one corner of his mouth quirking upward. "Au contraire." He spun his laptop around. On the screen, a hotel with crystal chandeliers listed job openings.

"Fancy, where's that?"

"California."

Mac's mouth fell open. Then she squealed. "You're going after Quinn?"

Trent took his laptop back but couldn't stop his smile from growing. "Yeah. There's nothing around here that's the right match for me. I knew that years ago, part of why I started cruising. But out near Quinn…there are options. It's a gamble. We didn't have the time together like you and Cole. If the job is right, it'll be worth it."

"So that's why you weren't going to visit her."

"I'm hoping to call her up and beg a favor of needing a place to crash for an interview. Fingers crossed I get one soon."

Susie leaned forward and grabbed Trent's hand. "I know I've only met you recently, but I'm so happy for you."

Trent laughed.

Susie leaned back, then forward again, sniffing Mac's cup.

"Mackenzie, why does this smell like my tea?"

Mac grabbed her cup. "Because I wanted tea."

"Since when do you like ginger tea?"

Since her stomach started acting up a few days ago. "Susie, is this really important?"

Susie didn't say a word but didn't stop looking at her.

She sighed. "I'm having some not-so-fond memories of food poisoning. If Dani wasn't fine, I'd think our takeout went bad."

Susie rubbed her stomach and eyed Mac. "What kind of memories?"

"Upset stomach, nausea, an overall off feeling. I'm hoping the tea kicks it to the curb." She was so over feeling crappy.

Susie tapped a finger to her belly. "Funny, sounds like me

the first trimester."

The words rang in her head, bringing with it a vivid image of Cole under Mac when she forgot protection. She opened her mouth, then closed it.

"Shit," Trent muttered and closed his laptop.

Mac studied him. "What did Cole tell you?"

Susie raised her eyebrows.

"He already said he thinks you're pregnant."

Mac tugged at her collar, in a sudden need for cool air. She'd nearly put her life back together and didn't know how this potential curve ball would alter things.

"Wait, why would he think you could be pregnant?" Susie asked, a questioning hand in the air.

Mac sighed. "We skipped protection one day."

"When was this unprotected sex?"

"I don't know, close to two weeks ago."

"When's your period due?"

Mac's cheeks flamed. The coffee shop didn't have that many patrons, but she felt every ear tuned into their conversation. "Mixed company, Susie."

"Wah. My world is placentas and vaginal discharge as I wait for my body to expel a child. If you're pregnant, you better get used to it."

Mac rubbed her forehead. "Would it make sense? It's been two weeks."

Susie shrugged. "Everyone's different. I know of some women who claim they had symptoms the moment the sperm met the egg, and others who had nothing for a while. For me, yeah, there were some early signs. But I'd been trying for almost a year; I was looking for those signs. And lucky me, my morning sickness has lingered. You'd be considered four weeks, though, so the timing is right."

Mac groaned. "Great, with how they count pregnancy, I'd be four weeks pregnant with a guy I've known for two weeks."

Trent laughed.

Susie nodded. "Yup."

This was more messed up than most of Mac's life. "I don't think it's a good idea to have a child with someone I met two weeks ago, especially if the pregnancy somehow predates him in archaic timing."

"Then you shouldn't have had unprotected sex with him. Cole's lemonade, sweetie. At least he's not one of those rotten lemons you dated."

Mac tried to control her breathing. "What are you saying?"

"The timing might be off, but the guy is right."

Mac opened her mouth. Then closed it. Her heart surged, agreeing with Susie's statement. Her mind held onto rationalization, protesting that maybe her period wasn't due. She grabbed her phone and accessed her calendar app. She found the current date, did some math...

Fuck.

She shoved her phone back into her pocket.

"You okay, sweetie?" Suzie asked.

Mac took a deep breath, then another, then some tea for good measure.

"Forget about dates or timing or any of that, because in the end, none of that would matter. Think of the man himself, because we all know you've been missing him."

God help her, she had. She'd wanted to ace that interview tomorrow, then invite him on a date, one final point for Mac getting her life on track before welcoming in someone destined not to be her rebound. If she was pregnant, it changed things, and she wanted to freak out, but a sense of calm came over her. Maybe it was the tea, maybe not. Facts were facts, and nothing she did now changed whether or not the test would be positive.

Mac packed up her laptop. "I need to get a test and go to his office." Nerves broke free and tried to consume her, and she knew only part of that was the weight of the test itself.

"Good luck, sweetie," Susie said. "I'll refrain from texting Dani."

Mac let out a breath. "You better." She leveled a finger at Trent. "Not one word."

He mimed zipping his lips.

She grabbed her belongings and tossed her tea in the trash.

Outside, she grasped the handle behind her back and took a deep breath. Time to find out what kind of a mess her first instinct granted her.

...

Cole emptied a filing cabinet into one of the many boxes around the office. Across the room, Dani did similar to brochures. Sure, many things were digital these days, but they still had some paper trails, and physical advertising had served them well in the past. The future might be a different story.

It felt bittersweet. Closing one chapter of his life, opening up to a new one. He had most of the details set for the transition and a timeline of how to make things as smooth as possible, thanks to Dani. He hoped other things, or rather, a specific person, would be part of this new chapter, and he pushed the thought aside. Mac needed time. He'd give her all the time she needed. This caring for another person thing had shifted his view on life. For so long, it didn't matter what happened to him. Now he had a reason to live. And he still suffered the loss by messing things up.

Time. He had it. He'd give it to her, too, and hope she'd come around. Hope this ache in his chest meant that she felt it as well. That their connection truly was deeper than the length of time they knew each other. Dani didn't give him a ton of updates, neither did Trent, but since both were in contact with Mac, he knew she was okay for now. And he also knew she saw his texts, even if she hadn't responded. He didn't know how long he'd keep that up, but maybe it made her day a little brighter.

The door chimed, and as if his thoughts had finally conjured her, Mac stood in the doorway. He hadn't seen her in nearly two weeks, and he soaked her in, taking in the way her hair hung loose, the skin still peeling on her nose, the bulky jacket and jeans. He straightened in his chair. It was either that or run to her. But he didn't know if she was here for him or Dani. The way her eyes held his, he dared hope she wanted to see him.

More importantly, relief washed over him. She was okay. He knew this, but seeing it with his own eyes loosened one of the tight knots in his gut.

Mac waved to Dani without taking her eyes off him. His heart picked up to a gallop as she walked right up to his desk, a second knot beginning to unravel. She held up a box. "I was hoping to have a few more things in order first, but if this is positive, that changes things."

He blinked, then blinked again, her words not making any sense. He leaned forward, as if that would help decode the mystery. "Positive?"

She dropped the box on his desk. A pregnancy test. His heart stopped. "I haven't been feeling so great the last few days, and Susie pointed out it sounded like morning sickness."

He studied her face, her round blue eyes. The time had come to find out if her instinct, and his, was correct. He wanted to see her again, to get a chance to talk to her. But not like this. "What do you mean by a few more things in order first?"

A small smile crossed her face, and he catalogued every shift in her features. "Meaning I wasn't ignoring you to be mean. I just needed to feel like I'd succeeded at something before," her cheeks pinked and he nearly crawled to her, "starting a relationship with someone."

The final knot unwound, and he no longer could keep his distance. He stood and took a step toward her. "I'll give you all the time you need. While this does change things, I can wait." He'd hang on a wire if it meant she'd give him, them, a chance together.

Her breath hitched, as though tears were about to fall. He took a gamble and pulled her into him, wrapping his arms around her. She felt good in his arms, like she belonged there. It had been so long, and he wanted to hold on and never let her go. "You have good instincts, Mackenzie-Mac."

She leaned her head on his shoulder. "We met two weeks ago."

Unable to stop, he kissed the top of her head. "I'm not going anywhere." If only she'd let him back in.

She picked up the test. "Where's your bathroom?"

It occurred to him she could have done all this on her own, and yet she was here. "Thank you for including me."

A soft chuckle escaped her lips. "It did take both of us to get here."

"What's your gut say?"

"That this test right here will tell us the answer."

Her eyes held his, a connection thriving between them. He pointed down the hall to the bathroom.

Dani had stayed quiet with her box, but the moment Mac turned the corner, she broke the silence. "What. The. Hell? I mean, yay, she's here. But what?"

He held up his hands. "Mackenzie instinct."

"So you get off her and grab a condom."

His lip twitched at the memory. Wasn't happening. "She

had me pinned."

Dani groaned. "I asked you to leave my friend alone. You didn't. You somehow got your luggage into her room and now may have impregnated her? I told you not to hurt her." She whacked him in the shoulder.

He blocked her hand from a second attempt. "The luggage was not my fault, and I'm not going to hurt her."

Dani raised her hand.

"I love her." His heart pounded, but the words were true and hadn't budged since the first moment he admitted them to himself. He knew they would be true for the rest of his life.

Dani dropped her hand, studying him. "Damn. You mean that." She crossed her arms. "If you mess up…"

"You can still decide how I kick my ass. Only I'll do it twice."

"Good." Dani returned to her desk.

Cole stared down the hall, toward the bathroom where Mac was taking a life-changing test. In a matter of minutes, he'd know the results of that early morning romp. In a matter of minutes, their lives were going to change, one way or another. He needed to tell her how he felt, let her know he was in this with her. One hundred percent.

If she was pregnant, he was marrying her. Two weeks or not.

• • •

Mac washed her hands in the little bathroom and stared at her face. She looked the same. Not that her face should look different. No glowing, not like Susie. But if she was pregnant, she wasn't very far along.

She'd add another moniker to her life status: unemployed, homeless, broke, pregnant. At least she knew who the father was, right? And at least the father wasn't Chad. The shiver down her spine ran deep and cold, and she squirmed. Cole was a better choice for a potential father, even if the timing was downright ridiculous.

A little flutter of something akin to hope bloomed in her heart. A child did not decide to be brought into the world, this decision was hers and Cole's. She wouldn't let timing get in the way of that. And she'd already done a lot at putting her life together. This wouldn't be a wrench in her story; it would be a shift.

Her hand went to her stomach, as though comforting a being that may or may not be there. She wanted it there. Preferably in a year or two or when she graduated with her degree in architecture. Life didn't always go as planned. Hers certainly didn't. Either way, she'd make it work.

She took a deep breath and picked up the test. Back in the main office area, she dropped it down on Cole's desk along with her phone set to a timer app. Two minutes to go.

"No one looks until the timer is up." She held out a finger to both Cole and Dani.

Cole grasped her hand. She squeezed him, then released in order to pace the office.

"I can't believe you're risking bringing little Coles into this world," Dani said, shaking her head.

Mac laughed in spite of herself. "I had just gotten off the phone with Chad, who was a raging asshole. Cole isn't."

"No, Cole's better than Chad. I'll definitely give you that."

Mac pulled her hair off her face and looked around the office. Boxes were strewn about, most pushed to the sides in a manner that said, "We're packing and doing business as usual." She knew from Dani they were going remote, and Dani was thrilled. She hadn't thought about it too much beyond that. The boxes would take up a decent amount of space somewhere in Cole's home, and she wondered where he planned to put it all. She also wondered why he still had photos on his desk, namely one of Cole and her from the cruise. She picked it up.

"You put this on your desk?"

He raised a single shoulder. "I like seeing your face."

Mac's aching heart wanted to reach out and touch him. She dumped him, and he had her picture on his desk, like they were an ongoing item.

She searched his green eyes. How was he lemonade? She opened her mouth to say something but couldn't find the words. Her throat closed on her. He'd been nothing but supportive, even while giving her space. She could keep finding herself and putting her life back together with him in it. The next step belonged to her.

"I'm glad you're getting the running prosthesis."

He shifted his stance. "I meant what I typed. You helped me get here. And I'm excited. It's going to take work to adjust to, but it will mean running again, and not in a way that wears out my regular prosthesis."

A soft smile covered his face, a sense of peace shining through. Her heart filled for him, happy to see him get here, and to be part of the cause.

He needed to know he helped her, too, that this time apart wasn't a fight. She took his words and support and made her life better than it had been before.

"You helped me, too. You and your first choice theory. I don't know how you saw it so clearly, but you did, and I've been doing my best to follow it. More than that, you've given me this unconditional support, even while we were separated. You've been there for me more than people who've known me much longer. And even though I needed to do these past few weeks on my own, I've thrived having you in my corner like that.

"I have an interview tomorrow. And I've been applying

for school." Her hand went to her stomach. "Oh no, how am I going to go back to school if I'm pregnant?"

Cole left his desk, the test, and the timer and rested his hands on her shoulders. "Look at me. It's going to be okay. I'll be here to help."

She nodded. He'd proved that, as foreign as it still felt. She wanted to fling her arms around him. It had been so long and she missed him, missed having him nearby. Missed having his support be in person.

His green eyes searched hers, and he brushed some hair behind her ear. "I want to say this now, before the timer goes off, so you know it to be true." He paused and bent until he was eye level. "I love you, Mackenzie-Mac."

The intensity of his eyes confirmed his words. Her already fast heart rate doubled, though a warmth washed over her. Regardless, the timing of everything had to be record breaking and so not healthy. "You barely know me."

"I know you have a thing for lemons. That your brother's teasing caused you to doubt yourself. That you have killer instincts if you would only trust yourself. That you are my lemonade, and two weeks or twenty years, I'm still going to want you by my side."

Mac's heart beat wildly, her pulse racing. He loved her. Her cruise fling loved her. He really was her—

The timer went off.

Cole remained in front of her, searching her eyes, not moving. Mac's chest tightened, but she kept looking at him.

The beeping stopped, and they both looked over to see Dani by the test. "Want me to check?"

Mac managed a nod. Dani picked up the test, her face an impassive fortress. She stared at it for what felt like much too long before turning it around to face them. In the little oval box was one word.

Pregnant.

A slow smile curved Cole's lips, but she couldn't register what the word meant. Her heart pounded. "Well, Cole, you've got yourself forever more wrapped up in an epic Mackenzie decision."

He grabbed her and held her to him. "Not a bad decision. Timing questionable." He tugged on a lock of her hair. "I love you, Mackenzie-Mac. Marry me."

She stepped out of his grasp. This was all too much, everything happening at once. She already had to rush into the pregnancy; she couldn't fathom rushing into anything else. "Whoa, do I need to remind you it's been two weeks? And I've already broken us up twice?"

Dani bent over Cole's desk, eyeing the test. "How many women have you dated who wanted you to propose? Tons. Yet you ask Mac to marry you. No ring, not even a knee. Classy."

"Do I need to send you home?" Cole asked.

"She's right," Mac began. These next words might hurt, but she needed to hold on to some sense of normal relationship time scales. "I'm not marrying you, Cole. Not after two weeks. I'm sorry." She closed her eyes against the shattered look in his. "I don't need to be married to have a baby. If we do get married, we'll do so when the time is right, regardless of a kid."

He wrapped his arms around her again. "I was raised to accept my responsibilities. But I want to marry you because I want you to be my wife, not because you're pregnant. Because I love you. And if you sprout anything about rotten lemons, I'm having your head checked."

She managed a laugh and rubbed her face into his shoulder. She dug deep, searching for her first instinct here. Way too soon came first. Second? Yes. She'd marry him, one day, when the time was right. "I love you, too," she said before she kissed him. She fell into his familiar warmth and taste and knew that one kiss would have had her back in his arms.

"I'm serious about marrying you."

She shook her head. "Not yet. Before or after the baby is born doesn't matter. We'll get married when and if the time is right."

"Will you at least come home with me and let me help care for you?"

She brushed his hair off his forehead. "I can take care of myself. But I think I'll take you up on that first offer."

Epilogue

SIXTEEN MONTHS LATER

Cole stretched under the gray sky. A light drizzle coated the land, and he shifted his left leg back and forth. He'd had the new running prosthesis for a year now. Didn't stop him from remembering what waited for him at the end.

The last spot he walked with two legs.

His group included other survivors. Trent stretched a few feet down. And Cole wasn't the only one missing a limb. Just when he wanted to call himself foolish and stop before any further calamities befell him, the sun poked through the clouds. The light hit his wedding band.

He wasn't doing this for himself. He ran for Mac. He ran for their eight-month-old daughter, Ada, the best souvenir he'd ever brought home from a vacation.

"You ready?" Trent asked, bouncing on his heels.

Cole nodded. "Yeah."

"Worried more about the run or the finish line?"

Cole studied his friend. Trent's bouncing wasn't warm-up

related. "What do you think?"

Trent forced a laugh. "We'll get through this. And then we'll see our three loves waiting for us. All of us safe."

Mac, Ada, and Quinn would be there for them when they finished. Not at the finish line for many reasons, of which Cole and Trent were grateful.

As they began the run, he kept his mind in the game and on his family. It took him six months before Mac had agreed to marry him and until three weeks ago for them to make it official. They took a small band of family and friends on a cruise. Third trip for Cole and Mac. First trip for Ada.

During the reception, best man Trent, ever the supportive asshole, made a joke about cruise romances never lasting. Quinn got upset and tried to walk out, so Trent proposed. Cole would have called it a smooth recovery if Trent hadn't produced a ring and already ran the plan by Cole and Mac.

Cole had things to look forward to. Watching his little girl grow. Living life with Mac. Flying out to California whenever Trent and Quinn picked a date. He had a life now. The last marathon he'd visited had taken a lot from him. But he'd bounced back, found his purpose again.

He focused on his running, on the curved spring of his prosthesis. Not the same as two legs, never the same. A good different. For the first time, he wondered if his life had turned out exactly as it was meant to be.

But the shadows always lurked, and crossing that finish line would be both relief and fear. He had more to live for now than he did at twenty-two. He needed to make sure he stuck around. For Mac. For his redheaded daughter. They'd be waiting for him when he finished. And he would finish.

• • •

Mac waited in the family meeting area at the end of the race.

She had an app tracking Cole's progress and figured he'd be finished in another ten minutes or so. She bounced Ada on her hip, pushing aside the unease in her stomach. Security was high, had been since the bombing. Yet she couldn't help but remember what had been. To think, she hadn't even known the love of her life was affected at the time.

Various friends and family had staked out along the course, and she'd gotten texts filled with pictures of Cole and Trent running. He ran better on one leg than she did on two. He claimed she helped him get back to running, and maybe she had a hand in his recovery. But in the end, it was all him. Whenever he got grumpy, she forced him to change prostheses and go running. It had a calming effect on him.

Ada squirmed, and Mac put the baby back into the stroller. Cole often ran with Ada, pushing a jogging stroller. Mac wondered if Ada would start walking or go directly to running.

With Ada strapped in, Mac stood and rubbed her side. Juggling motherhood, work, and college took a lot out of her, but true to his word, Cole helped out as much as he could, allowing her the ability to balance all three. And with him working out of the home, he'd been able to care for Ada without issues, freeing her up to follow her dreams. Life had been busy, and chaotic, and she wouldn't change a single thing. They never did anything the easy way, it seemed, since on their honeymoon they'd skipped protection. After Cole left for the marathon, she took a test and confirmed both of their suspicions.

Ada squealed and grabbed at a hanging toy before shoving it into her mouth. After the test turned positive, Mac made a quick shopping trip before coming to support Cole. She smiled down at her daughter wearing a "big sister" shirt.

After this, she needed a more permanent form of birth control.

Quinn returned and handed Mac a bottled water. "I can't believe you're surprising him this way," she said, looking down at the kicking baby.

Mac laughed and took a sip. "Like he doesn't already know the possibility."

Quinn looked around. "You think they're okay?"

Mac put a hand on her friend's shoulder, noting Quinn twirled her ring around her finger. "You've seen the pictures. They are fine. Sweaty and smelly, but fine."

Quinn laughed and squeezed Mac's hand. She pulled out her phone and held up the tracker app. "They're close."

"I wish we could see them live."

"Me too. But they'd be too freaked out if we were there."

Mac picked up Ada. "Get ready to congratulate a very tired Daddy."

Ada clapped her hands and grabbed a fist full of Mac's hair.

The energy was high around her, full of waiting families and tired but happy runners. And then Mac saw Cole and couldn't stop the grin. He staggered a bit, and she bet he had a few new blisters from running twenty-six miles in a prosthesis. But his smile was large and full.

"You did it," she said once he got close.

Cole picked up Ada, who had her hands outstretched for him, and held her close. He didn't notice the shirt. Then he pulled Mac in for a kiss. "Yeah," was all he said.

Beside them, Trent had Quinn locked in a long kiss.

She chatted about the marathon updates she'd gotten while Cole held Ada and drank water. Trent eventually came up for air and joined in. Then she couldn't take it anymore. "Look at your daughter's shirt."

Cole's eyebrows drew in, and he held the giggling baby out, blinking at the shirt. Then he tilted his head back and laughed. The tiredness fell straight off him. "Oh, Mackenzie-

Mac, only you."

Yeah, only her. About to juggle a job, college, and two kids. And she wouldn't have it any other way. Thanks to him believing in her. And from the peaceful look on his face after completing his race, that belief ran both ways.

Acknowledgments

Back in 2014 I got the idea to write a cruise romance. My skills were still very green, but I had fun. I later went back and revised, and revised, and revised, my characters morphing and growing along the way (Cole was not originally an amputee, or named Cole!). This story grew along with my skills, until it reached this final form.

I couldn't have gotten here on my own. Thank you to Lydia Sharp, for always giving me such amazing edits that allow me to take my stories to the next level and make them shine. I've learned so much from you! And thank you to the entire Entangled team, including Liz Pelletier, Molly Majumder, Bree Archer, Curtis Svehlak, Riki Cleveland, and everyone who has helped make this into a book worthy of its final form. You are all such amazing and talented people and I feel honored to work with you!

To my agent, Lynnette Novak, you jumped in to take this project under your wing, helping with all the speed bumps, and not so speed bumps, along the way. I feel honored to have you in my corner!

A story this long in the making has multilayers of readers to thank. Rion Phillippi, you gave this novel some early love, and gave me some great feedback. I know Trent was your favorite, and I hope you still enjoy him in his final form! Heather DiAngelis, you read this years ago and always give such great advice, and continue to be a top notch cheerleader! Kari Mahara, Gwynne Jackson, Jami Nord, you've all given me support in one way or another with this novel and I would be lost without your support!

Rochelle Karina, how can I ever thank you for reading and rereading parts of this, for the lengthy messaging as I tried to tweak out different parts of this novel. You jump back and forth from real life drama to story drama with a blink of an eye and I'm so honored to have you as a friend!

A special shout out to Celeste Cochran. You took time out of your life to chat with an author about your experiences in the Boston Marathon Bombing, and as an amputee. You gave me such valuable information and I did my best to write Cole with accuracy and respect for the horrors you and others experienced. I hope I have done the character justice. Readers, any errors are purely my own and if you would like to learn more about the actual events check out the HBO movie *Marathon: The Patriots Day Bombing*. This is a documentary following many of the survivors, with actual footage and follow up on how their lives were changed that day.

To my parents, for instilling an early love of cruising in me. I've been on many ships and had the privilege of exploring different areas of the Caribbean. You can still be found cruising multiple times a year, which made research on this novel very easy!

To my family, thank you for always being there for me. For putting up with my long hours on the computer and deadline chaos.

And, as always, to my readers. Whether this is my first book you've read or not, I appreciate you taking the chance to read my stories and enter my worlds. I hope you enjoyed the journey!

About the Author

After spending her childhood coming up with new episodes to her favorite sitcoms instead of sleeping, Laura Brown decided to try her hand at writing and never looked back. A hopeless romantic, she's been drawn to love stories since an early age. She lives in Massachusetts with her family. Laura's been hard of hearing her entire life but didn't start learning ASL until college, when her disability morphed from an inconvenience to a positive part of her identity. At home the closed captioning is always on, lights flash with the doorbell, and hearing aids are sometimes optional.

Also by Laura Brown...

MATZAH BALL SURPRISE

ABOUT THAT NIGHT

THE UN-ARRANGED MARRIAGE

Discover more romance from Entangled...

The (ex) Spy Who (maybe) Loved Me
a novel by Christi Barth

At the end of a trip away from her small town home, scientist Blake Montgomery wants a sexy fling before returning. And the hot stranger at the airport bar looks like a perfect one-night stand. Until he shows up in her town the very next day. Wyatt Keene is just an average guy—now. But four days ago, he was a black ops intelligence agent who spent fifteen years being anyone except himself. Wyatt and Blake are not only stuck in the same town together, but also sharing the same office. Wyatt's trying to convince everyone, especially Blake, that he's just a normal guy—whatever that means. But nothing spells danger like trying to start a relationship with an ex-spy who hasn't quite left his old life behind...

Miles and Miles of You
a novel by Jennifer Bonds

Lucy Gonzalez hitched up her grandma's bitchin' vintage Airstream and is hitting the road with all the best places to find on a shoestring budget—with company along for the ride: billionaire Miles Hart. True story, he used to be Lucy's boss until she quit on him. Now, you have front-row seats to the hottest trip of the year. Sparks! Fireworks! Unexpected smooching! And you won't want to miss the jaw-dropping surprise that will make this destination totally worth the hilarious journey...

THE MATCHMAKER AND THE COWBOY
a Windsong novel by Robin Bielman

Somehow, every person who's worn one of Callie Carmichael's dresses has found love. *Real* love. But for Callie, love is way too dangerous—especially when it comes to her best friend's ridiculously hot brother, Hunter Owens. Cowboy, troublemaker, and the town's most coveted bachelor. Now Hunter wants Callie to make him a "lucky for love" best man's suit. But what happens if she makes the suit and he finds true love…and it isn't her?

LOOKS GOOD ON PAPER
a novel by Kilby Blades

Zuri Robinson is done with terrible dating apps and split-second hot takes. She wants something real. So now she's exchanging letters—*incredible* letters—with an impossibly charming Italian named Alessandro Fabricare. But when Zuri decides to travel to Italy to meet the good-on-paper man of her dreams, she's about to discover Alessandro is not exactly who he says he is…